THE CHARMING BILLIONAIRE

THE BALTIMORE BOYS
BOOK 1

SAMANTHA SKYE

Copyright © 2023 by Samantha Skye

ISBN 978-0-6457144-0-1 (ebook)

ISBN 978-0-6457144-1-8 (Paperback)

ISBN 978-0-6459897-5-5 (alternative Paperback)

Cover Design: Angela Haddon

Editor: Nice Girl Naughty Edits

Proofreading: Kimberly Dawn

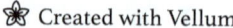 Created with Vellum

CONTENT INFORMATION

This book contains spicy scenes, swearing and descriptions of violence. It also contains kidnapping.

It is an opposites attract, workplace, billionaire romance that will have you hot under the collar and keep you on the edge of your seat.

Enjoy.

1

BETH LONGMERE

BREAKING NEWS

Rumors are swirling that Baltimore's poster boy billionaire, Harrison Langford, will be announcing his run for governor of Maryland.

Harrison, well known across the East Coast for his stance on economic reform, is Harvard Law educated and heir of the Langford dynasty, along with his three brothers. Often nicknamed "The Charmer" for his dazzling smile and like for the ladies, his lavish lifestyle and connections put him as the main contender for the top spot.

But will the boy from Baltimore, born with a silver spoon, receive the votes he needs from the general public? Many of whom say he is out of touch with what the real people want.

Affordable housing, advanced infrastructure, and investment in jobs are not something our poster boy has ever had to worry about before.

More to come.

"You know I spilled a tray of champagne on him once," I mumble to my dad as we both relax in the living room, watching the nightly news.

"Hmm?" His eyes remain focused on the TV, even though the picture is slightly black in spots from where I accidently hit it with the vacuum the other day.

"We had a charity event for his mother, the one where Issy was kidnapped," I continue as I scoop out a spoonful of ice cream from the tub of chocolate chip sitting on my lap. It is my Sunday night reprieve after a hectic week, the only luxury I give myself and, even then, only on pay weeks.

Dad side-eyes me. He doesn't like me working in the city at all hours for my job managing events for the rich and famous of DC. Even less so after Issy was kidnapped. But it is our only income and I get medical, so he can't complain. Besides, Issy is fine now. She got her happily ever after with Jake and is loving life in the country. It all worked out.

"I turned and crashed into a waiter. The drinks went flying straight onto his Italian loafers. His mother was furious. I've never felt more insignificant than in that moment when I dove onto the floor to mop up his shoes while he and his mother looked down their noses at me." I continue the story, the image still vivid in my mind despite that night taking a different turn. The ice cream drips onto my sweater from the spoon, creating a big brown splotch, and I quickly scrape off the remnants, internally cursing myself. *This is why I can't have good things*, my mother's voice, although distant, rings in my mind.

I work with many of the elite, yet in reality, I couldn't be further from them if I tried. I struggle to make ends meet to look after Dad and me. The opulence I see and create on a daily basis is in complete contrast to our bland, mismatched living room, where the carpet is so worn there are dents in the floor from my dad's wheelchair tires. The marks around our home are lovingly referred to as his racetrack.

But there is no racing. Our home is so small, we struggle to navigate his chair. We have only what we need and nothing more.

"Those pompous idiots have no idea how the real people live. He will run for governor, and he will win too because of his name, because of his connections. Not because of the difference he can make to the community," Dad says, clearly unimpressed with the boy from Baltimore despite everyone else loving him endlessly.

As I see images flash across the TV screen of him with a stunning brunette on his arm, the wind outside picks up and I hear the roof lifting a little, the air howling through the rafters. My eyes immediately focus on the dampness seeping through the ceiling in the corner of the room. Little black patches of mold have appeared, so I make a mental note to look into it.

My eyes flick back to the TV, which is now showing

Harrison Langford shaking hands at some industry event, flashing his smile. I watch his commanding presence, feeling it through the screen.

He didn't say anything to me that night when the drinks stained his loafers. He didn't have to. His mother was ranting at me and anyone else who would listen about my incompetence, loudly reminding everyone within earshot of exactly how expensive her son's shoes were. He, on the other hand, just looked at me. His eyes pierced mine. He had a little crease in between his eyebrows, and his jaw ticked, which made my cheeks flush and my hands shake. I am clumsy, yes, but not usually so flappable.

But he was something else. And I was glad to see the back of that event. I didn't miss his gaze on me as he left, though.

"Are you coming to the center tomorrow?" Dad asks me as I scrape out the last remaining spoonful of ice cream from the tub.

"Yep, I'm doing yoga with Marci at nine a.m. Do you want to catch the bus together?" I ask him, knowing that he wouldn't miss a day at the center for anything. Especially the daily game of chess he plays with Larry. The two of them are trouble when they get together at the local community center where Dad spends most of his days.

"That would be good," he grumbles.

"Are you alright, Dad?" He looks a little more worn out than when I was here last Sunday.

"Fine. Don't worry about me." I am used to his grumpy old man attitude by now, but it does make it difficult to tell when there's actually something wrong. That is why I am so upbeat. I have to be. We both can't be sad day after day. We both can't live in the past and have our hearts filled with worries.

"Have you been working with Jeff this week?" I ask, trying to dig a little deeper.

Jeff is the new community manager at the center. He arrived six months ago and has gotten everyone in order and has started new programs. He is even assisting Dad with trying to secure additional support and financial aid because of his disability, even offering to drive him to appointments.

"Yes. But Larry and I can see straight through him," Dad mumbles, raising a brow as he glances my way.

"What do you mean?" My head tilts at the look on his face.

"Jeff is sweet on you."

"No, he isn't," I scoff. "We are just friends, Dad. Two adults of the opposite sex can be just friends, you know."

"Oh, I know. And I also know that *friends* is not what that young man wants to be with you." There's no doubt in his tone, only resolve, as he shakes his head.

"How do you know?"

"Larry and I watched him last week when you did yoga. His eyes didn't leave your backside for a moment."

"Dad!" I screech, feeling my cheeks heat.

"Well, they didn't. Plus, he follows you around like a lost puppy and bends over backward to help me. He is infatuated with you, Beth."

"Oh, he just doesn't know many people yet." I try to

wave off the accusation Dad has put into the air, settling back in my seat.

"Why don't you go on a date with him? He seems nice."

"Because I don't feel anything more than friends for Jeff. There are no butterflies. My heart doesn't beat a little faster when he's around. I don't care to spend more time with him. Didn't you feel all those things when you met Mom?" The minute the words leave my mouth, I know I shouldn't have said them.

Our jovial conversation now feels like tar inside my body. The slow build of dread hits my stomach as the air of uncertainty hangs between us. I hold my breath, wondering what response I will get, too scared to say anything else.

"I'm going to bed," he says gruffly, and disappointment fills my chest. I feel sick. Sunday nights are our night, and I spoiled it. It's what I do. It is what I always do. Spoil things. Spill drinks. Upset Dad. I can't have nice things.

"Good night," I say to him quietly as I watch him maneuver his chair and push down the narrow hallway, listening for his bedroom door to close as I let out a sigh.

Dad is right. The boy of Baltimore has no idea how the other half lives.

2

HARRISON LANGFORD

I sit in my den, looking at my mother, my brother, and my newest staff member. Excitement swirls in my stomach. I have been waiting for this day my entire life and it is finally here.

As a kid, my dream was to be president. I have worked hard over the last year building connections, readying myself for a bigger role in politics. Now the governorship is so close, I can nearly taste it. I am ready. I am ready to lead this state and make a difference.

"When will you announce your intention to run for governor? I want to organize the event. I don't want you to worry about anything!" Mom says, clapping her hands together, the smile on her face the widest I've ever seen.

Clearly, she's happy to have a son on the national stage as governor for Maryland. Dressed in her signature matching Chanel tweed suit with her fresh blow-dry, I can see she has had some recent cosmetic work done. Her eyes are a little tighter and her cheeks a little sharper; she no longer looks like the woman I grew up idolizing.

"Oh, imagine it, Harrison! You will be amazing!" Lilly gushes as she flutters her lashes. Even though she is one of our oldest family friends, I am under no illusion. She wants more from me than I am prepared to give. Like my mother, she is freshly primped, her large designer bag sitting on the floor at her feet. Her lips are bright red and glossy, more swollen than last week, and I wonder not for the first time if it is possible for them to overtake the lower part of her face entirely. My eyes flick between the two of them, trying to understand their agenda.

"Mom, seriously. Harrison can manage this. He can hire his own events team, you know," my brother Eddie pipes up. His and my mother's relationship has always been strained and even though he is the youngest, he is the most protective of me and I him.

"Edward. Now is not the time," my mother huffs, and I raise my eyebrow, not needing them to get into it here in my home office.

"I'm ready," I state. "I'm committed to serving the people. I want to make a difference, and that's my priority." Taking a deep breath, I give my mom and brother a pointed look, leaning back in my leather chair.

I'm already thinking of the changes I can make and how I can position Maryland to be more. My mother's lips thin as she looks at my stance. I know she wants me in the main seat to further her position in society, not for the greater good of the people. I, on the other hand, think differently. She just fails to hear it.

"Of course, of course." She waves her manicured hand around, her mind no doubt filling with who to invite and who to strategically leave off the list. "Darling, throwing parties is what I do best so let me handle this one. You and Lilly will be the biggest stars of the night."

Taking Lilly to an event isn't new, but I am not keen on the idea this time around. She is a friend, nothing more, and that won't change—much to my mother's outrage. She has been trying to set us up for years and can't seem to see that we are not a match. Not in any way.

Eddie rolls his eyes, as he hates all this ceremonial extravagance.

The penny drops for me as I watch my mother and Lilly share a smile. This is yet another tactic of my mother's to push Lilly and me together. She gives me her *your father died and left me surrounded in the chaos of his infidelity* sad eyes, and I give in.

"Fine," I grit out, really preferring her to take a step back from my life now that running for governor is in the cards. "But I want real people in the room, not just your society friends. And leave me and my team to the politics. I do not need your meddling." I leave no room for questions, and with a curt nod, she's back to chattering with Lilly.

My new chief of staff, Oscar Barone, sits in the large leather chesterfield, looking over everyone in the room with his assessing eyes. He is a strategic pit bull. He takes no shit from me or my mother. As someone who has led key political campaigns for some of the country's biggest representatives, Oscar is the key to my campaign. He is what will help me win. Not my mother and her rich friends.

"Oh, what will I wear!" Lilly jumps up, gushing. "I want to look perfect for your big night, Harrison!" She smiles wide, looking at me with her big brown eyes, the same ones her father Ronald has. One of the biggest funders of my campaign. My brother curses under his breath, but she doesn't falter as I grit my teeth.

"Come, Lilly darling, let's start the party planning and leave the boys to work," my mother says, knowing she has pushed me as far as she is going to today and that her next move needs to be out the door.

The three of us watch as the two ladies walk and talk with such excitement it is already giving me a migraine. As the door closes behind them, Oscar opens his mouth.

"Your mother will plan a great party, and I am sure Lillian will look great on your arm," he states diplomatically, knowing how important her father's money and support are for my campaign.

"She is trying to get a ring on her finger. I love her like a sister, but seriously, she needs to know that you are not going to be marrying her," Eddie says, sitting forward and placing his elbows on his knees, looking at me accusingly.

"I've told her," I reply with a groan, running my hands through my hair in frustration. "I can't make it any clearer without taking out a full-page ad in *Society News*. She is practically already part of the family. But between her and our mother, some wires have been crossed and before I know it, she'll be expecting a diamond that I have no plans on giving her. It is something I have no plans on giving *anyone*." They both nod their heads in silent understanding.

"You will need to take a date to the event, though, and

she is a good choice," Oscar continues, leaning back in his chair, assessing me.

"No." I have no desire to make that kind of public statement. I have no romantic feelings for Lilly at all and have no intention of leading her on by having her on my arm during the campaign or after.

"You are well known for your bachelorhood and love for the ladies, but that is not going to win you votes. Your father did not leave a good legacy in that regard. You need to look all-American. You and Lillian have known each other for decades, played together in the Hamptons as kids. The press has practically already written you off as married." He just won't quit.

"No," I grit out, swallowing my growing irritation.

"Who then?" he challenges.

"No one. I don't need the distraction," I say firmly, committed to being focused on the campaign and not my sex life.

I need to ensure that my father's philandering history is not something people think I will repeat. I am seen out and about with women. I love women. But right now, I need to focus. It is my one and only shot at putting myself on track for political success, and I would prefer to be judged by the new policies I plan to implement, not by the woman I take to events.

"He is afraid of commitment," Eddie adds, and if looks could kill, he would be mush right about now.

"You have to have someone on your arm," Oscar presses.

"No, I don't." I sigh. I may be in my midthirties, but I have no plans to marry or commit myself to one person for the rest of my life. My parents proved to everyone that never works out.

"Yes. You. Do." He punches the words out to further emphasize his never-ending point. He is right, of course. But taking Lilly will make a firm statement. A statement that she will be by my side not just during the election campaign but through life. It makes a statement that *together*, we will look after Maryland and make it better. That is not a statement I want to make. She is not my forever.

"Let's announce it some other way," I say, rubbing my chin, thinking of a way to get out of this situation, dreading the alternative.

I am staying away from women during this campaign. I have worked too long and too hard to get this chance, so for the first time in my life, I am going to remain single and concentrate on my future. I will be a man for the people, so my dick just has to fall into line.

"But your mother is already organizing the party," Oscar reminds me.

"I think we should work out what our key focus point is and then announce my running at a place that's relevant," I suggest, and as I say it, I know it's the perfect solution.

"Good idea," Eddie jumps in, giving me a nod.

"Somewhere in the community, then. Somewhere with the people," Oscar states, sitting forward with renewed interest, and I can already see his mind turning.

"Who is telling Mom?" Eddie asks, looking right at me with a smirk. I ignore his look of question because we both know our mother is not going to like this one bit.

"Great. I will investigate venues. Now that we have that sorted, let's talk about the key points of your campaign. Inflation, jobs, and infrastructure investment." Oscar talks specifics, and we get down to business. I want Maryland to flourish. I want to help the communities who need the support, and most of all, I want to make a positive difference across the entire state.

It is a big challenge, trying to keep everyone happy, while also supporting those who can't afford to support themselves. That's why Eddie is here with me. Out of all my brothers, he is not as enamored by the wealthy as the rest of us have been brought up to be. In fact, he purposefully rebels against it. Having backpacked around Asia for six months, living off two dollars a day, and surviving on cheap street food, there was more than one occasion when his travel insurance was needed due to hospitalization over food poisoning. Aside from that medical luxury, he didn't live like the billionaire he is, and still doesn't.

"So I have mapped out the state, and you have most of the areas in hand, which is good. Obviously, you're well known and loved in Baltimore City and most outskirts. However, you have some work to do in the southeast, particularly toward DC. Some areas have high poverty rates and high unemployment rates, so we really need to get our messaging on point before we delve into those areas."

Oscar opens a map on my desk and the three of us look over it like a military tactical team, assessing the segmentation of areas that Oscar has already done, color coded in a traffic light system. The areas of the state that are colored red are those that I need to be more active in;

green are the ones that I already have a good following in. And amber are the ones that can go either way.

I go to DC often, although I live and work in Baltimore City. DC is the political capital of the country, where all the big players are, many of whom I am friends with. If I want to continue to climb the political ladder, it is where I will need to be spending my time, eventually.

"What do you suggest?" I ask him as I look over the map.

"Infrastructure. Investing in large-scale infrastructure will build jobs and a better life for many people in some of these areas. It will keep the labor market happy, unions satisfied, and as long as your family property and construction company doesn't benefit directly from it, then it will make the construction industry thrive as well."

"So new hospitals, schools, that kind of thing?" I ask, already liking the idea, with healthcare being one area I do want to focus on.

"They are too involved. Too expensive. Think large-scale residential development or commercial, in terms of shopping precincts to kick-start the local economy by way of retailers."

"You don't think schools or health facilities would be a better investment?" I question. I know they would be welcomed.

"What about the people?" Eddie asks.

"What about them?" Oscar counters.

"Has anyone thought about asking them what they want?" Eddie asks, and I nod in agreement.

"They don't even know what they want. It is up to us

to build a vision and they will come. Harrison here will be like the pied piper and all the people will follow him, no matter where he goes." Oscar sits back with a satisfied smile on his face, and I wish I felt his confidence. It will be a tough race for me. My competitor is someone who has been eyeing the governorship for years.

"You do realize the pied piper took all the children, right? And left the town bereft?" Eddie asks Oscar mockingly.

"Wait and see, young man, wait and see," Oscar says, rubbing his hands together.

3

BETH

I finally take a breath as I see everyone seated, well fed, and happy. With only thirty minutes to go before the guests are due to leave, I can finally take a small breather. This is the time when you know ninety-five percent of the work is done and even though there is still a lot to do with debriefs and budgets behind the scenes, the event itself is complete. This is my last event for a while, so I take it all in. The beautiful flowers, the distinguished guests, the plates of lobster, and glasses of champagne. Opulence of the highest caliber, nothing is too much for this high net worth cohort of businessmen.

My boss, Kelly, is about to have her first baby, and while the event agency can work without her, she has decided for us all to have a small break for three months. We have been busy. Being one of DC's most in-demand event companies has us working almost twenty-four seven, and while Kelly is slowing down, wanting a quieter life, my need to continue to provide for my dad and myself burns under my skin.

Some of the team are taking extended vacations, Paris and London seemingly the most sought-after locations. But that is a luxury I can't afford. Thank goodness I'll still have a job. Kelly has kindly let me work throughout the next few months, but it will be reduced pay and hours, more admin than event management for a little while before we gear up again just in time for party season. It isn't ideal, but I still get my medical benefits, and I hope I can pick up something else part-time to help with the bills.

Looking around the room, I spot the usual suspects. Many of whom I speak to so regularly for event logistics and RSVP management that they are now good friends. It is nice. Others, though, still treat me like I am their servant and those people I steer well clear of, not wanting to give them any more reason to dislike me or our business.

My eyes flick to table four. Harrison Langford sits tall and confident, talking with the other businessmen around him. I wonder if the rumors are true and if he is going to announce his run for governor soon. He was a last-minute addition to the guest list today.

I take a moment to look him over. I haven't seen him since the champagne incident. His thick, dark hair falls slightly across his face, and his broad shoulders are covered in a well-fitted navy suit. He looks like he doesn't have a care in the world, yet he's firm and focused on the conversations around him. I admire his strong posture and commanding nature. He looks to be in control of the entire table. It is very appealing to a girl like me whose life is always sitting on a knife's edge and could spin totally out of control at any moment.

"Beth. I need you." I hear my boss Kelly's panicked voice in my earpiece.

"Where are you?" I ask her quietly as my eyes sweep the room. Now that I think about it, I haven't seen her in a while.

"Down the hall, in the corridor near the kitchen."

"On my way," I tell her as I walk with purpose to the other side of the room and quickly duck down the hall.

"Beth!" Kelly pants, her hand holding the wall, her other hand resting on her very pregnant belly.

"Are you okay?" I ask, my eyes roaming her body, panic starting to well inside me.

"The baby is coming," she says on a breath, and I just about scream.

"What?!"

"The baby is coming, Beth. My water just broke."

"Oh my God! Do I call an ambulance? Do you need to sit down? Do you need water?" I'm not the one about to have a baby, but with the nerves running through me, you wouldn't know that.

"John is on his way. He will take me to the hospital," she says too calmly, and I thank God her husband will know what to do.

"Let me get you a glass of water." I turn quickly and slam straight into a waiter coming from the kitchen down the hall. My body propels backward, and I fall to the floor, landing on my butt as the tray full of champagne flutes she was holding flies through the air. I watch them float, like they are hot air balloons moving in slow motion. All would be fine, except at that moment, a man walks around the corner into the hallway.

He steps backward quickly, but the glassware still catches on his white shirt, which is now saturated with a delicious bottle of Dom Perignon Vintage 1992.

"Shit," he curses as the tray and glasses fall to the floor. Thankfully, it's carpet, so nothing breaks and there is no loud clatter to disrupt the formal proceedings of the event in the main room.

As I survey the mess of glasses and champagne that now decorate the floor, Kelly's breath hitches behind me. I look up to the man to apologize, and it is then that I see his face and my stomach drops. Not again!

"Kelly!" John, Kelly's husband, rushes down the hall, grabbing Kelly, who is panting through what appears to be a contraction.

"I'm so sorry," the young waitress says to me as I scramble off the floor and grab Kelly's handbag, passing it to John.

"You two go; I will finish up here," I tell Kelly and John, wanting this to be the last thing Kelly worries about in her condition.

"You sure?" Kelly asks, looking between me and the man behind me.

"Yes, of course, go. I will wrap up here, then head to the hospital to check on you." Looking at John, he gives me a nod before walking Kelly toward the kitchen, then out the back exit. We planned for this. John was on speed dial for the past few weeks as Kelly's due date got closer. And while she isn't due for another few weeks, one of the contingencies of our event today was to run it like Kelly wasn't even here. What we didn't plan for was her water breaking at the actual event, or for my awkwardness and the tray of champagne landing on one of our guests.

"I am extremely sorry, sir," I say quickly as I turn to look at Harrison Langford, who's trying to mop himself down with a napkin. My eyes catch on his now see-through shirt, and the very clear outline of some well-formed abs, and I swallow quickly.

"It's fine. It was an accident, no harm." He's being kind, too forgiving, even though I see his jaw clenching. I cringe, tentative as I wait for his wrath, but it never comes.

"Follow me. I can get you sorted with a new shirt and organize the dry cleaning," I tell him in the most professional tone I can muster. Spinning on my heel, I don't wait for his response as I hightail it farther down the hall, stepping around the waitress who is cleaning up the mess, to a discreet cloakroom that is prepared for just such an occasion.

Pushing open the door, I flick on the light.

"I'm guessing a size thirty-eight?" I ask, my back still to him, but I know he followed me into the room. His masculine scent wraps around me, giving me goosebumps, and I rub my arms to create friction so they disappear. The door to the room closes, shutting out any noise, and the quiet is suddenly startling. You can hear a pin drop, and I am scared he can hear my traitorous heart as it thuds harder in my chest.

"Yes. Thank you." His voice makes my nerves dance in my stomach, my body warming at his proximity. I need to pull myself together; it isn't like I haven't spilled champagne on him before.

"Of course." I'm feeling breathless, but I'm trying to keep it together, my hands shaking a little as I grab the new shirt from the rack.

"Here," I say as I turn to face him, proud that we have a Hugo Boss white dress shirt in his size. This is what sets our event agency apart from all others. We go the extra mile. We think of everything. Including a dressing room full of clothes in case people need a quick change.

"Thank you," he says as he takes the shirt from my hand. Looking around the room, his eyes rest on mine again. "You have quite the wardrobe in here. The whole event is extremely professional and well organized. One of the best events I have ever been to, and I have been to many."

His voice feels like warm honey down my body, and I'm hoping I'm not obviously blushing. I quickly turn and give him my back again as I grab a laundry bag to put his wet shirt in to dry clean it for him. We are standing close, and I can feel the heat radiating between our bodies. All I would need to do is step back and we'd touch, and my body hums for the connection. It's been a long time since I have been with a man.

"We like to ensure we are prepared for anything. It is why we are one of the best event agencies in DC. We look after every last detail. If you would like to put your wet shirt in this..." My words stop on my lips when I turn back to face him again. He is standing there half-naked, his wet shirt in his hand. Those abs I saw momentarily before are now right in front of me and my eyes cannot move away from them. There is a smattering of dark hair that runs across his perfect chest, leading up to his solid shoulders and down to a trail that's extremely enticing to a single girl like me.

It's unavoidable now... I feel the heat flame my cheeks. *Stupid cheeks.*

"Oh my God!" I gasp as I right myself, my hands flying to my face, and I cover my eyes. My cheeks flame even hotter as I shake my head, trying to pull it together. I turn around again, drawing on every professional bone in my body, nearly losing my footing in the process. *Why do I have to be so awkward?*

I hear him chuckle. "It's fine. I didn't mean to startle you. I apologize." Even though my eyes are covered, I know he is grinning. He is clearly confident in his body, and he should be. It is like it is sculptured or airbrushed or something. I gaze down at my very average physique. Sure, I have curves, but they are not what I would call desirable by any stretch of the imagination. I flaunt them, regardless. I am not totally inept.

"Please put your wet shirt in this bag, and I can organize the dry cleaning," I say, throwing the bag behind me at him without looking. I think I hear his faint chuckle again, but I am too embarrassed to look. His closeness almost suffocates me.

"I will give you some privacy." I move quickly toward the door, tripping slightly on the line of spare shoes in the process. My hip hits the clothing rack, which is on wheels, and it runs down the length of the room, banging on the end wall.

"Shit!" I hiss under my breath.

"Are you okay?" he asks as my heart thumps through my ears, and I just want the world to open up and swallow me right now.

"Yes. Absolutely. Never been better. Please don't worry about me." The words rush out of me in a fluster. I look everywhere but at him, trying to find an escape route to get out of this situation.

"Wait, you're caught!" he tries to warn me, but in my haste, I pay little attention until I am falling. My foot capturing the side of a box, my body twists, and the floor comes toward me at a rapid pace.

"I've got you!" I hear him say before I feel his hand wrap around my waist, the warmth from his grip spreading through my body. I gasp as I continue to fall, the momentum pulling us both to the floor, and he lands on top of me, the two of us in a tangle. His one hand remains around my waist, keeping me close, the other holding him up slightly, yet his face hovers mere inches from mine.

Mortification doesn't come close to the feelings welling in my body, not including the warm tingling that is happening down below. His half-naked form pushes against mine, his strong pecs brushing my breasts, hearts meshing together. If anyone were to walk in right now, our position would be seen as extremely unprofessional and would be front page news on the local gossip websites.

I squeeze my eyes shut. My hands are stiff and straight, remaining by my sides as a flush colors my cheeks, and I bite my lips and hold my breath, waiting for his wrath. But it doesn't come.

"Are you alright? You seem to prefer the floor. This is the second time in five minutes I have found you on the carpet." His rough voice speaks with concern, yet it's laced with some humor.

I peek open one eye to look at him, seeing him smiling above me. Slowly, I open my other eye and get the full picture of his blindingly white smile. I can't help but drink him in. He is hot. Like a model hot. His eyes search my face and when our gazes meet, I am certain I see his deep blues twinkling.

"Yep!" I say, popping the *P*, my breathing shallow. I once again notice the small wrinkle in between his brows, and I squeeze my fists tighter so I don't reach out to smooth it away.

"Who are you?" he asks, almost in wonder, looking at me like he is seeing me for the first time.

"I'm Beth. The event planner." Could I sound any more pathetic? My heart sinks because now I know for sure that his mother is never going to be a customer of ours again and Kelly is going to kill me.

"Beth..." he says slowly, like he is tasting the flavor of my name on his tongue. "The event planner... Have we met before?" His eyes crinkle at the sides as he assesses me, and I want to close my eyes and disappear.

"Yes. Once." I grimace. Might as well get this over with. I'm mentally preparing my resume for the job hunt I will be on once he fires the agency from ever working with him and his family again.

"You have spilled champagne over me before, haven't you?" The smile on his face fades to one of awe, and I'm not sure if that's a good thing. His memory is much better than I thought it would be.

"You remember?" I ask, horrified, but I'm also a little intrigued that I made an impression.

"Hmmm," is all he says, making no move to get off me, his body heat melting into my bones, and I suddenly understand why women fall at his feet. He is looking at me like I am the only woman in the world. Like I am special.

His cell phone vibrates in his pocket, startling us both. He jumps up off me then, offering me his hand to help me up. I take it, trying not to look at his body and pretending that the brown carpet is the most interesting thing I have ever seen.

"Yes?" he says as he answers the call.

"Fine, I will be there in two minutes. Don't let him leave."

I pick up the laundry bag and put his wet shirt inside while he finishes dressing in the new shirt I gave him.

"So, Beth, you work with Kelly at DC Events?" he asks me, his tone friendly as he fastens the last button.

"Yes." I give him a one-word answer, too scared of the verbal diarrhea that may explode out of my mouth at any moment and really not wanting to make this situation any worse than it already is. I ruin everything. It is why I can't have nice things. This is why I don't have a boyfriend. It is why no one could possibly want a girl like me.

"The dry cleaning can be returned to my office," he says while pulling on his jacket.

"Okay. No problem."

"Great. Good to meet you, Beth..." The way he says my name makes my stomach flip. His lips quirk at the sides as his eyes find mine once more before he steps around me and out the door.

What the hell just happened?

4

HARRISON

I strut away from the dressing room like it is on fire. Clearing my throat, I pull at my collar.

Beth is someone I didn't think I would see again, but a face I have never forgotten. When I saw her earlier, I knew the universe was playing a joke on me. The minute I declared I am staying away from women, Beth showed up and a flood of instant admiration flew through me like never before.

I watched her all day as she was organizing the media scrum like a pro and walked around the room taking care of everyone, her professional attire doing nothing to hide her voluptuous body as she managed the event without breaking a sweat.

Straightening my tie, I try to get my growing dick under control as I walk down the hallway back into the event room to meet Oscar.

I am days away from announcing my run for governor, and I don't need her as a distraction, yet my thoughts have been on her for most of the event, my attraction instant. I also wasn't the only one to spot her. Every man in this place had his eyes on her, and I can't blame them. I'm here for work, to mingle and meet; she is the last thing I need, yet the vision of her ample body underneath mine is now seared into my brain.

I rub my eyes, my vision fuzzy and my pulse at a rate it hasn't been for a while.

She isn't my usual type. She looks too young and too innocent for starters. She can't be older than early twenties, and I don't make a habit of dating younger women. There have been enough political assholes playing around with barely legal women over the years, and I don't need to add to that list. Although the way she handles herself is with more maturity than any woman I have come across in years. That thought alone confuses me.

I smirk, thinking about how she was looking everywhere but at me, even though I was hunting for her eyes. I wanted to see if they were the same perfect sparkling blue that I remember. They were. But she is the only woman I have ever met who doesn't seem to like the look of me. The only woman to see me half-naked and not touch me or attempt to take a photo and sell it to the gossip magazines. Both are a rarity in this city for me, unfortunately.

I walk out to find Oscar looking panicked. The room today is full of all the key people, a gold mine for garnering support for my soon-to-be announced campaign. I crack my neck as I strut toward him, pushing my thoughts of her to the back of my mind. I need to focus.

"Where is he?" I ask, knowing that the entire purpose of me being at this event is so I could catch Arthur Stratten to appeal for his support. Aside from my family and Lilly's father, Arthur is one of the biggest landowners in Maryland and has his hand in many businesses. He is also a ruthless old bastard. He and my father were arch-nemesis in the old days before my father passed away, but now he remains mostly out of the limelight, preferring to count his millions at home, it seems. Oscar got word that he was at this event and managed to get us tickets on short notice so we could get an audience with him.

"He said he had to find someone, but I can't see him anywhere," Oscar says, frustrated, as we both look around the room frantically for him, knowing that the event is about to wrap up.

Then I spot him. Laughing and smiling. Which are two things he never does.

"He is over there," I say, nodding to the far right of the room, near where I just came from, and Oscar's eyes follow mine.

"He's laughing?" Oscar gapes, his eyebrows hitting his hairline, and the two of us take a few steps in his direction before I stop. I see who he is with and what is making him so happy, and it is the same woman who put a smile on my own face moments ago.

Beth.

Oscar pushes me along, but my feet are already moving of their own accord, my eyes firmly on her. She is laughing too. Her shoulders are back, her eyes sparkling. Her lips curve up in a way that has me thinking all sorts of things I definitely shouldn't be. She looks different from the woman I was just with in the darkened cloakroom. Vibrant and full of life, standing tall, looking radiant.

I observe her some more, seeing her interact with Arthur. I am impressed that she seems to have such a friendly relationship with one of the wealthiest men in the country. In fact, I see many people walking past her on the way out, all of whom say goodbye or shake her hand. She has DC wrapped around her little finger.

As we step up to them both, Beth looks up, and her beaming smile fades as she sees me.

"Arthur, good to see you," I say, pushing my way into their conversation and trying not to let her obvious dislike for me sour my mood.

Arthur turns and looks at me as Beth excuses herself, her sprinkle of freckles highlighted by her pink-tinged cheeks. "I will leave you to it, Arthur."

"Let's do lunch and chess later this week, Bethy. I will send my car to get you," he tells her fondly, and I watch her smile at him as she takes a step back. I appreciate her professionalism.

"I would love that, Arthur. But you won't win chess, you know that, right?" Looking at her, I wonder what I need to do to get a smile from her like that.

The two of us watch as she turns and merges back with the crowd. Her red hair flows over her shoulders with her stride. And I don't miss the way her ass looks in her black dress or the way her legs extend from her black patent high heels. Arthur clears his throat, and I whip my head toward him.

"Keep your eyes off her. She is far too good for the likes of you," Arthur says in warning, and I raise my eyebrows at him. For a man pushing seventy, he still has a lot of fight left in him.

"You can have any woman you want. Beth is not the one for you," he continues, his eyes narrowing on me.

"Just like your father, looking at every pretty girl in the room," Arthur mutters, shaking his head, and I look at him. He is the first person to mention my father to me in a long time, but given their history, I shouldn't be surprised.

I clench my teeth, but smile. We both know that my father was a philanderer. A playboy. A name that is often associated with me due to the myriad of women I date. But unlike my father, I didn't marry a woman twenty years my junior, then cheat on her every chance I got. To be honest, the thought sickens me, and I have no plans to invest in the institution of marriage after the mockery he made of it.

"Arthur, I want to chat with you, perhaps take you to lunch?" I state, ignoring his previous remark. There is no point making small talk; Arthur is a straight shooter and so am I.

"You want my money? My support? Is that it?" Arthur, like the businessman he is, gets right to it. I remain silent, waiting for him to give me the answer I want to hear.

"We can meet. But not for lunch. I only have lunch with friends, and let me be very clear, we are not friends,

Harrison. But I will hear what you have to say. Call my office, they will set it up."

"Thanks, Arthur. I will call and arrange something for next week." I appreciate that he shakes my hand this time as I extend it to him again.

"We'll see, boy. We'll see." Turning away from me, he slowly walks out the door. The event is now finished, and the room is starting to clear.

"Well, that went well. Who was he talking to just now?" Oscar asks, his head still whipping around the room, seeing if there is anyone else we need to speak to while we are here.

"Why?" I question as my own eyes roam the room, hoping to catch a glimpse of the woman who has twice now crashed into my life, shocking me with cold champagne, before flowing out again.

"Who is she to you?" Oscar asks, and I turn and see him looking at me. His accusing eyes crinkle at the sides. He must read something on my face as his look turns serious.

"You said it yourself; we don't need distractions, Harrison."

"I'm not distracted. I am one hundred percent focused. Let's go," I grit out, not liking that he is questioning me about a woman and already making assumptions.

We make our way outside and into our waiting car. Slipping inside, my body sinks into the soft leather seat as exhaustion nips at my heels. It has been a long week, and I haven't even publicly announced my running yet.

"I am serious, Harrison. Lillian is a great girl. If

anyone is on your arm during this campaign, it needs to be her," Oscar continues to push, and my jaw clenches.

"Whom I date, whom I spend time with, is not up for debate. To be clear, I have no intention of stringing Lilly along for my own political gain."

"You are running for governor of Maryland. You need to have someone by your side. You can't be a playboy bachelor during the campaign. The people need to see a stable, in control, dependable leader. They need to see family values, strong ethics, a perfect picture."

I am not my father. I enjoy the company of women, but I am not a playboy. Not like he was.

"I don't need Lilly by my side. I won't portray something that simply isn't true. I don't want to start this campaign with a fake state of affairs," I retort, my frustrations starting to turn into anger.

"You also don't need distractions, Harrison, and I wouldn't be doing my job if I didn't point these things out to you," Oscar says, obviously sensing he is hitting a nerve.

"Oscar, let me make my position on this really clear. Lilly, in no way, shape, or form will be the woman by my side. For this campaign or ever. Do not question me on that again." My words have bite, but I need him to know that Lilly and I are not an option, even though I know presenting a united front would help win votes.

"I also don't plan on being a *playboy bachelor* as you put it. I have dreamed of this opportunity for most of my life. Do I love women? Yes, who doesn't. But I am focused and committed. I can do this without drawing any unsavory media attention. I know the game and I know how to play it."

I take a breath and rub my eyes, trying to erase the bright-blue ones from my memory. Oscar is right, and this is why I hired him. I need to remain focused. I don't need distractions.

Especially one as beautiful as Beth.

5

BETH

After a heated discussion about me wheeling him versus him managing his chair on his own, Dad and I are on our way to the community center. We both slept terribly last night, a regular occurrence for us when thunderstorms roll through. Reminders at night are never good and we have been bickering with each other all morning.

As I walk along, half-asleep, my cell vibrates, and I see it is Kelly.

"Kelly! How are you?" I ask with glee. She is currently back home from the hospital and is deep in her love bubble with John and their new little baby boy.

"Beth. I just got off the phone with Harrison Langford," she states, and I stop walking, dread filling my bones. Here it is. I am about to lose my job. I am about to lose the only income my father and I receive. I look at him, and like he can sense it, he lowers his head. I'm even surprised my father still loves me at this point due to the amount of anguish I cause him every time he looks at me.

My face is a clear reminder to him of the night our lives took a turn no one was expecting.

"Look, Kelly, I am really sorry about the incident last week…"

"Beth. Stop. I trust you. You are amazing at your job. So amazing, in fact, that apparently you made quite the impression. So much so, Harrison has asked that I offer you as a secondment to assist his team for the next three months to help his campaign. He is announcing his run for governor today."

"*What*?!" I practically scream into the phone, needing to hang on to Dad's wheelchair in case I faint on the spot.

"He has given me twenty-four hours to get back to him with our answer. I want you to think about it today, Beth. Speak to your dad and call me with your decision by tomorrow. I know it is quick, but it gives you a chance to keep a full-time income, and technically, you will still be working for me, so if it doesn't turn out to be something you like, you can always come back to me on reduced hours and shuffle some paperwork at any time. Anyway, I have to run, the baby's awake, but call me later once you have decided, okay?" I squeak out a nonsensical reply, and she ends the call.

I jump when a car horn honks in the distance, and I try to center myself and refocus on Dad. Even though I feel like a walking zombie, Kelly's call just now has my head spinning. *Harrison Langford wants me on his team?*

"Did you lose your job?" Dad asks, and the sorrow in his face says it all. He thinks that I did. I told him all about the champagne incident after the event last week because I wanted him to be prepared in case I became unemployed.

"No, I got offered a different one..." I say, lost in thought, and he breathes a sigh of relief and doesn't ask any other questions. I walk along silently as my mind races, then I try to snap out of it and focus on him. My eyes home in on his wheelchair. For the last block since we got off the bus, I have been watching Dad glide ahead of me, and I've noticed one of his wheels wobbles in a way it isn't meant to.

"Dad, is there something wrong with your chair?" I ask. He never said anything, but I can now see clearly that it is bothering him.

"No. It's fine," he grumbles.

"But your wheel looks..."

"Stop it, Beth, I said it is fine!" His tone leaves little room for questions. I may now be an adult in my early twenties, but I still keep quiet when my dad is stern with me. So I clamp my lips and keep walking.

I continue to watch the wheelchair, and I wonder if the wheel is going to come entirely loose. He has had the same chair for years, but he doesn't want us spending any more money on it.

We have had the same argument for weeks now. He hates the fact that as a young woman I am spending all my money on him. He hates being dependent on me. The guilt he feels for what happened to my mother continues to eat at him, even though deep down, I know I am the one to blame.

Growing up through my teenage years without Mom was hard. Trying to help Dad as he went through his physical and mental health decline on top of that was stressful. But we have come out the other side and we make our way in life just fine.

"So does this new job mean you will be home bothering me more now?" he grumbles, changing the subject back to focus on me rather than him. He obviously still thinks I will be on reduced hours and reduced pay as Kelly takes her time away from the business to focus on her family.

"You will love having me around more!" I joke with him. My father would hate to have me around all the time, but he will probably hate me taking this new job with Harrison more.

"I have a routine and I am sticking to it. You will have to find your own things to do. Maybe go on that date with Jeff," he suggests, and I stumble a little on the jagged sidewalk before righting myself with the handle of his chair.

"I'm not dating Jeff, Dad," I groan. I would do anything to please my dad, but dating Jeff is one step I really don't want to take.

"He is a good guy. Smart. Good-looking. You could do a lot worse than Jeff," he says, and I sigh. What he means to say is that I should be happy that a man is showing interest in me. No one else has in a very long time.

Dad is right; Jeff is all those things. But I don't feel it. And I really want to feel it. That heart-thumping, panty-melting, *I need you more than the air I breathe* kind of love. The one my parents had. Before I ruined it all.

"What's all the commotion this morning?" Dad grumbles, pulling me from my thoughts as we push through the doors of the center to see people running around in all directions.

"Larry, what the hell is going on?" he yells to Larry who is waiting patiently for him by the chess table at the front window. As we dodge the racing people, many of whom we know, but some we don't, we make our way closer, watching Jeff barking orders near the offices at the back, clipboard in hand.

"Apparently, there are some dignitaries coming today," Larry says as he shrugs. A veteran, Larry spends his days here at the center with my father, and the two of them have become close over the years. Larry ensures Dad is looked after when I am not around. It is good to have him in our lives.

After a beat, Dad wheels over and takes his usual place around the table and the two of them start playing their game without batting another eyelash. Their attention to chess is unrelenting. They don't even keep score, yet they are here every day, playing all day to pass the time.

"Hey, Beth. Crazy, huh?" Jeff says close to my ear, his warm breath skirting across my neck, and I jump, startled, having not expected him.

"Yes. What's going on?" I ask, my hand resting on my thumping heart as I take a small step away from him, shielding my personal space, not wanting him in it.

"Last-minute call from the head office. We have a team of politicians coming through this morning. Nothing major. Just your usual walk and talk, I'm sure. Yoga is still going ahead as normal." He smiles at me as he clicks his pen, ticking off an item from his list. I don't miss as his eyes skirt down my body and back up again when he thinks I am not looking. I swallow, not sure how I feel about his eyes on me like that. He is not it for me, and deep down, I know it.

"Well, I will leave you to it, and I will go and join the class!" I say, trying to sound jovial, when all I want to do is crawl back into bed and sleep for the day.

"Are you feeling alright? You look tired, Beth. Is there anything I can do for you?" Jeff asks, and my shoulders tense. Why can't I just like him? He is good-looking, nice, caring... yet there is something about him that doesn't feel right. I give him a brief smile as I try to feel upbeat.

"Oh, I'm fine. I just didn't get much sleep last night," I say, trying to act nonchalant, brushing off his accurate observation.

"Oh, the thunderstorm. I get it. It was a wild one." I don't think Dad would have told him, but they have become close, so maybe Jeff knows about why thunderstorms are not welcome in our lives.

I give him a brief smile before taking another step back.

"Good luck with the morning, Jeff." Offering a brief wave goodbye, I mark the end of the conversation. I'm not able to get away from him fast enough this morning as he stands there looking at me with a weird smile on his face.

Morning yoga at the center is run by a wonderful middle-aged lady named Marci who, despite her electric-blue hair, tight attire, and bright-red lipstick, is a ball of cosmic energy. She brings along healing crystals and incense, and I don't miss the way she flirts with my father after class. She is the only woman to bring a smile to his face ever.

"Well, hello sugar," Marci says warmly to me, and I am amazed by her. Pushing the top end of fifty, she is as fit as she is flexible.

"Hey, Marci," I say before my mouth breaks out into a yawn.

"Rough night?" she asks, and I just nod, glassy-eyed, and she squeezes my shoulder before closing the door and calling the class to start.

"Morning, everyone. Thank you for joining me this morning. Given the activity that is happening in the main area of the center, I have decided that this session will be power yoga, where we can really move our bodies and get a great workout since meditation and relaxation is totally out of the question." Marci's calmness centers me, and as I sit tall, legs crossed, I start to feel calm and my breathing begins to slow.

"Let's start with our sun salutations." Her voice floats through the air and my limbs automatically move, and I am now grateful for coming to class this morning. My body needs it. I stretch and relax into the poses, feeling my body lengthening and the stress starting to leave me. I haven't done power yoga in a while and soon feel out of breath, yet grateful for the workout.

Before long, I am cursing myself for wearing my old thread-bare yoga pants and crop top as they stick to my sweat-covered body. Again, I am behind on my washing, and I mentally high-five myself for taking a spot at the back of the class, highly doubtful that anyone would want an eyeful of my big backside in my nearly see-through pants.

As we move into a downward dog, I let my head fall down and melt into the pose. I take a deep breath and sink farther into the stretch, really feeling my muscles pull, then the door to the class opens right behind me.

I see Jeff's sneakers and jeans appear in my vision between my legs, alongside three pairs of shiny black shoes and tailored black trousers. Dammit. The last thing I need is Jeff looking at my butt. My thong is no doubt on full display, and I groan as I slowly stand up, wondering why I can't just at least look like I have my life together for once.

But as I turn to look at the men, I come to understand that luck is not something that is offered to a girl like me.

6

HARRISON

It's hot. There are sweaty bodies everywhere, but my eyes are glued to one.

"No distractions, remember?" Oscar grits out to me under his breath, and I look at him sharply, not thrilled with his unnecessary reminder. I hold his gaze until he looks away, then my eyes lock on to the most perfectly round ass I've ever seen. I look up at her body, follow the vibrant red hair in a tight braid that runs down her back, and as she turns around, our eyes meet. Her cheeks flame, matching her hair. My cock jumps in response, and I swallow.

Beth. *What the hell is she doing here?*

The class ends abruptly as we stand in the room. Clearly, we are an interruption, as Jeff, who runs this center, was giving us a tour. Beth's eyes are darting between mine and Jeff's as he stands next to me. We purposefully left it to the last minute to notify anyone and had Jeff and his management team from Baltimore City scrambling, but I wanted the media scrum, and

Oscar said last-minute surprises are what will make a mark in the media today.

Plus, we didn't want my mother ruining it. This way, she can still have her party as a celebration, but I won't need to have Lilly on my arm when I present myself to the state. I can be with the people whom I want to represent.

"What are you doing here?" Her voice hits my ears, and my eyes refocus on her.

"I could ask you the same thing," I say, trying to get my bearings, keeping my eyes on hers and not on the curves of her breasts in her skimpy workout gear.

"I'm doing a yoga class. Or rather, I *was* doing a yoga class," she sasses back, and I smirk. She looks even younger out of her corporate attire. Fresh-faced with no makeup, she is even more beautiful than I remember. There is now no doubt that I am at least a decade older, and I should be pushing my thoughts of her far from my mind. But they remain, as do my feet that are glued to the floor right in front of her. Unmoving.

"My timing was impeccable then, wouldn't you say?" I grin at her because my timing couldn't have been better. Her cheeks flame a little more, and I rub my jaw to prevent the genuine full smile that threatens to emerge.

"Your timing seems to always put you in the middle of the action," she murmurs, and I see her take in a deep breath, her chest moving up and down, causing my eyes to leave hers briefly as I take her in.

"You look good out of your corporate attire..." I leave the remark to linger between us for a moment before I get interrupted.

"Ahh, Beth. This is Mr.—" Jeff starts to say, but she cuts him off.

"I know who he is, Jeff," she retorts, her eyes still not leaving mine, and I watch as a bead of sweat runs from her hairline down her shoulders and chest before going in between her breasts in the tight crop top she is wearing. I fight the sudden urge I have to trail it with my tongue as I shoot my eyes back to meet her bright-blue ones.

"The media scrum is here. We need to go out the front," Oscar says beside me.

"What media scrum? What is going on?" she asks, her hands now on her hips, looking between all of us.

"I'm announcing my run for governor this morning. Looks like you get a front-row seat," I answer as Oscar turns toward the door to start proceedings. Eddie and Jeff follow him out, but I hold back, intrigued and wanting more time with Beth.

The plan is that I will stand out front on the steps and make my official announcement to run for governor. Oscar chose Riverside because it is one area where I need the numbers. It has higher unemployment, lower household income, and we're thinking of investing in some infrastructure projects here. But any productive thoughts went out the window the minute my eyes rested on Beth's body. Voluptuous. Curvy. Flexible. So very fucking flexible.

"So you're announcing it here? Kelly didn't mention that..." she says, taking a step toward me. I look over her flaming-red hair sticking to her head, then my gaze lowers, obviously so, down to her yoga pants that are doing little to tamp down my imagination of what is underneath them. I clear my throat as the last of the class members step around me and out the door, only the teacher remaining at the far end of the room.

"I'm glad she spoke with you. I hope you consider the opportunity. So aside from yoga... what are you doing in this area?" I ask her, my brow lowering in question. Taking a quick look around the room, I notice peeling paint, scuff marks on the walls, and a broken window at the back taped up with thick black electrical tape. It is a dump in need of urgent repair.

"I live here," she states, and I watch as her arms cross against her chest.

"But you work in DC?" I ask, tilting my head in confusion, keeping my hands in my pockets so I don't do something stupid, like touch her.

"Yes, I commute."

"From here? That must take hours in the traffic. Why don't you move closer to the city?" I ask in surprise. *Is she mad?* That commute would be horrendous during peak times.

"Did you get your shirt?" she asks me, tactfully changing the topic.

"Yes. Thank you. I appreciate the swiftness of the dry cleaning. I had it the next day. Very professional." She smiles at the compliment, her defensive body language relaxing slightly.

"Harrison, we need you out front," Oscar interrupts as he pokes his head back into the room, and I nod to him.

"You're announcing it right now? At the center?" Beth

asks, her eyes wide, obviously just putting two and two together, looking at me as though I am crazy.

"Harrison," Oscar says impatiently, stepping farther into the room again, his tone not leaving me any chance to argue. My eyes remain on him for a beat, giving him a silent look to leave and he takes the hint, albeit with a sigh of frustration.

"So are you coming out with me? I could use the support. You're my lucky charm after all." I'm feeling greedy, my smile growing, already wanting her nearby for what is without a doubt one of the most important days of my life.

"Your what?" she questions, her eyes squinting up at me.

"My lucky charm. You saved me from a long night with my mother a year ago when those drinks spilled on my shoes. Last week, you saved me from an uncomfortable face-off with my soon-to-be opponent at the luncheon. That's twice you have saved me, so I am calling it lucky," I state, firm in my assessment. The vision in my memory of that night over a year ago is now brightly lit. I was hating every moment of being at that event and Beth gave me the perfect opportunity to escape.

"I am not lucky, and I can't go out dressed like this." Her arms spread wide, looking herself up and down.

"You look beautiful to me," I murmur, just loud enough for her to hear, and I let my eyes sweep down her body and back up again, clear for her to see, committing her to memory. I watch her blush once more, and it's becoming my favorite sight. She's cute when she's flustered.

"Harrison! We need you out front!" Oscar says again from the doorway, his voice now strained, not happy whatsoever that I am taking my time. He is stealthy, because I didn't even hear him come back in.

"Shall we?" I ask her, sweeping my hand to the side toward the door.

"So chivalrous, Mr. Governor," she says with a lift of her brow before strutting past me and straight out the door.

"You have no idea..." I murmur again before following her out of the room and walking toward the media pit outside.

It is frantic, with journalists and cameras everywhere. As Oscar and Eddie try to get a handle on things, I stand waiting for everyone to calm down. It takes a moment until I hear a sigh behind me and my redhead steps forward.

"Okay, everyone, take your spots. It is about to start, and I need you in your final positions," Beth yells to the crowd of reporters, her hands on her hips. My eyebrows raise at her take-charge attitude. I like it.

The media scrum listens immediately, all shuffling into position, getting ready, and my eyes rest on her again. *She is good.* I see Oscar scowling, which is in contrast to Eddie's smirk, my own thoughts now running a million miles a minute in a direction they really shouldn't be.

"Hey, Red, what are you doing out here?" one of the photographers says to her, and I watch with interest as it appears she knows a few of them.

"Hi, Max. Someone has to keep you all under control.

Are you ready?" she sasses them, and everyone stands still, looking directly at me.

"The floor is yours, Mr. Langford," Beth says, then she retreats behind me to join her yoga classmates and watch the proceedings. I smile at her. A genuine, beaming smile that shows just how impressed I am by her. Stepping forward, flashes of cameras go off in my face, just before microphones and a myriad of cell phones are shoved under my chin.

"Thank you, everyone, for being here. I am at the Riverside Community Center this morning to officially announce my run for governor of Maryland," I begin the practiced speech, keeping my shoulders back and my head high.

"I have been working toward this for my entire life. Even as a kid, I dreamed of leading this state. I want to serve the community, building the state to become one of the most fiscally sound in the country, ensuring that our communities are invested in, and bringing jobs and new infrastructure projects to the doors of many, including everyone here in Riverside. I want to thank Mayor Rogers for being here this morning and for all the amazing work he and his colleagues will do with me if I am elected."

I nod my thanks to the mayor and he replies in kind as my eyes roam the sea of reporters. I force my head to stay forward, needing to make a conscious effort not to look at the side, where I know Beth is standing.

"So along with my announcement this morning, I would also like to provide you with an introduction to one of our key promises that I will deliver if elected. Here in Riverside, we will be investing over fifteen million dollars into new infrastructure for residential and commercial purposes, creating jobs, economic stimulus, and breathing new life into the community. Starting right here at 45 Starling Street, we will redevelop this state-owned land to bring in new investors, increase the flow of money into the state, and provide a better lifestyle for everyone here."

Cameras continue flashing, capturing this moment, and there are murmurs from the media pack, along with a big smile on the mayor's face.

"I want to thank everyone who has supported me and continues to support me in making Maryland the best state in the country and, of course, I want to make a special mention to my team and my family for all their continued support. I will now take questions."

People shuffle before me as I point to one of the media scrum to take their question.

I skillfully answer the questions thrown at me, being as honest and open as I can, before Oscar calls a close to the press conference and we walk back inside.

"Great job. Well handled. We are now off and racing," Oscar says with a rare smile as he smacks my back like a proud father.

"Where's Eddie?" I ask as my eyes roam the people, and I shake hands with a few.

"Over talking with the people from the center," Oscar murmurs, his head buried in his phone.

I look over at the small crowd of people and see Eddie talking with Beth and my shoulders tense as an unfamiliar feeling starts to swirl in my stomach. I don't like the way he is looking at her. She is still in her yoga gear and the need I have to take my jacket off and put it around her shoulders to cover her up runs strong.

My younger brother makes friends wherever he goes, including this community center, it appears. He has a smile that makes most women swoon, but right now, my redhead looks like she is ready to punch him in the face. I walk over, wanting to talk with her again and see what is going on.

As I approach, she sees me and her body swivels toward me. My step almost falters as her eyes find mine.

"You cannot be serious!" Beth says to me, fire in her tone, her hands flapping around and her forehead crinkled.

"About what exactly?" I ask her, my eyes sweeping to my brother, trying to get an indication of what the hell is going on. He offers me nothing.

"You are going to demolish the center?" Beth questions in a high pitch as her hands find her hips, and I am glad most of the media scrum has gone. I grab her elbow, relieved to actually have my hands on her, and pull her over to the side of the room for more privacy.

"We will be redeveloping it. Expanding it. Making it into residential homes as well," I clarify. This is an issue that Eddie already raised when Oscar made the proposal of investing in redevelopment of this site.

"But that will take years," she says, not backing down, and I welcome the challenge. No one ever challenges me —not ever in public, anyway—and I see my brother's eyes widen.

"I can assure you, Beth, that—" She doesn't let me finish.

"If you can promise us all an alternative place to enjoy our community while the redevelopment is happening, then that would go a long way to appeasing the locals, Mr. Langford." I look behind her and see the small crowd she has in support all nodding and murmuring in response.

I smile, impressed with her enthusiasm. "We will ensure you have full amenities during the redevelopment." I notice her eyes flick to my mouth, taking in my grin, and she bites her lip in frustration.

"It has to be close to transport," she continues, her eyebrows rising in challenge, not backing down and pushing me for everything she can. I appreciate her standing her ground. She knows what she wants and is going for it.

"We can ensure that is the case." I try to remain professional, even though I smile wider.

"And accessibility for everyone." My eyes flick down to follow her gaze, toward a man in a wheelchair among the gathering small crowd behind her.

"I am sure that can be arranged as well. Anything else?"

"We all want a say in the redesign. We use the facilities, so we want a chance to make them suitable to our needs." Her demands nearly knock me over. She is cunning, smart, well spoken, and just what I need in my corner. She is a mix of Oscar and Eddie as well as someone with great contacts and project management experience.

I want her. On my team and in my bed.

I think about my next move carefully. I have already

offered her a job, but she hasn't accepted it as of yet. But there is no way I am leaving here without a yes.

"Fine. On one condition," I say to her, my eyes piercing hers, and her gaze doesn't waver.

"What is that?" she asks, her eyes narrowing, probably already knowing what I am going to say.

"You come and work with me."

7

BETH

What? What the hell did he just say?

I squirm a little because I can feel my father's eyes boring into the back of my head from where he is situated behind me. Guilt for not telling him earlier swirls in my stomach, making me clench it a little. I don't like keeping things from him, but I needed time to think about it all myself. I guess this is politics, though. Never a dull moment and everything moving at a rapid pace.

"Three months, Beth. Give me three months," Harrison says to me quietly as he steps closer. This is now the second time our bodies have been this close. Like magnets, the pull between us is starting to get stronger.

His scent envelops me, taking me down a whirlpool of rainforest and fresh summer breeze. *Why does it relax me so much?* With us being so close, it borders on unprofessional, and I wonder if he has lost his mind while my heart does a weird flip-flop movement that startles me.

Heat pours from his gaze as it settles on me. I watch as

his eyes flick down to my lips, and my tongue comes out, sweeping across my lower lip involuntarily, a movement that makes his nostrils flair, before his eyes meet mine again.

There is lust in his gaze. The way he is looking at me in this moment, I feel every inch of my female instincts pinging my skin, telling me that Harrison Langford is drinking me in. I'm not sure why, since I am not the kind of girl that men usually gaze at. Especially a man like Harrison. I find it confusing that he would have that type of reaction to a suburban girl like me. But my skin heats all the same, and my heart starts racing, my head saying one thing, and my body saying something entirely different.

"Why?" I ask him, challenging him some more. I still can't believe this is a serious offer. I want to know why someone like Harrison Langford would want someone like me working with him. I'm just an event planner. I'm a nobody.

He positions his body even closer, shielding me from everyone and everything around us so all I can see is him. I look up to meet his eyes, my hands remaining by my sides, my nails pinching into my palms. I'm too scared to move them in case they land on his chest, where I know I will find euphoria in his sculpted muscles. The very same muscles I have dreamed about ever since I saw them in the event closet last week.

"Because you are not afraid to speak your mind. You are immensely organized, seemingly prepared for anything. You are empathetic, yet firm and supportive. Plus, you already know the who's who of DC, and I really need someone like you in my corner," he states without missing a beat.

Boy, he is good. No wonder all the women swoon at his feet. I already want to give him my vote as well as my underwear.

The compliment is not something I was expecting, nor prepared for. It makes me feel seen. Like he is looking right into who I am.

I wring my hands together, suddenly feeling a little vulnerable, yet somehow entirely comfortable around this man. A throat clearing has both Harrison and me whipping our heads toward the noise. Harrison's hand comes to my waist instinctively, catching us both off guard. I swallow roughly, the humming feeling in my body way too new to comprehend.

"Beth, you can't work with Mr. Langford; the hours would be ridiculous," Jeff says flippantly, and my teeth grind together. I hate people talking for me. It makes me feel like he is undermining me. Like I am a child incapable of making my own decisions. Taking away my voice.

Then I look at where he is resting his hand on Dad's wheelchair and understanding washes over me. Jeff is right. No matter if we need the money, the hours a campaign like Harrison's would demand will be too much. The days would be long, and with no time off. My dad can't look after himself, so I need to be there.

Though, the money would be great... I might even be able to start putting some away into savings instead of living from paycheck to paycheck.

Looking at Dad, I see his shoulders already reaching

his ears. His neck is red, and he is grinding his teeth so hard I internally scream for him to stop because we can't afford to see a dentist right now. He is not happy.

"You don't have to worry about anything here, sugar," Marci says quickly, standing next to Dad, her hand possessively on his other wheelchair handle, making it clear that she will look after him and that has sparked my interest. I wonder if she and Dad do have something going on that I don't know about.

"Enough!" my dad barks, and I jump at his tone. Harrison's hand flexes on my waist, and he pulls me to him, offering me support. His body is already seemingly in tune with mine. Given the nervous energy running off me right now, it isn't surprising.

"Mr. Langford, my daughter is very talented and would be an excellent team member. So, Beth, if this is something you want to do, then do it. We'll work it out. As for the rest of you, stay out of Beth's business," Dad says before wheeling away, leaving us all looking after him.

My heart breaks a little, feeling his frustrations. He hates people speaking for him too. Just because his legs don't work like they should, that doesn't mean he is incapable of making decisions. Everyone here knows that, but some people seem to forget sometimes.

Looking back at Harrison, my eyes feel heavy with unshed tears, already knowing that the guilt of not being with Dad each day will be enough to kill any positives that the extra money can bring. We will make do. We always do.

"I'm sorry, I have to go," I say quietly, as Harrison

looks at me with what I think is concern. He goes to say something else, but I step away, out of his grasp, and follow my dad to the back of the center.

I push through the door and take a deep breath to gather my thoughts. The sun hits my face, and I pause for a moment. There is a lot to take in. I need sleep; I need to process; I need money.

"Dad?" I walk through the community garden and spot him digging around in the vegetable patch.

"Beth, don't listen to anyone. That is a good job. An asshole of a boss, no doubt, but a good job."

"But I won't be around much. Jeff is right; it will be a lot of hours," I say, confusion at what I should do eating my insides. My mind is working in overdrive, trying to weigh the pros and cons.

"You work a lot anyway. This won't be too different," he says, giving me a small but exhausted smile, and I look at him for a second, wondering if he is always this pale.

"Dad, are you sure you are okay?" I ask, reaching my hand out and resting it on his shoulder.

"Don't worry about me, honey. I am fine." He pats my hand, and it comforts me just the slightest bit.

"I don't want to interrupt the moment, but I need to go," Harrison says from behind us, and I see Dad stiffen. I turn and see Harrison standing there, tall and strong next to his brother, Eddie, whom I was talking to earlier. His eyes still look at me with concern, but he remains where he is, not coming any closer.

"Three months. I will double the wage you receive from Kelly's Agency. I will provide a town car to take you to and from home to lessen your commute. Additional medical and well-being benefits to support your care-taking needs." Harrison's eyes flick from me to Dad and back again. I need to grip on to Dad's chair because I almost fall over. Double my wage? The money alone would be enough, but a car at my beck and call and additional benefits... Now I am wondering if there is a catch.

"I can also confirm he is an asshole of a boss," Eddie says from beside him and his comment breaks the tension. I bite my lower lip so I don't laugh out loud. I watch as Harrison gives him a look that would tumble any grown man, but Eddie just shrugs.

"I'm joking!" he mumbles to Harrison. "I'm joking. He is great." He shoots me a playful wink, and I see Harrison shake his head and rub his eyes before he looks back at me, giving me a small smile. Stupidly, I melt a little.

"So, are you with me, Beth? We would make a good team." Harrison asks, his expression hopeful.

I hold my breath and meet his stare. His eyes search mine, and it is like he is looking into my soul. I can feel the energy hum between us, even from this distance, my traitorous heart beating even louder than before. I have no idea if it is the right thing or not, but in this moment, with our eyes locked, I say the only word I want to say to him.

"Yes."

8

HARRISON

"Have you totally lost your mind?" Oscar seethes now that we're in the car on our way back to my city office.

Perhaps I have. I offered her a bigger salary and more benefits than I have ever offered anyone else. I was so unsure of what her answer was going to be, I threw everything I could at her, desperately wanting her to say yes. When she walked away from me, I thought I had lost her. I couldn't help but follow her outside, my body on autopilot. When I saw her talking with her dad, the pull I had for her only grew stronger. It is something I haven't felt before. Yet it is there, so much so, I rub my chest a little from where I sit, wondering if, as Oscar said, I have lost my mind.

"I cannot wait to see the look on Mom's face when you tell her you have hired your own event planner!" Eddie says, gleaming.

"Project manager. She will oversee the events, but that won't be all she does," I growl, as I think of the beautiful redhead who seems to look after everyone but herself.

I offered her a job that anyone would jump at, and she was willing to reject it based on the feelings and thoughts of others. Only now am I starting to think how hard it is going to be to work with her twenty-four seven for the next few months. How looking at her beautiful body in my office every day is going to be one of my biggest challenges yet.

I am a go-getter, a high achiever. Whatever I want, I strive for it, including this governorship. I am beyond dedicated, but the laser-like vision I had on the role has now widened, encompassing Beth as well. I'll need to try harder at pushing her out of my mind, while also keeping her close so she can bring her full self to the team.

I want all of her—her passion, her professionalism—but I just need to ensure I don't touch her as the governorship will depend on it.

"What exactly are you going to have her do?" Oscar asks, still bewildered by my decision to hire Beth.

"Did you not see how well she handled the media scrum this morning?" I ask, pointing to the fact that she did a better job than he did. Oscar swallows, but remains quiet.

"She will be my right hand in addition to you. She will manage my events and appearances, work with you on my appointments and meetings. Take charge of the media. You will maintain your focus on the campaign, speech notes, and tell me where I need to be. Between you and Beth, I will be a well-oiled machine."

"Something will be well oiled," Eddie murmurs, and I

look at him sharply. Eddie is great fun, and our love runs deep, but he is still young, now only just getting a handle on working in such a professional environment. His cheap shots at me are something he needs to reserve for home life, rather than in the car with Oscar nearby.

"What? You were like Tarzan who had just found Jane. You went all protective of her even after she challenged you. She is not scared of you. I like her. *A lot.*"

"Eddie!" I growl at him again. A weird feeling of heat sprinkles up my spine. I don't want him to like her. I don't want any other man to even look at her. The fact that every fucking male within a hundred-yard radius seems to home in on her makes my blood boil just thinking about it. I pull at my collar. I need to get these intense feelings I have under control. It is ridiculous.

"I still don't think we need her. We have people to handle those responsibilities already," Oscar says again, but I am not changing my mind.

"She is a great addition, but remember she is only on secondment, so she can walk at any time. I want you both to make her feel welcome, show her the ropes, get her settled in quickly. She will have good thoughts on what the people want, great ideas on our events and appearances, and may even whip you both into shape," I snap, sick of having to defend a decision I made for my own fucking campaign.

"I will organize her car and driver and send over a laptop and phone tonight. Then I will get her to come in tomorrow for the event overview with Mom and Lilly," Eddie says, pulling out his phone, already getting to work.

Oscar sits quietly, looking at me.

"What?" I bark at him, wishing he would spit it out already.

"You told me that you don't need distractions..." he says in a final warning.

"Beth is not a distraction."

"Are you sure about that?" he smarts back, and I look at him, but don't answer. My silence is enough to tell him exactly what he already knows.

"You made your announcement this morning!" my mother shrieks as I step into my office after our drive back from Riverside.

"Yes," I state simply, trying not to groan at her tone, heading for my desk. Oscar and Eddie follow me in, and I wonder why both she and Lilly are sitting at my office conference table with swatches of colored fabric draped everywhere.

"But we have our event in a week! I have it all planned!" she continues to scold me, waving her arms around everywhere, the rows of gold and diamond bracelets on her wrist jingling as she does. Lilly sits nervously next to her, watching the interaction. Probably trying to assess what it means for her wardrobe selection. I stop abruptly as I get to my desk and look at them both.

"It is my campaign. I will run it how I see fit. We will still have the party, but the announcement has now been made," I tell them, leaving no room for questions. I'm still feeling wound up from Oscar's interrogation in the car.

"You should see the new girl he just hired!" Eddie says gleefully as he flops down on the small sofa near my bookcase, a big shit-eating grin on his face.

"You hired who?" My mother's voice rises, and I would imagine her eyebrows shooting to her hairline, but her forehead is frozen solid. It hasn't moved in years.

"Beth Longmere, from DC Events. She is professional and extremely passionate about her community," I say as I walk around, removing pieces of cloth from my desk and throwing them on the table in front of her. What the hell possessed my mother and Lilly to claim my office as their own?

We have about sixty other offices in this very building. Our family law firm, of which I am currently CEO, sits in the upper levels of this high-rise, our property and construction business just below. My brothers and I all have city penthouses on the top four floors, yet for some reason, my mother took it upon herself to command my office.

"Longmere..." my mother ponders. "I've never heard of them. What have you hired her for?" Her voice rises another octave, and as much as I love her, I'm becoming more and more frustrated by the fact that she continues to question my choices and appears to want to make them for me. I see Eddie smile as he watches, but Oscar, on the other hand, sighs and rubs his head like he is in pain.

"She is going to be working with Oscar and Eddie. She brings the best of both of them, and I think she will make a good member of my team," I state firmly, daring her to push me further.

Mom looks over at Oscar, and he shrugs. Her lips thin.

"Well, I am sure you know what you are doing, dear," she says in her condescending tone, and I grind my teeth together, then flash her my biggest, most charming smile.

When Dad died, she became a shell of herself before reinventing her life as a rich socialite only interested in climbing the social status ladder. She leaned on me the most, and I was always there for her, helping her with her business affairs in Dad's absence. But lately, her role in my life has become all-encompassing, and she needs to take a step back.

"Good. Now why are you in my office?" I ask, folding my arms across my chest as I look between her and Lilly.

"Well, I just wanted to get your thoughts on the color palette. I want to ensure that we match. I want my dress to be perfect," Lilly answers, giving me a smile, clearly clutching at anything to ensure she is the belle of my ball. It is my turn to sigh. My eyes flick to my mother again as I try not to let anger be the emotion that is about to pour out of me. Luckily, Eddie saves me.

"I have scheduled a briefing meeting tomorrow, so why don't we go through all the party planning then? Beth will be here, so it will be good to get her up to speed," Eddie says, sitting forward. I nod. It is the smartest thing he has said all day.

"Fine," my mother says, pursing her lips. "We will get out of your way and have everything prepared for tomorrow." And with that, the two women grab their samples and their matching designer handbags and walk out the door. No doubt to go somewhere nice for a long lunch.

"Well, that was entertaining. I am going to set up an office for Beth to use while she is here," Eddie says as he jumps off the sofa and walks to the door.

"Where are you putting her?" I ask him.

He stops and looks at me, his eyebrow slightly raised. I never care where my staff sit, only about their outcomes, so my question has obviously intrigued him.

"There is a spare office next to mine," he offers, by way of suggestion, shrugging his shoulders.

"Put her in Mindy's office," I murmur to him. My assistant, Mindy, left a week ago to travel the world. I have been using the other administrators on the floor to help me with my admin while HR finds a replacement. I watch as both his eyebrows shoot up and a small smile curves onto his face.

"You sure? That is right next door to you. She won't be a... distraction?" he asks sarcastically, quickly looking at Oscar to see if his statement elicits a response. It doesn't.

I nod, which Eddie returns, before he opens the door and walks out, leaving me alone with Oscar.

"I know you don't see my point of view on this, but I need you to trust me and to trust Beth. Give her the courtesy of your time and patience," I state, looking at him.

"Of course." Oscar nods and sits forward, clearly unimpressed, but knowing his place and picking his battles.

"Great. Now, what's next?" I ask, relaxing behind my desk and looking through the messages that I have from this morning.

"We need to talk about your speech for the event your

mother is planning, as well as go through the plans for our scheduled visits early next week."

"Okay, first let's look at what the next week has in store for us, as that may influence some of what we say in the speech. Where are we going?"

"We are going to an elementary school where we will discuss educational requirements for the county. We have an afternoon with our funders, and then I am trying to set up a briefing with the police, going through the statistics around Maryland's crime rate and hot spots and so forth," Oscar says as he looks over his calendar.

This is what he does best. He knows what industries and sectors we need to be in and when. He knows who I need to talk with and what the key topics are. If he sticks to this, Beth can assist me with the logistical elements and the media and support Eddie with community relations.

It will be perfect.

As perfect as her ass in those fucking yoga pants this morning.

9

BETH

After a brand-new phone and laptop arrived at my house last night, along with a full schedule for the rest of this week, I knew I had to put on my armor today. My long bright-red hair is blow-dried and styled. I've done my makeup softly with precision, and I am wearing the best suit I have—albeit, one I grabbed from the bargain bin at the thrift store a few months ago. But it is a brand name, even though it is a few seasons old.

To say that Kelly was supportive of my three-month secondment was an understatement. Apparently, on top of doubling my wage, Harrison also offered Kelly a secondment bonus of her own, in appreciation for loaning him my services. It appears that everyone wins, even though I still have no idea what I am in for.

But I know I deserve to be here. Working on a political campaign was never something I imagined doing; it wasn't my dream to be building a man up to lead the state, but I always wanted to give back to my community.

The same community that rallied around my father and me for most of our lives. I am good at my job, and I am going to take every opportunity presented to me, not just for the paycheck, but to give back, regardless of the nagging voice in my head that continues to tell me I am not good enough.

As the elevator opens to the thirty-fifth floor, I am hit with bright lights that shimmer off glass walls so clean that my reflection is sparkling, and my nerves creep back in. I don't belong here. Everything is so nice, clean, and expensive. My eyes search the beautiful foyer, trying to notice anything out of place, but I come up empty. It is perfect. The only thing out of place is me.

"You're here!" a chirpy male voice says from the side, and I turn to see Eddie, whom I chatted with briefly yesterday.

"Good morning," I greet and put out my hand to shake, just as he thrusts his forward, handing me a hot coffee. As our hands collide, the coffee flies out of his hand and off to the side, smacking against the bright-white wall, the cup breaking on impact. The porcelain shatters into a million tiny white pieces as black liquid splatters against the wall, staining the white paint. It would look like a crime scene if it was red.

"Oh my gosh, I am so sorry!" I gasp, internally cringing. I could not keep it together for more than five minutes... seriously? They will fire me before lunchtime, I am sure. I step forward and begin to squat down, attempting to pick up the porcelain pieces from the ground.

"No. Don't worry about it. Sandra, call the cleaning

crew to get this sorted, please," Eddie says, looking around at the woman standing near reception who nods while she takes a call.

"It is fine. I don't want you cutting yourself or anything," he assures me with a smile. "Great to have you here! I did wonder if you would show up this morning, actually." It appears that the charming gene runs in the family. He is broad and confident, just like Harrison, but more relaxed, almost jovial. And, of course, he's good-looking too, although not as handsome as I find his older brother.

"Oh, really? Why is that?" I ask, shaking his hand, trying to act professional and feeling anything but as I side-eye the mess I created. The impact of the coffee on the wall is a very real reminder to me that this is not a world where I belong.

"Harrison is my brother and I love him, but when he sees something or *someone* he wants, he goes for it. I know this is all probably a bit sudden and new for you, that's all."

"I look forward to the challenge," I say, ignoring his reference to Harrison wanting *me*, and grip my handbag a little tighter, my nerves already out of control. I need to try to stay focused. I need my mind on the job, not on the man whose face still features in my daydreams.

"Great! Sandra. This is Beth, Harrison's new project manager. Beth, Sandra works here as part of our admin team. She is a tough cookie; nothing gets past her." Eddie winks at her while making the introductions, and I smile at the casual nature. The older woman greets me with a big smile, while juggling a phone call and signing for a courier who just walked in.

"Great to meet you, Beth. Eddie, I will call the cleaning crew to sort that out. You two better get moving. I know you have a busy schedule today," Sandra says with a smile, and my tense shoulders relax a bit.

"Right, let's get started, shall we," Eddie says with a flick of his head, and I follow him down a hall.

We pass a few offices, all with fantastic views. The office space is huge, taking up the entire floor, with floor-to-ceiling windows in every office we pass.

"This is my office here. Oscar Barone, our campaign manager, is right here next to me, and the staff amenities are farther down that way." I eagerly look around as he gives me the tour, and my eyes widen as I take in the cleanliness and luxury of it all. I have visited a few city offices in DC, many well-established ones, but I don't venture into Baltimore much. This office is new, state-of-the-art, and without a chair out of place.

"So you work with Harrison too?" I ask as we take a turn and walk down a hallway that is a little quieter. I try to take some deep breaths to steady my nerves, the mere mention of his name making my palms sweaty.

"For the moment. I just got back from traveling around Asia, so I said I would help him out for a few months before I take over our real estate portfolio."

"Oh. That's great." I try to sound enthusiastic at their lifestyle. I can barely afford the rent on our two-bedroom cottage, which is crumbling down around us. A real estate portfolio is something I have no concept of at all.

"Well, I am lucky. My family has a few businesses,

and I had a lot of benefits growing up," Eddie says and then stops walking and looks at me. "We are privileged. We know that. Harrison, my brothers, and me. But we also work hard and try to give back where we can." He is serious for a moment, and I stay silent, but nod. It is good that they can at least acknowledge it.

"Well, we're here!" he says as he opens an office door, and we step inside. It is not dissimilar to his office down the hall, this one with great city views and a small sofa along the wall. A large desk sits in the center and one wall of the office is a full double sliding door that opens into another large office.

"Wow, this is great!" My eyes hurry to take it all in. It is different from DC Events, where I have the privilege of working in a large open-plan workplace. It feels nice to have my own office.

"This will be all yours to use when you need to, for the next three months. Feel free to make it your own. Mindy, Harrison's assistant, is taking an extended break overseas, so she normally sits in here, but it is now all yours," Eddie continues as I take a few tentative steps to the desk, reaching out and skimming the light wood, feeling the silky varnished surface under my fingertips.

"You have direct access to Harrison, his office being the one through there," he continues, pointing to the huge office that I can see through the open double doors. It is currently empty, but there is a clear line of sight of his desk from mine.

I try to swallow, even though my mouth is suddenly very dry, and I brush the hair out of my face and begin to fidget. The nerves that had started to dissipate from before are now back in full force. How am I meant to work for the man when all I have been dreaming about is his hand on my waist, the desire in his eyes, or his rock-hard abs? It is something I haven't reconciled yet. But I am many things, and a professional is one of them. Besides, they are stupid dreams that will never be my reality, so I pull my shoulders back and force myself into work mode.

"Oh, here you are, Eddie." A man walks in, dressed in a black suit, a stack of paperwork in his hands.

"Hi, Beth, I'm Oscar, Harrison's campaign manager. We didn't get to meet formally yesterday," he says, extending his hand, and I take it in greeting.

"Great, now you're here, let's start the briefing!" Eddie says as he takes a seat in an armchair in my office and pulls his laptop out, getting down to work.

"Of course. Great," I say, remembering that this was my first appointment on my schedule today. Oscar takes a seat in the armchair next to Eddie, and I position myself at my desk, opposite them. Grabbing a pen and my notepad, I start to settle in. There is nothing like hitting the ground running.

Oscar kicks off the meeting by going through Harrison's key talking points, upcoming speeches, and what areas are no-go areas that we need to stay clear of. There is nothing too out of the ordinary, so I pick it all up quickly.

"Harrison will be giving a speech next weekend at the party," he says, handing over a copy of the speech that he has already prepared.

"This is draft one. There will be a lot of changes

between now and then, but it gives you an overview of the key points he will be making on the night, in case you have any ideas or issues."

"So what is the party again?" I ask, my eyes already scanning the schedule for this month, trying to work it out. I did see an event next Saturday, but since I wasn't sure if I was to attend, I paid little attention.

"Our mother has organized a party to kick off the campaign. We have a briefing with her and Lillian Harper today. There will be a lot of key people in the room, our funders, key businesspeople and the like, but also friends and family," Eddie replies, jumping into the conversation.

"Oh. Great!" I say, faking a bright smile while mentally wondering what the hell I am supposed to wear. While I do have some nice work outfits, I have only one formal dress, and I am not sure that will zip up anymore. It has been a few years since I wore it last, and my love for chocolate ice cream runs deep.

"Okay, so I am familiar with Mrs. Langford; I have done an event for her in the past, but who is Lillian?" I ask, looking at both Eddie and Oscar, trying to understand all the players.

"Lillian Harper. She is the daughter of Ronald Harper, one of our biggest funders," Oscar explains.

"Ronald was good friends with my father back in the day. Our families have been close for years," Eddie adds, and I make some notes. I haven't met Lillian Harper before, but I have heard her name. She is a socialite, I think, so it makes sense that she is close to the richest family in Baltimore.

We talk some more before there is a knock at the door, and Sandra walks in with some lunch.

"I saw you guys were busy, so I organized a working lunch for you," she says as she places a tray of sandwiches down on the table next to the small sofa before retreating just as quickly.

"Brilliant! I'm starving," Eddie says, jumping up and grabbing one.

Sandra rolls her eyes, closing the door behind her, and that's how my afternoon continues. Eating sandwiches with Oscar and Eddie, going through the key talking points of the campaign, and an overview of Harrison's opponents. Within a few hours, I feel like I have been here for a decade and am well versed in the basics of Harrison's campaign strategy.

We are mid-laugh about something Eddie is doing when I feel him. Harrison walks into his office, and my eyes wash over his form, beyond my control. His arms are firm in his well-fitted navy suit, and his perfectly styled hair and shiny black shoes finish off his luxury look, even though his face is in deep concentration as he talks into his cell at his ear.

But it is his presence that captures me. That sure and steady stance. He doesn't even have to open his mouth for people to find him dependable. Solid. Someone they can count on. Something that I crave. He lifts his head, and his eyes meet mine immediately, and I feel the heat flood my cheeks.

"Great. Thanks. Talk later," he says, his eyes still on mine as he pulls the phone down, putting it in his pocket and walking in our direction. His eyes haven't wavered, remaining on me until he reaches the doorway and sees both Eddie and Oscar sitting across from me.

"How's day one?" he asks, his mouth turning upward slightly at the corners, and my throat dries up immediately. Damn, he looks good with a smile.

"Great!" I say too quickly. I need to take a steadying breath. *Pull yourself together, woman!*

"We have gone over everything, and she is up to speed on our key points so far," Oscar reports to him as both he and Eddie stand. But Harrison merely nods in their direction, his eyes still on me.

"I'm great, bro, thanks for asking. We will wait outside for you both," Eddie pipes up sarcastically and both Harrison and I watch as he and Oscar walk out of the office, the door closing slowly behind them.

"I knew you would have it all in hand right from the start," he murmurs, taking a few more steps in my direction. I stand up then and straighten my dress, trying to get my nerves in check.

"You seem so assured of my abilities, Mr. Langford." Where does he get this confidence in me?

"I know good people when I see them, and you, Beth, are one of the best," he says, coming to stop right in front of me. We are not touching, yet I can feel his body next to mine. I grip the desk subtly before I lose my footing.

"Is assessing people a skill you have picked up recently, or something you have honed for years?" My voice almost betrays my nerves. He smiles as he looks down at me.

"Believe me when I tell you, I had to work through

the weeds in order to get to the flower..." he says, his eyes remaining on mine, and I watch him swallow.

"Speaking of weeds, we are meeting my mother at two p.m. Are you ready?" Clearing his throat, he takes a step back, giving us some space, the two of us now out of our trance.

"Yes, of course," I say, smiling. My nerves have all gone and been replaced by a feeling I remember having back in school, whenever the good-looking, popular guy would look my way. The one that was way out of my league, and even though my heart races and my palms sweat, romanticizing being with a man like Harrison is just asking for trouble. I shake my head, pick up my cell and notepad, and follow everyone out the door.

It is only halfway through day one and I am already losing my thoughts, something that I need to reel in. I am good at my job; that is why he hired me, so I need to wipe any swoony notions I have of Harrison from my mind.

I am here for three months to support his campaign, give back to the community, and to make enough money to keep Dad and me afloat for a while. Nothing more, nothing less.

10

HARRISON

O scar was right. She has been here for half a day, and I have only seen her for merely five minutes, and I already know she is going to be exactly what he said. A distraction. Dressed impeccably, her long hair is loose, flowing down her back, and as she walks in front of me to the conference room, I can smell her rose scent waft over me and I want to drown in it.

I clear my throat and flick through my emails on my phone, doing anything I can not to stare at her round ass or think of the ways I want to undress her and discover what lies beneath her attire.

My smile may be charming, but my thoughts are filthy.

Pushing through the door of the conference room, I notice my mother and Lilly are already here, sitting at the table next to each other in matching Chanel suits. I silently groan. They have colored fabric swatches again, a flower arrangement on the table, and their designer handbags perched on the seats next to them. Eddie rolls his eyes, Oscar sighs, and Beth gives them both a small smile before introducing herself.

"Great to see you again, Mrs. Langford. I'm Beth. I managed the charity function you held in DC a little while ago." Her voice is strong, confident, and I feel the stress of the day already dissipating from my shoulders just from her tone. I relax knowing she is in charge of things, already holding her own in front of my mother. I wish I could say the same for some of my other staff members, all of whom usually walk the other way when they see her coming.

My trust in Beth comes easily. It throws me for a bit because I don't trust a lot of people. Not since my father made a fool of us all. I take my seat across from my mother, as I see Beth stretch out her hand to her. My mother doesn't move an inch and looks at her like she is diseased, and I grind my teeth together.

My mother wasn't always the sour woman she has become. Before Dad died, she was the life of the party. Loved everyone and everything. But when he died of a heart attack a few years ago, the news got out pretty quickly about exactly how many women he had affairs with, and she plunged into a dark pit of hatred for any woman not on her best friends list. Unfortunately for Beth, she hasn't made that list yet.

"Oh, really? I can't recall," she says in her condescending tone, waving her off like she is already bored. I watch as Beth's smile doesn't waver, but I see the hurt in her eyes.

"This is Lilly," Eddie says, making the introductions,

and Lilly stays quiet, but shakes Beth's hand half-heartedly. But I am impressed, because despite the cool reception, Beth remains professional, giving Lilly a big smile before taking her seat next to me, opposite them. Eddie sits on the other side of her, both of us obviously aware we need to guard her against the onslaught that our mother will no doubt throw today.

"Let's start. Mom, give us an overview." She eyes me suspiciously before she starts telling us all about the event she has planned.

I sit back and listen to my mother talk through the logistics of the event, informing everyone about the venue, music, and catering, none of which I care too much for. I am here just to discuss the guest list. As she talks, Lilly is acting like her assistant, showcasing the various imagery and color palette. I have no idea what the hell is going on and why the two of them feel inclined to be so involved in my campaign, but I assume it is good for their image. I promised Mom this one event, and that is it, so I grin and bear it, knowing it will all be over by next weekend and she can go back to long lunches at the country club or shopping and spending Dad's millions.

As my mother drones on about steak or seafood, my nose starts to tickle, and I rub my eyes as they water. I grab my handkerchief just as I sneeze three times in quick succession.

"Seriously, Harrison, what has gotten into you?" My mother's voice irritates my spine, and I sit up to answer her, but before I can, Beth pipes up.

"It's the flowers," she says, not looking at anyone and making notes on her notepad.

"Excuse me?" my mother questions, rearing back like she has been slapped.

Beth stops what she is writing and looks up. Noticing that all eyes are on her, she continues.

"It's the flower arrangement. You have baby's breath in the arrangement, and it causes rhinitis. It is a flower often used by florists as a filler in arrangements like this one, but they give off a strong aroma, which can trigger the onslaught of allergies, even if you have never had allergies before. They are a beautiful flower, but for something so small, they really pack a punch. I steer clear of using them at events; otherwise, the whole room will walk out within an hour," she states, and we all look at her with a bit of shock.

As if to back up her point, Eddie then starts to sneeze, and I see Oscar brushing his nose. I push the intercom for Sandra.

"Sandra, come in and get rid of these flowers, please." I'm not sure how much longer I can stand to be in the same room as them.

"But these are the arrangements I have ordered!" my mother says, bewildered.

"Oh, the florist should be okay to tighten up the bouquet and just remove the baby's breath. It won't be a large change for them," Beth says, answering my mother's concern.

"How do you know so much about flowers?" Lilly asks Beth in a tone I do not like, as Sandra walks in and grabs the vase silently before walking out with them.

"Oh, I love flowers," Beth says, smiling, and Lilly gives

her a half smile in return. I decide to get this meeting back on track.

"What flowers, Beth?" I ask her, and her head flicks to face me in surprise. Her blue eyes widen, her lips part, and I start thinking things that I really shouldn't be in this meeting.

"Oh, um..." She ponders, looking quickly at my mother's deadly eyes and then back to me.

"Roses. Always roses," she states confidently with a nod. My eyes remain on hers for a beat, the room quiet. She isn't saying it as a question, like she is asking permission to have her opinion like most of my staff do. She says the words with finality. Like this is how it needs to be done. Like she is in charge. The first person in my life since my father to have that ability with me.

"Great. Swap them out for all roses, Mom. Next," I say, my eyes not leaving hers. I break our stare and look at my mother when she doesn't continue. I am getting impatient, my time better spent elsewhere, even though I would never leave Beth to deal with her alone. My eyes flick back to Beth who is still watching me, and my lips quirk when she glances away.

Mom huffs before clearing her throat and starts on the list of catering options, decorations, music, and gifts that we will give guests.

"And that's it," Mom says as she finishes her rundown, and I see Beth's eyebrows raise.

"Beth?" I say, referring to her again. My opinions on this event are no longer mine to verbalize, but Beth's. She already knows exactly what I need and when I need it.

I shuffle a little in my seat, my dick becoming aroused

from having her this close to me. I wonder briefly what it would be like to clear the room and make her scream my name from this very boardroom table.

"Seriously, Harrison, I know how to throw a party, much better than Beth, I can assure you," my mother retorts. I ignore her.

"Is there anything we are missing, Beth?" I ask again, prompting her to talk, and she gives me a look. I know without speaking to her that she has something to say.

Beth clears her throat. "This is all great..."

"But you have some questions," I say, finishing her sentence, and I don't miss it as my brother's head whips toward me.

"Go ahead." I sweep out my hand and offer her the floor.

"What is happening with security? When I went through the guest list, I noticed that there will be a lot of high-profile people attending, so I wondered what firm you had booked for security?"

Mom remains silent and looks at her as though she is stupid.

"We have our own team we will use." She punches her words heavily so they make a mark. To ensure that Beth understands we are a family with means.

"Oh, of course," Beth says, looking down at her notepad again, and I admire her stamina. Anyone else would have broken under my mother's gaze already.

"Also, in terms of media, will they play a part and, if so, who will be managing the media scrum?"

Mom looks startled, and I realize this is something she didn't consider.

"We are looking into that at the moment," she says, saving face, and I see Lilly scribble something down in her notebook.

"Great!" Beth says, remaining professional.

"And one last thing," Beth says, and Mom sighs as if this is paining her, but Beth pushes on.

"The photographer and emcee run sheet doesn't match and the menu doesn't match the guest list dietary requirements. Also, you mentioned the music is a three-piece jazz band, but in this venue, a five-piece may provide a better atmosphere; otherwise, the room can look too big when everyone is seated, and the acoustics jump around the space, creating echoes."

When Beth finishes, once again, the room is quiet. I see Eddie's eyebrows rise and Oscar look at her in disbelief. I knew she had this in her and a feeling of pride washes through my chest. She is beautiful, there is no doubt about it, but her take-charge attitude, all delivered with a smile almost as charming as my own, is what really makes me pay attention.

"All good points, Beth," I say, backing her up, and our eyes meet briefly. I notice a soft pink tint come to her cheeks before my gaze lands on Mom and Lilly. They wanted this gig; they wanted to be responsible for managing this event, so they need to make sure it is in line with what we need. And Beth is what we need.

Lilly looks between me and Beth before she pipes up. "This isn't our first event, Beth; we know what we are doing." The sharp tone of her words is meant to maim, but Beth continues to smile. The passive-aggressive attitude that Mom and Lilly are giving off is uncalled for, but

Beth is handling it with grace. I smirk at Oscar across the table, giving him an *I told you so* look.

"Of course, I'm just crossing the t's and dotting the i's. We want to ensure that this event is a terrific night, given it is kick-starting the campaign. A statement really needs to be made," Beth replies, her eyes flicking to me, and I nod, giving her a smile in agreement to everything she says. She seems to like the silent praise, her posture and smile telling me that she is relaxed in her decisions as long as I approve. And I do. Very much so.

"Oh, Harrison and I have color coordinated our outfits, so we will make a grand entrance together that I am sure the cameras will love!" Lilly gushes. Eddie covers his laugh with a cough, and I think Oscar groans. Lilly just tried to mark her territory, even though I am not hers and never will be.

"I am taking Beth to the event," I announce, sitting back with confidence, my eyes homed in on one person and one person only. I hear the collective gasps from around the table.

"You are?" Lilly and Beth both ask in unison.

"Yes. I am." My eyes now lock with Beth's, and I see her shimmery blues sparkle, flickering, appearing to be happy with my suggestion. I look around the table to see Eddie's eyes widen, matching his smile, while Oscar covers his mouth with his hand, and my mother looks like she is going to jump across the table and slaughter me.

All in all, it was a good meeting.

11

BETH

Day two at the new job and my driver Tom is taking us to the first appointment of the day.

"I can't believe we are meeting with Arthur this morning!" I say cheerily, because this is not work for me. I have been to Arthur's office a few times, and have spoken to his secretary a lot, so I am looking forward to seeing them both.

"Yes. First Arthur, then a press tour at the elementary school. I haven't spent a lot of time with Arthur over the years. He hates me, but I am trying to find some middle ground so he can support my campaign," Harrison says from beside me in the car. We are sitting close, and it feels electric.

My senses continue to heighten whenever we are together. The humming in my body only grows, and I wonder if he feels it too.

As the car turns and weaves through the city traffic, my heart feels like it is going to thump right out of my chest. The dream I had of him last night isn't helping, my mind racing with all sorts of inappropriate scenarios.

It is just the two of us this morning, as Oscar and Eddie are meeting us at the elementary school later, where Harrison is having a photo op with the media as part of his education policies that he will introduce if elected.

I feel good. After his confidence in me at the meeting yesterday, I feel like I am on cloud nine. The way I catch Harrison looking at me, however, has my stomach fluttering, as does the fact that I am his date to the event next week. Something I still need to talk to him about.

"Why does he hate you?" I ask, curious, not believing that Arthur actually hates anyone, especially someone like Harrison.

"He and my dad had a huge rivalry decades ago, always competing for the same business and trying to rule the city. I guess that is a legacy that was passed down to me; however, I don't really see Arthur much these days, so it is more of a hangover from the old days rather than anything current."

"Arthur is great. I think you might get along pretty well if given the chance," I state as I lean back in my seat, getting comfortable as our conversation continues. This ease between the two of us is nice, even if my body is traitorous, ignoring the sane signals from my brain and making me feel things I haven't for a very long time. The more time I spend with Harrison, the more I am starting to warm up to the boy from Baltimore.

"How do you know Arthur?" he asks as his lips turn

upward, and I know he is enjoying our conversation as well. His phone rings in the background but he doesn't move an inch. His focus remains on me, like I am the most important thing in the world.

"We met through the events I run in DC. He has the same meal at every event and is the only guest that is ever given exactly what he wants—medium rare steak and mashed potatoes—regardless of whose event he is attending. We just hit it off and became friends. He is like a grandfather I never had, in a way. We meet up every couple of weeks and play chess. I always enjoy spending time with him."

"You play chess?" Harrison asks, and his smile widens. It's his trademark, the large watermelon smile that makes women swoon. Including me.

"Sometimes. It is my father's favorite pastime, so I learned from him. It is something we do together at home," I say, grinning back. His questions about my life make me feel special. Like he cares. I could count on one hand the amount of people in my life who have expressed an interest in me.

"So you play chess, love yoga, are an expert event manager, and can handle a media scrum with your eyes closed. What else don't I know about you?" Harrison asks, his head tilting. There's a playful curiosity in his gaze, a small smile teasing his lips.

"Oh, there are many things you don't know yet, but I'm a pretty simple person." I smile, thinking of a few things to share as his eyes stay on mine. "Hmm... favorite color is pink, and I love giraffes. I could live entirely on

Italian food, and I have an unhealthy obsession with chocolate chip ice cream." I giggle at that last admission. "What about you?" I ask quickly, keen to learn more about the man and what makes him tick.

"Well... I have a weekly golf match with my brothers. Ever since I was a child, I wanted to be president. That was after I wanted to become an astronaut, though, because we all know that space is awesome. And I have a small addiction to Milk Duds." He quips the last bit, and I laugh.

"And now that you are running for governor, president doesn't seem too much of a dream anymore, does it?" I ask, because I can certainly see Harrison being president one day.

"One step at a time," he says, chuckling softly, the sound soothing me from the inside out.

"So you get along well with your brothers?" I ask, already knowing Eddie, but I don't know much about the other two.

"My brothers and I are best friends. We are a strong family unit." I feel him shuffle a little, something like pride in his tone.

"What about you? Siblings? Your mother?" he asks, and my chest drops.

"No siblings, and my mother died years ago. It's just me and my dad," I say quietly, pressing my lips together in a smile. The words feel odd to me because I never talk about my mother. To anyone. I have never trusted anyone with my family history before. Yet I don't hesitate to let Harrison know, the words coming easier than I ever imagined. I should feel uncomfortable; I should want to steer the conversation in a different direction, but the way he looks at me has me opening up to him like it is as easy as breathing.

Like Harrison can feel the pain, he covers my hand with his, giving it a small squeeze.

"I'm sorry for your loss; it isn't easy losing a parent. I can't imagine it happening as a young child," he says, and I stop breathing. For a moment, the world ceases to spin as Harrison and I sit in the back of the car, circulating in each other's orbit, not rushing to escape.

Having not had a man in my life aside from my dad, ever, the thoughts I have been having about Harrison are borderline schoolgirl crush and stalkerish, yet he is not pulling away either. His hand is firm, and his thumb skirts across my skin. It is not a friendly touch; it is more than that.

"I lost my father a few years ago. Heart attack." It is something I knew, of course, but I didn't have many details.

"That must have been hard for you." His thumb continues to caress my hand, and he nods.

"It was. It was sudden, so that makes it worse, I think. Then we had a lot to deal with in the aftermath."

"I did see some things in the news," I admit. Everyone heard how one of the richest men in the country died and then how multiple women came out with all sorts of demands for money, saying that they were his mistress or other partner.

"I can't say any of it was pleasant, and it was hard for

my mother, obviously, but I think we are out the other side now. It is still hard to come to terms with their entire marriage being a sham, though," he says honestly, and I feel for him.

"My mom and dad were so in love; there was just no way they would even look at another person. When Mom died, my dad's heart shattered the same day and all these years later, it is still not back together. I don't think it ever will be. I am sure it was really hard for your mom." I can't imagine the man you loved and married and had a family with having multiple lives with other people.

"It was. It goes a long way to explaining her poor behavior toward you yesterday. I apologize for her being a little intense at the meeting."

"It's fine. I have dealt with worse." I shrug and notice his eyes crinkle. I like his eyes on me.

"You shouldn't have to and won't with me." His words of protection wrap around my heart. He says them self-assured in the fact that there is nothing that would stop him. We hold each other's gaze, and I swallow, trying to find the words, yet not knowing exactly what to say.

The car hits a bump in the road, and I clear my throat.

"So, Arthur?" I question, getting our conversation back on track. Harrison smiles, moving his hand, but not before his thumb caresses my skin again so softly that I feel the tingling shoot up my arm, spreading warmth throughout my body. His smile is infectious, making me grin even wider.

"Well, hopefully, we can get his support. It would

mean a lot. He is well respected and admired, and I think it could really move the needle for me in terms of garnering public support."

"Arthur is a smart man. I am sure he will either be supportive or have good reasons not to be. Either way, I guess we will find out soon." He nods, taking in my words.

"So do you have any questions about the party next Saturday night?" Harrison asks, looking at me. I shift a little in my seat because I am still not sure what the hell I am going to wear. I went through my entire wardrobe last night when I got home and there really wasn't anything worthy.

"It should be great. I just need to find something to wear," I say jovially, covering my nerves with humor in my tone.

"I will organize a stylist. Will early afternoon work for you?" he says as he grabs his cell from his pocket and starts typing, all while I sit stunned.

"Harrison, no! That is too much. I am sure they are busy. I can find something to wear, no problem," I say, not quite believing he would offer me a stylist. A luxury that I certainly can't afford.

"It is my event and we invited you at the last minute. I have a team who can dress you and provide hair, makeup, and anything else you need. I can have them come to your house." He ignores my pleas, his face still buried in his cell.

"No, I am sure I can find something. I am thinking I will stay in the city. Hotel Providore has a great deal at the moment, and I can just go shopping between now and then. It will be fine. I can sort something out." The words rush from my mouth, trying to act nonchalant, even though my palms are sweating.

He looks up at me then, searching my eyes.

"Beth, I need you with me and focused on the campaign at all times. Things such as event attire, a driver, city accommodation, and anything else you need, I will handle. If you need something special for the event —clothes, hair, makeup, *anything*—I will get it for you. Any request, I will arrange for you. Anything you need, I will provide it for you. Do you understand? No worrying about any of it."

"Okay, if you say so..." I reply quietly, not comfortable accepting such extravagance, but it is *his* campaign, so I will be a team player.

"Give me a minute," he says as he types into his phone.

"What about your dad?" He pauses what he is doing and looks at me with concern, making my heart melt a little. Even though he has a myriad of things to be worried about, my dad comes to his mind. The two of them haven't even formally met, yet Harrison is already taking him into consideration.

"He is fine. Jeff will look in on him. They are trying a new medicinal program for his legs, so they are all into that at the moment," I tell him just as his cell phone dings.

"Medicinal? Is it safe?" he questions and, to be honest, I hadn't even thought about it. Dad trusts Jeff, and throughout the years, we have tried all sorts of things to help Dad through his disability and mental struggles.

"Yes, it's a new juice cleanse or something. Jeff has my dad trying all sorts of weird and wonderful things to get some muscle improvement back into his legs since ongoing physio is not within our reach."

"Does he not have regular support? Medical or anything else?" Harrison asks, and I appreciate his interest.

"No. I have medical through work, obviously, which helps a lot, but we can't really afford all the top care that he needs. We make do."

Harrison looks at me, taking in my smile, but doesn't say anything.

"Alright, all organized. I have booked you the suite at the Four Seasons, and I have a team coming to you at the hotel at four. I will pick you up at seven," Harrison says with finality.

"Wait, what? Harrison. This is too much," I do not want him spending more on me than he has to. I can make my own way; I always have.

"Beth. Listen to me. You are a professional who does a damn good job, and I want you with me. I need to introduce you to people, and you will have to work the room as well. I want you by my side for this event and the next one, so it is the least I can do. Call it a work perk."

Harrison's eyes focus on mine before he pockets his phone, turning his body slightly to me like he is challenging me to continue, knowing that I won't win. His charming smile is back, and I don't miss his eyes as they flick to my lips and then back again, something he has a habit of doing. The back seat of this car just got a whole lot smaller.

"If you're sure?" I say, still not convinced. No one has ever bought me anything like that before, but I guess he does have an appearance to uphold, and it is important for me to look a certain way in public at such a well-attended event.

Harrison also wants me by his side. I didn't miss that comment and now my heart is thumping loud enough for my throat to vibrate. He lifts his hand and brushes a stray hair from my cheek and pushes it back around my ear, and my skin tingles from his gentle touch. I need to bite my tongue to remind myself that we are in work mode. But it's hard to tell sometimes with him.

"I'm sure," he murmurs, our eyes hooked on each other, then his lower to my lips once more and flick back to meet mine again. *Is he going to kiss me?*

I'm nervous, and my body feels hot. We shouldn't be looking at each other like this. Like we are wanting to be more than we are.

We sit like that for a short time, the air getting thicker by the second, my heart jumping from my chest. It is not inappropriate, but intense. If he were anyone else, I would ease into him, the moment just right for me to get closer, and seal our fate. My body is strumming with need for more of his touch. But he is my boss, so I refrain, not moving a muscle.

Tom clears his throat from the front seat, and we pull apart quickly.

I whip my head around, noticing that the car has stopped, but Harrison's eyes remain on mine for another few seconds before he pulls back, the cool air from his absence making me shiver.

"We're here, sir," Tom states, then he steps out of the car and walks around to open our door.

"You okay?" Harrison asks with slight concern on his face. I smile, and his wrinkles ease.

"I'm more than okay."

12

HARRISON

Everbright Elementary School. The place where I'll deliver my educational policies that I will enact if elected. Turns out, it is the same place where I watch a particular redhead get down on her knees in front of me, a sight I was not ready for.

I watch her play on the carpet with a small group of six-year-olds whose little faces light up like Christmas trees the minute she gives them attention. Not dissimilar to my own, I am starting to learn.

With Beth by my side, my smile is even wider and now reaches my eyes. I shake my head, thinking about how I almost kissed her in the car, not believing I came so close, knowing that if I started, it would be very fucking hard to stop. Not to mention, that I am in the middle of my campaign and gunning for the very job I have dreamed of having for most of my life. The deep-seated desire to be governor hasn't waned. It just doesn't seem to be the only thing that gets my blood pumping since she popped into my life.

I can feel the tension between us growing stronger by the day. Every time we are together, I see her fingers fidget, her chest rise and fall faster, and I know this is not one-sided. I can almost feel her putting up a professional wall when we get closer, the urge we both have to jump over it becoming very hard to stop, but I respect her for it. She is showing just as much resistance as I am; I can feel it. Personally, I need a fucking gold medal for my self-control, because the more time I spend with her, the more I want to uncover.

I finish up the coloring I was working on with a small group of kids, cameras flashing in our faces every two minutes. When I looked through the pile of drawings on offer, one stuck out immediately, and I eagerly got to work. It was almost relaxing sitting here in the chair way too small for me, chatting with the kids. I learned all about how cool slime is and how doing a front flip is harder than a back flip.

As I stand, I take my picture with me, holding it in one hand as I walk around the room with the school principal.

"Everbright is a great school, Mr. Langford. We are in the lower socio-economic part of town, as you know. We are a small school, with three hundred kids in total. I have been here for close to ten years, and it is a great community; we just need some additional resources and support," Principal Robert McNash says as he gives me a small tour of the school. I look around as he talks, yet I always go back to Beth, watching her smile and play, the kids totally enamored with her. Just like I am.

It isn't just the kids either. She has given her time to

all the parents and staff in the hour since we have been here, listening and chatting. She was made for this, talking to the community, listening and being empathetic to their needs. It is where she shines.

"Tell me about the teachers you have on staff," I ask Robert, and as he explains the staff cohort, I nod and smile, observing the few journalists who have turned up today. Oscar and Eddie are talking to other support staff, getting more information on the school and current education system that we can unpack later.

"Education is something that I think is extremely important. I was afforded the best, but many people don't have that luxury. Robert, today I will be announcing that schools just like Everbright will be able to access a teachers' fund, additional payments, and support to teachers who work in community schools, along with new programs helping children through additional learning pathways, such as tutoring and support for children with learning difficulties." My heart warms when I see his smile widen.

"That would be very appreciated, Mr. Langford, and something that I think would benefit the children greatly." The two of us turn to watch the kids in the classroom, and the first thing I see is Beth now with more kids around her as she reads a book to them all. I can't help but smile as I watch her get into character, pulling funny faces and changing her voice to fit the storyline, just like my mother used to do with me as a kid.

I join them, sitting on the old carpet next to a small boy who seems to be an outlier. Beth watches me and smiles briefly before continuing with her story.

"You're too big to sit here," the young boy whispers to me.

"Do you want me to move?" I ask as I look down at him. The small scruffy boy gives me a smirk before shaking his head.

"My name is Harrison, but you can call me Harry," I say. It is a nickname my father used to use, one that hasn't been said since he died.

"My name is Charlie, and you can call me Charlie," he whispers back with a small nod, and I smile at his spunk. We sit together like that, both watching Beth as she continues to tell the story, her eyes lighting up, her beaming smile taking over the place.

"Are you her boyfriend?" he asks me, and my eyebrows rise in surprise.

"That's a pretty adult question to ask."

"It's a yes or no answer, Harry," he says deadpan, and I try not to laugh.

"Why do you want to know?"

"Because if you are, I will leave her alone, but if you are not, then I am going to ask her to be my girlfriend because she is pretty." I chuckle, but his expression couldn't be more serious.

"I can't argue with you there. She is pretty. But she might be a little too old for you. What about that girl over there?" I say as I point to a cute little blond girl sitting down in the front near Beth, hanging on her every word.

"That's Emily," he says as his cheek flush. "She doesn't like me."

"Why is that?"

"I accidentally spilled paint on her clothes last week and she got upset."

"Did you apologize?"

"Yeah, but she doesn't like to sit next to me anymore," he says sadly. I look up in time to see Beth finishing the story and decide to help my new friend out a little.

"C'mon, I will introduce you to Beth." His eyes light up as we walk toward Beth who is now talking with little Emily.

"Hello!" Beth says excitedly, seeing Charlie next to me.

"Beth, this is Charlie," I introduce them, hearing the click of cameras from the side of us, bringing me back to reality. Beth squats down to his height to greet him, and I look down at her, gritting my teeth at how perfect she looks.

"Hi, Charlie, I'm Beth. Pleased to meet you," she says, and the two of them shake hands. Her smile is contagious as I watch their interaction, more cameras clicking from in front of us now.

"Charlie spilled paint on me last week." Emily pouts at Beth's side.

"Oh, well, sometimes that happens. I spill things all the time!"

"You do?" Charlie asks, eyes wide.

"Yes. I am extremely clumsy. Just ask Harrison, he will tell you all about it," she says as she stands, her eyes twinkling as she contains her giggles.

"She is. She has spilled drinks on me twice now," I say, holding up two fingers.

"And you are still friends?" Emily asks, surprised.

"Of course, she is my best friend," I say, and all three of them look at me in awe.

"Charlie, do you want to be best friends?" Emily asks him, and Charlie gasps.

"Yes! Best friends." And they shake on it.

"Best friends, huh?" Beth says quietly as she stands beside me, and we watch the kids run off to play.

I look down at her, our arms brushing, and notice her pouty lips. My eyes flick down farther, taking in the curve of her breasts under her corporate attire, before I move them back up to meet her vibrant blue eyes. Her lips part, and I silence the growl in my throat that is crawling to get out.

The things I want to do to this woman have me completely out of the friendzone. So much so that I can't even see the border of it.

The urge to kiss her again flows up my body, and when she swallows roughly, I know she is struggling too. But I keep my spine ramrod straight, not giving myself an inch, knowing if I do, the cameras here today will be reporting a totally different story than what they came to capture.

"Here. For you," I say, handing her the picture in my hand. She grabs it and unfolds it, and I hear her intake of breath and watch the pulse in her neck as it speeds up.

"You did this for me?" she asks, stifling a giggle, and I grin as her eyes light up.

"Do you like it?" I ask, suddenly feeling a little vulnerable.

"Harrison! It is a pink giraffe, what's not to love! I am

going to stick it in my office. Our space needs a bit of color," she says, laughing, and my smile widens.

"That's great, you two!" one of the photographers yells, and Beth and I both look at him, mid-laugh, seconds before flashes go off in our faces.

"Hey, Max!" Beth says, stepping forward to greet the young photographer.

"Boy from Baltimore got you working for him now? Best decision he has made so far in this campaign," he says jovially to us both as he gives Beth a small hug. He isn't wrong.

"Harrison, this is Max, a freelance photojournalist." He is a short chubby man, with a stubble of hair gracing his chin, and a headband wrapped around his forehead, encasing his curly yellow hair.

"Pleased to meet you. Thanks for stopping by," I say, extending my hand, remaining professional as I size him up. His hand is on Beth's arm, and I want to flick it off, but I refrain.

"Anytime. You both look like you are having a good time here today?" he asks, looking between the two of us, and I am careful with my response. He might take the photos, but he is still a journalist.

"It is a great school, and they are doing amazing things," I state, keeping my tone level and my answer simple.

"The kids are so much fun!" Beth says, her face lighting up.

"Sorry to interrupt, but it is time to make your announcement, and then we need to go," Oscar says as he and Eddie meet us, and we get down to business. Max steps away to join the media scrum, and Beth gets them all organized.

I step out to the courtyard and address the school staff group, media, and my team, and deliver my education policies. It is warmly received, and a few cheers go up in the group. I smile at their excitement, but it is Beth's approval I look for, and her smile and sparkly eyes give me everything I need.

13

HARRISON

I watch Beth as she sits at her desk and wonder what the hell I am doing. I need to be reviewing these healthcare policies in front of me, but I have read and reread the same sentence for the past half hour as my eyes are more connected to her than the funding requirements for the busy Baltimore hospitals.

I thought I could keep it together. I knew she would be an asset for my campaign, and she is, undoubtably, the best hiring decision I have ever made in my entire career. She is worth every penny I threw at her, but now I want to keep her. Permanently.

But in moments like these, where I sit here at my desk, watching her, I begin to question my logic. I watch as her hands fly across her keyboard, her fingers dainty, yet determined. I have observed the way she takes time to think and process. Her head tilts a little to the left whenever she is mulling over scenarios, and she bites her bottom lip when deep in thought.

Those lips are plump and pouty and on my mind a lot.

She works with the radio on, something that would usually annoy me, but has become such a part of our workday routine that I don't even notice. But I do notice the way at the end of the day, she starts to dance in her seat to the music. A hundred percent out of time and uncoordinated, but her face is stress-free, happiness radiating from her, thinking nobody is watching.

I'm watching.

Our days together are long, often eating dinner at our desks, something I never did before, but enjoy now, especially as it gives us time to talk about other things outside of work. Like how she has never been to a zoo to see a giraffe in real life, or how I burn water, not having the first idea how to cook. These extra moments are worth the late nights. Where the policies I need to review are often read closer to midnight when she isn't such a distraction. The more I get to know her, though, the more I want her with me at midnight. In my bed, naked, squirming underneath me.

"Harrison!" my mother's voice squawks through the air, making me jump as she barges into my office, with Oscar and Eddie hot on her heels.

"What's going on?" I question her as I stand from my desk, looking suspiciously at Eddie behind her, him only rolling his eyes.

"What's going on? I will tell you what is going on!" my mother says, her array of gold and diamonds catching the sun and lighting up the office wall as she waves her hands around, a habit of hers happening more and more frequently. I see Beth jump up from her desk and walk over, standing next to Oscar at the side. Of course, I see her. I always see her.

"Mom, you cannot just walk in here, yelling and acting like a demanding diva." I sigh, rubbing my eyes, because this is the last thing I need. I am up to my eyeballs in paperwork. I have meeting after meeting scheduled for the next few days, and that is merely just scratching the surface of my to-do list.

"I was talking to Annabelle VanCleef at the country club over lunch today. She mentioned to me, confidentially, that your opposition is releasing a new policy to state that they will fund a new development over at Ellwood Grove." My mother purses her lips, and I wait a beat.

Ellwood Grove is *the* wealthiest suburb in all the state. Investing in infrastructure there doesn't make sense to anybody. Why do the wealthiest people need state government money to provide anything over and above the basic requirements?

"He's buying votes," Beth says, looking right at me, her arms crossed over her chest, answering the question that was on my mind. My nostrils flare because she is right. He is.

"Pretty overt way of doing it," I add, as I move from the back of my desk, walking over to Beth, my sounding board. The need to be closer to her is now nearly as natural as breathing.

"But he obviously needs them; otherwise, why would he commit funds to something so..." she starts, and I can see her mind ticking over, her brain just as beautiful as her body.

"Ridiculous," I finish her sentence and put my hands on my hips as I think over the scenario. Our stance is close, the energy bouncing off the two of us, like we are the only ones standing in the room.

"It means he is scared. He's..." She bites her lower lip.

"Playing games," I say, my eyes homing in on her lips. I forget where I am for a moment.

"Let me call Arthur," she states suddenly, looking at me with fire in her eyes.

"I will call Ronald," I say in unison, and we both turn swiftly. It isn't until I am sitting back down and pick up the phone that I look up. Three pairs of eyes stare down at me. Eddie smirks, Oscar frowns, and Mom looks like she is about to blow a gasket.

"Is that all?" I ask, looking at all of them.

"I can see the two of you have it handled," Eddie quips, his eyes dashing between mine and Beth's and back again with a smart-ass smirk on his face, before walking backward slowly and out my office door.

"Let me know if you need anything. I'm heading down to police headquarters to submit our election night plans," Oscar says, and I nod before he retreats as well.

My mother is the only one left standing, and I can see it in her eyes, there is more she wants to say. I look over at Beth, who is already on the phone with Arthur, smiling and pacing her smaller office near her windows. I notice her outfit today for the hundredth time. A black pencil skirt—my favorite one.

"Harrison!" my mother hisses, and I whip my head around to face her.

"What else, Mother?" I ask as I flick through my phone to find the number I am looking for.

"Be very careful, Harrison. You don't want to turn out just like your father." She seethes the words, disgust written all over her face as she looks over at Beth, giving her a stare that would bring anyone to their knees, although Beth is too busy in her conversation with Arthur to even realize that my mother is still here.

"What is *that* supposed to mean?" I ask her, gritting my teeth. She has my full attention now.

"Chasing the cheapest, ugliest, and in this case, fattest skirt in town," she quips.

"Be very careful with your words, Mother; they can't be taken back once they are said. I will not tolerate you speaking about Beth like that," I say to her quietly but with a bite, not wanting Beth to hear.

"Seriously, Harrison, she is a baby, for God's sake. She even has that ridiculous picture on her wall. That is not how a real woman behaves." My mother refers to the pink giraffe I colored for Beth at the elementary school. She said she was going to hang it in our office, and she did. It brings a smile to my face every time I look at it.

"I think it is time you left." She must see the seriousness in my eyes because she scoffs at me, then turns on her heel and leaves before more words can be spoken.

I fume silently and unclench my fists before rolling my neck, trying to let go of the cloud of tension she always seems to bring with her whenever she is in my space.

"So, Arthur said it was true. He got a call just yesterday from our competitor who said that he has put a policy together and is showing everyone who is anyone of the plans, while following it up with a request for support to his campaign," Beth says as she walks up to my desk, handing me a glass of water.

I grab it from her, taking a gulp. She reads me like a book. I often come into the office bright and early in the morning and already have a steamy cup of coffee on my desk, or a file magically appears when I need to work on it. Water just now to get rid of the bad taste my mother left is yet another thing Beth does, knowing what I need before I do.

"Fuck," I murmur, standing and making my way to the window, needing to move my body now that my mother has made me agitated.

"It's actually a good thing, Harrison," Beth says, coming to stand next to me as we both look out the windows at the city.

"How's that?" I ask, acutely aware that she sees a silver lining in every cloud. Even the darkest ones.

"Well, he is committing state funds to the wealthiest part of town, to build what? A community center? A community pool? None of which any of those kinds of people will want or use. So he will immediately lose about seventy percent of the voting public from the outskirts just on that move alone," she says and she isn't wrong.

"The fact that he is also committing funds to the freeway that he plans to run alongside the golf course in the very same area, well, that knocks out at least another five to ten percent of the votes he would hope to capture in Ellwood," I add, looking at her, our end game the same.

"If you ask me, he is handing us the election on a silver platter." She gives me the side-eye and a cute grin to match.

She is right, of course. Just like she is right about everything else. The tension I felt before leaves my body as I think through what she has just said. I love that golf course. It is where my brothers and I play every week. Many people have come to speak to me on a weekend when I am there to air their frustrations at having a new motorway so close.

"How did you get to be so amazing at this?" I ask, acutely aware I am stepping into unsafe territory the more I want to know about her. But I want to know everything. Every inch and special quirk.

"Oh, I studied political science as a minor at college," she quips, and now my interest is piqued even more.

"Really? Why? What drew you to politics?" I ask, turning to face her, giving her all my attention.

"I think my desire to do better for the people. So many people miss out, Harrison. They fall through the cracks. And all the red tape that comes with working with the state on healthcare support, education support, any support, really, that struggling families need is a nightmare."

I know immediately she is talking from experience. The urge I have to take care of this woman jolts me a little.

"I'm sure you never have seen that side of things?" she

challenges me, her eyes resting on me, waiting for my answer.

"No. Never. But I do know about them. I am aware that there is a lot of work we can do to make things easier. Fairer, for everyone in the community. It was the main driving force for me wanting this job. This as a career," I answer her honestly.

I was born into wealth. The articles about me, saying I was born with a silver spoon, are accurate. But my father ensured all us boys grew up knowing the realities of life. We all had to work in community support growing up. Some of us volunteered, and Ben and I do a lot of pro bono law work through the firm.

"Why didn't you mention your political studies earlier?" I ask her, intrigued, because that is yet another feather in her cap.

"The real world can't be learned in a textbook. Only life lessons can teach us the real things we need to know." Her words are heavy, and I let them seep into me.

"I hope I can make a difference in this role..." I murmur as I look out at the city through the window, feeling the weight of the position for the first time.

"Well, I think you will make a fine governor of Maryland. You will make a lot of people proud." Her compliment washes over me, giving me a sense of power, accomplishment, and motivation to do better. Better for her.

"Even though I make you work late almost every night? Including tonight?" I ask, grinning at her like I have won the lottery.

"Only if I can choose what takeout we get for dinner?"

she sasses, lifting her brow. We have had takeout a few times this week, our day never really finishing at five. Her smile is now wide, matching those perfect sparkling blues I can't get enough of.

"Why do you always choose Italian? I know it's your favorite, but don't you ever get tired of it?" I say with a pretend groan, even though I love it too.

"My mother always made me lasagna every week when I was little. It makes me think of her," she says, her tone now more subdued, her gaze looking out at the city.

My body is telling me to touch her, but my mind is telling me to sit back down at my desk and get to work. It is the same state of flux I have been in since meeting her. I have tried to rein it in. Tried to keep these growing feelings under control.

"I got you something," I say, and I see her head tilt to her left and can't help but smile.

"Really?" she asks in wonder, her eyes lighting up again, her smile matching mine.

I pull out the card from my wallet. Something I grabbed yesterday, thinking that it would be a nice token, but now the impact on her might be something else entirely.

"It is a year's worth of Italian takeout from Giuseppe's, so if you want to eat Italian every lunch and every dinner for the rest of the year, you just show them this card and it is on the house," I say, handing over the small laminated card that the restaurant put together for me. When I handed over my Amex for it, they almost lost their minds. It seemed a silly thing at the time, but now I know it means so much more.

"What?" She half laughs, half chokes out, taking the card from me and looking it over.

"You can have all the lasagna you want," I offer with a little laugh of my own, putting my hands safely in my pockets so I don't pull her to me. Her body stands close to mine, and I look down at her as she is taking it all in.

"Harrison! This is ridiculous!" she says with a giggle, and I feel like a king for making her smile.

"No. It just means you can buy us all dinner from now on." My smile widens as her laugh rings through my office, and just like that, my mother's visit is a distant memory.

14

BETH

BREAKING NEWS

The campaign for governor is off and running, with Billionaire Harrison Langford and his team out and about in the community, visiting schools, small businesses, and local sporting facilities.

His team has increased with the addition of Beth Longmere, a long-standing event expert from DC. Beth is familiar with many of the media on Harrison's campaign trail, some even saying that she brings a positive new light to the campaign and is complimentary to the charming smile we are all familiar with.

There are whispers that the two of them are a force to be reckoned with. This journalist is questioning whether it is all business, or if there is more than meets the eye.

More to come.

My new job is just as busy as I imagined it to be.

This week, Harrison and I have visited local communities, spoken at policy meetings, and visited sporting clubs, all to introduce ourselves to the people. While he was the star of the show, I stood back with Eddie and Oscar, taking notes and watching and learning. Often, he finishes my sentences, or I already have the paperwork he needs. The way we work together is impeccable and not going unnoticed by the side-eyes Oscar continues to give us.

His compliments are frequent. He tells me how well I am doing, providing positive feedback on a daily basis, the attention only stoking the flame that started flickering when I started this job. I knew I was capable, and I am proud that I have managed to not only do the job, but exceed expectations on many fronts. This new confidence I have in myself, growing daily, is all because of him.

My feelings for him are developing with every smile he gives me, every brush of his hand, or the overt displays of chivalry, like helping me from the back seat of the car and holding my fingers for a beat longer than he needs to. The constant camera flashes from the media scrum are the only reasons he seems to let go. Which has done nothing for my daydreaming, my thoughts now permanently in overdrive.

Today, however, we are visiting Elmwood Senior Citizens Center, and I am currently being challenged to a game of chess. All bets are off. I am a fierce chess player, and the chess pieces in front of me have my undivided attention. I want to win.

"Your move," Garry, the older man who sits opposite me, says, as I see Harrison and the team wandering around and shaking hands, talking to people, doing all the things that I should be doing, yet I can't step away from a chess challenge. My father would never forgive me.

I look at the board and bite the inside of my cheek. Garry is good. We have been at it for around twenty minutes now and are starting to draw a crowd. He has a solid strategy for combating every move I make, but I am confident, and even though I have been holding back a little, I know I need to wrap this up soon.

"There," I say, by way of a small challenge. He still has another move to make, and we can both see it clearly, the twinkle in his eye telling me he knows what I am up to, but he is happy to play along.

"Hey, Red!" Max, the photog, shouts, and both Garry and I look up just as he takes his photo.

"Don't you get sick of those damn photographers?" Garry mumbles as he looks back at the board.

"Comes with the territory. I am kind of used to it now." Whether it is working in events or now working with Harrison, the media is something that I have had years of experience managing, so much so that many, like Max, are good acquaintances to have.

"I didn't know you played chess, Red," Max says, looking down at our game on the table.

"It is one of my favorite things to do!" It is the one way Dad and I connect the most.

"She is a shark," Harrison says as he approaches from behind me, and I can feel him at my back. We aren't touching, but I know he is there.

"That she is..." Garry says, his voice petering out as he makes his move. I watch where he places his piece. He makes the only move he can, the one whereby I am able to snatch his king and seal the game.

"Checkmate," I say as I knock his king over and end the game.

"That's my girl." Harrison's smooth voice skirts down my neck from where he leaned over to my ear. His words make my body shiver involuntarily, and his hand comes to my shoulder. He squeezes me gently, and I look up at him, my lips parting. I try to be professional around him, but his words have left me breathless.

The two of us have been edging closer to our business boundaries for weeks, the urge between us building. His voice just now was deeper than his usual tone, full of insinuation that I am sure was just for me. His eyes twinkle in delight as they bore into mine, and I don't miss as one of his eyebrows quirks or how he rolls his lips subtly, biting his bottom one. I feel a flush of desire and heat swirls in my body in places it has no right to in this environment.

We are lost in each other's stare until I hear a click, the camera lens bringing us both back into reality with a jolt. His hand leaves my shoulder instantly, and he takes a small step back, looking at Garry on the other side of the table.

"Good game, Garry," I say, putting out my hand for him to shake while a big shit-eating grin is plastered on my face.

"Good indeed. If Beth's chess game is anything to go by, then I'd say you have this election in the bag, Mr.

Langford," Garry says to Harrison as he shakes my hand and stands.

"She's my lucky charm, Garry. She keeps me in line," Harrison says with a smile, his smooth tone shooting through my veins as he smiles at Garry, and they both shake hands as well.

"Well, if you ask me, we are in need of a change of management. Maryland has been okay over the years, but some fresh blood like the two of you would do the state wonders." He nods at me.

"When we win, you will most certainly get fresh ideas and new policies to help the community, as well as sound fiscal management to ensure the wealth of the state grows." The political themes roll off Harrison's tongue like they are gospel, everyone around us hanging off his every word.

"You just need to promise me that when you win, you'll bring Beth back here so we can play another game. I haven't had this much fun in years!" he says, his eyes shining as he looks at me. He sits back down then, his eighty-year-old body preferring the soft lounge chair to standing upright for so long.

"It's a deal. I will bring her back here for game two as soon as I can," Harrison says, smiling, his hand settling on my lower back, ready to move us on as we need to get back to the office. My blouse is loose, covering his fingers where they are splayed against my skin, and I can feel them as he caresses me with his thumb, our bodies close as we start to move as one.

The more we are together, the harder it is for me to not touch him. The heat from his hand skirts across my back and up around my chest. Every step we take, I can feel him, and the wall I have built to try to keep him out is crumbling. We have been dancing around each other for too long; there is no way I could ever walk away when all I want to do is run to him.

"I can't wait, Garry. I look forward to it," I offer, trying to keep my cool. Feeling the air change around us, the mood has shifted, and I'm already thinking about what is going to happen when we get back to the office.

Garry squeezes my hand again before Harrison and I walk away. Both smiling and shaking hands before slipping down the hallway to our car. All the while, his hand remains on my back, as his fingers curl into my side, ensuring I am close.

Too close for it to be classed as entirely work appropriate.

BACK IN THE OFFICE, I am sitting with Harrison, looking over the schedule for next week. It is the first time we have been alone for a few days, and after this morning, I am trying to concentrate on the paperwork in front of me, rather than his wandering hands from earlier. His schedule is grueling, meeting after meeting, with limited time for anything else.

"Is this normal? This schedule is insane!" I ask, looking at him like he is crazy, because by the look of his calendar, he is.

"Unfortunately. I want the top job and it isn't going to land in my lap. I have to work for it," he says, standing and walking toward his floor-to-ceiling window, pondering his thoughts while looking over the city he will soon rule.

"I understand that, but this schedule is locked in from eight a.m. through to ten p.m. almost every day. You even have working lunches, not even half an hour to yourself?" I question him as I stand and walk over to meet him, the schedule paperwork in my hand.

"It's the job," he says, looking down at me, and as I meet his gaze, the air in the office evaporates.

"You will burn out." I remain calm, trying to keep my mind focused, even if my insides are starting to betray me.

"It has to be done." His words are almost a whisper as he moves his body, now facing me, the two of us standing closer, barely an inch between us.

"You need to carve out some time. It is too much," I say, worried that he will get too exhausted, that we both will.

"Are you worried about me?" he asks, one eyebrow raised. His hand comes up, brushing away a nonexistent hair from my face, the feeling of his fingers grazing my cheek almost making me buckle at the knees.

"Of course I am worried about you. I worry about everyone. How are you even going to get through all this?" I continue, as my eyes search his for answers, not just to this question but to many others now skirting around in my mind.

"With you." His words are so self-assured, they are almost startling.

"Excuse me?" I pull back a little in question, wondering how he thinks I can help him.

"With you. With you by my side." He closes the remaining distance between us again, and I feel his hand grab mine at our sides.

"Harrison, I can't do anything to support you other than tag along, meet and greet, manage a few photographers..." I say, acutely aware of our hands, our fingers intertwining. No longer the friendly squeeze, but something more intimate that I long for.

"And be with me. Every step..." I know his words mean more than they seem to as his eyes bore into mine.

"Harrison, I can't be you. I can't woo the people like you can." I feel good in this new job, and I feel good with him. But I can't command a room, not like Harrison.

"I don't need you to be me. I need you to be you. You don't give yourself enough credit. You are great with people. You walk into a room and everyone smiles immediately. Including me. Your presence alone relaxes me and makes me want to do better," he says softly, looking serious. His eyes graze over my face, and my heart sounds like it is punching out into the room so loudly that I am waiting for the walls to start vibrating.

There is no denying his feelings. His words push straight through the protective wall I had developed for keeping this daydreaming idea I had under wraps. I swallow as I watch him, standing firm, his body language reiterating exactly how sure he is. My fingernails pinch into my palm that's not held in his, and I feel the sting. This is definitely reality.

Harrison Langford is saying he needs me. In his campaign and outside of it. I am stunned. At a loss for words.

"You are beautiful, Beth, inside and out..." he whispers as his hand reaches out and cups my jaw. I momentarily stop breathing, my stomach dips, and it is only due to my sheer will that my legs keep me upright.

"Harrison..." I breathe out as we both edge closer, our faces now only inches apart. My heart is racing because we are in his office, meant to be finalizing his schedule. This is work and anyone could walk in. And I really need this job. I don't need office gossip about our governor elect and his project manager to be the topic that kicks me into the unemployment line.

"Goddamn, I want my lips on yours," he grits out like he is barely hanging on, his thumb moving to trail across my lip, pulling my bottom lip down a little, and a moan leaves my throat all on its own. He growls then, his nostrils flaring, his fingers on my jaw tightening. His other hand comes up and he cups my face, and his eyes are running from mine to my lips and back again, over and over. He is acting like he has been holding back his desire for a long time, like he is almost at the breaking point.

"Harrison, we can't..." The words are weak as they fall from my lips. I don't believe them and neither does he. Because right here, right now, even though it is the last thing the two of us should be doing, kissing Harrison Langford has never felt so right.

He leans in just as I do, our lips meeting softly in the middle, and I hold my breath.

"Harrison!" Oscar says as he opens the office door and strides into the room, thankfully looking down at his cell phone. I jump three feet into the air and almost fall over, except Harrison's strong hand grabs my elbow, making sure I am alright before I step away. I'm hoping we both look professional, even though only two seconds earlier, we almost certainly weren't.

"What is it?" Harrison asks, looking at me with concern, yet his words are voiced to Oscar.

"Looks like the photogs had a field day this morning at the senior center. Let me bring it up," Oscar says, as he lifts his head up to look at us. He pauses mid-stride, his eyes flicking between me and Harrison, no doubt seeing the guilt written all over my face. Harrison stands tall, but his eyes remain on me.

I pull my shoulders back and nod to Harrison before looking back at the paperwork in my hands and shuffling them, pretending I am putting them into some sort of order, but they are all haphazardly bound together— much like the thoughts in my mind right now.

Oscar starts moving again, still eyeing us both suspiciously as he makes his way to Harrison's desk, tapping on his computer. Harrison and I stand behind him as Oscar brings up the *Society News* website, and there, right on the home page, is a large photo of... me.

The colors are vibrant, the lighting just right, and it looks almost airbrushed. I look over Oscar's shoulder and take it in. It is me playing chess with Garry, but looking up at Harrison behind me. Harrison is looking down at me, his hand on my shoulder. The image itself shows nothing but a friendly game of chess at a senior center, but the look in Harrison's eyes as they bore into mine offers an alternative that I hope the public doesn't investigate.

"What the fuck is this?" Oscar barks, and I startle.

"Watch your tone," Harrison says, giving Oscar a look I haven't seen from him before. Oscar nods before moving on.

"Harrison, you know what image we need to portray. Beth, I mean no disrespect, it is a great photo. A great story. But they are starting to really capture you both a lot more. The media is starting to have a field day about how good the two of you are together, even going so far as to suspect something more. I suggest that Beth hangs back on the next few visits, staying here at the office instead. Just to create a little space." I give him a small nod in understanding, because I don't want anything to over-shadow Harrison's campaign. But Harrison bristles beside me.

"No," Harrison states, taking a seat behind his desk as Oscar stands. I look at Harrison, his face stern, his jaw clenching.

"Harrison, as staff members, our jobs are to ensure you are in the limelight, not us," Oscar pushes, and I watch their exchange with interest as Harrison's eyes flick to mine before resting on Oscar again.

"I said no. Beth comes with me. Everywhere." Harrison leaves no more room for questions as he looks at me again. I take a deep breath, letting the words slip over me, and I swallow. The confidence Harrison places in me is almost as attractive as the man himself. Oscar gives me the side-eye, but I remain impartial, not knowing what to say or do.

"Fine. But perhaps less chess games next visit, Beth?" Oscar says to me, his tone sounding resigned.

"Sure. No problem. I can blend into the crowd more, but still offer a friendly face," I say, smiling, hoping that pleases both of them.

"Oscar, give us a minute," Harrison says, almost dismissing him, and I still, watching Oscar as he nods and silently leaves, closing the office door behind him.

"Beth," Harrison starts as he stands from his desk and walks toward me. "I don't, in any way, want you to feel uncomfortable on this campaign, or with me—" he says, but I cut him off before he can continue.

"I don't." The words are swift from my lips, and a smile pulls at his. He doesn't make me feel uncomfortable; he makes me feel wanted.

"How do you feel about being with me twenty-four seven? Because my words earlier are true. I want you with me. Every step of the way."

I know he is asking me for more than just work. He wants to spend time together, a lot of time, and I can't help the smile that is now forming on my lips, because I want that too.

"I think I can manage you," I say, my eyes meeting him in a challenge. His nostrils flare, and his Adam's apple bobs as he swallows. The tension in the room escalates... again.

"We will have cameras on us all the time. They will be relentless. You will be judged. Fairly or unfairly, the media will comment on your appearance, what you do, what you don't do." He looks worried, a little crinkle in his forehead showing me his concern.

"I can handle it." And I can. I have already been to

hell and back in my short life—a few photos with a billionaire is child's play.

"I will protect you. Whatever you need, I will give it to you. I will always have your back." He nods to me, ensuring the words penetrate, and they do. He's got me. He won't let me fall. I feel that truth deep in my core.

"I believe you. I will have your back too," I offer, wanting him to know that I will do whatever I can to support him.

He steps closer to me, just as close as we were before, and leans down to whisper in my ear. "And tomorrow night... I want you with me. At the event and after. Tomorrow night... you are all mine," he grits out, his warm breath teasing my sensitive skin, the sensation reaching my nipples that peak under my blouse. As he pulls away, I look at his smile, which almost disarms me this time. I swallow then, letting his words soak in, anticipation for what he is promising seeping into my bones.

"Tomorrow, I will be all yours..." I say back to him, and his eyes alight. His jaw clenches slightly, and I hold my breath. The words we both say leaving no room for questions. He wants me and I want him.

There is a knock on his office door, so I take the opportunity to grab my things and leave them to it. I need air, coffee, and to swap out my panties, because one more look from Harrison, and I will be a puddle on the floor.

15

BETH

A s the afternoon sun hangs low in the sky, the makeup artist finishes up my look with a swipe of gloss on my lips.

"There, all done and looking ah-mazing!" she gushes.

"Thank you so much, I really appreciate it."

"You haven't even looked at yourself! Here," she says, stepping to the side so I can get my first glimpse at myself in the full-length mirror. I am momentarily stunned as I look at the woman staring back at me.

"Wow..." is all that comes from me as I stand in shock because I do look amazing. Natural, yet glamorous. Like an enhanced version of myself. My hair is so shiny and vibrant; I had no idea it could ever look like this. It is striking as it falls down past my shoulders in soft waves that rival any shampoo commercial. My body is held tight, wrapped in a classic black gown which covers everything but makes my curves so smooth that even I want to touch them. My shiny lips are reflecting the lights from the ceiling, and my black lashes are so long they throw shadows on my cheeks.

"Wow is right. When Harrison calls, I run, but on this occasion, I am glad I did. You look perfect! Such a natural beauty." I smile at her kind words.

"Does he call you to dress women often?" I ask and internally cringe as the question leaves my lips.

"No. Never. Usually, it's for his brothers' dates or maybe his mother. But you must be special, because you are the first woman he has ever let me near!" she says, laughing, and I laugh with her, even though my stomach is doing crazy flips right now.

"I just can't believe this is me!" I peer closer into the mirror, wondering if I can see anything remotely obscure, but I don't. I am styled and everything is in place and exactly where it should be. No frizzy hair, no ice cream stained top. From the tips of my toes to the top of my head, I look and feel beautiful.

As the makeup artist leaves, I grab my cell and snap a photo to send to my dad. I am surprised I get a decent shot at all because my hands are shaking, my nerves running sky high. The thought of being with Harrison has been on my mind all night. *I want you with me. At the event and after*, his voice replays over and over in my head. I shaved every area of my body for tonight, and I smell like I bathed in roses. Although I want him, I am a little anxious. And given the fact that Harrison and I nearly kissed in his office yesterday, I am a ball of nervous energy about to unravel.

We effectively remained professional over the last day,

being together and both remaining focused, but his parting words still linger regardless.

I grab my bag, checking for the third time that I have everything as I try to sort through my racing thoughts. This event is something that needs my full attention, and I need to make it my priority. Harrison and I both do.

My hotel room phone rings and reception tells me that my car is here. Not wanting to keep Harrison waiting, I rush out and get in the elevator, all while trying to act professional. This is work, not a social event, and I'm praying that my heart will stop racing so I can appear elegant for once in my life.

It takes approximately two seconds for that to fly out the window, though. As I rush out of the elevator, I run straight into a hotel staff member carrying a room service tray. Red curry, by the look and smell of it, is now all over the floor. I gasp, my hands rushing to my chest.

"I am so sorry!" The words rush out of me almost without thought, the need to constantly apologize for my clumsiness almost second nature.

"Not your fault, ma'am. I wasn't looking where I was going," the young waiter replies as he and another staff member begin to clean up the mess. I look at my dress to survey the damage, and as if someone is looking down on me tonight, I don't even have a splash on me. The black dress and shoes are still perfect, the hotel foyer floor less so. My hands are shaking a little, my nerves about seeing Harrison in a tuxedo coming to the surface.

I am about to apologize again when the staff jump up and help me step around the mess, apologizing profusely, and I quickly walk away, seeing the black limousine waiting at the front hotel entrance. I quicken my pace, which matches my breathing, and as the doorman opens the car door, I slide in and see Harrison's eyes alight like fire, staring right at me. There is no turning back now. The heat radiates from both of us, the urge to slip closer to him along the seat so strong that I grip on to the car door handle to prevent me from moving. I underestimated how hard this was going to be. To be with him, but not touch him is almost painful.

"Wow, Beth. You look great!" Eddie says with a big grin, the younger Langford brother growing on me by the day. He is more relaxed than his brother, seemingly without a care in the world. Harrison, in contrast, seems like he has the world on his shoulders, but can carry it all and then some.

"Thanks, Eddie. You too," I say with a nervous chuckle as I fidget with my clutch, my hands sweating. All I get is a small smile and a nod from Oscar while Harrison continues to stare at me. Our eyes lock, and I watch him swallow. His look is steaming as his eyes slowly lower, obviously so, taking in my full appearance before they rest back on my face. Eddie and Oscar get into a conversation about a new bill passing through Congress, ignoring us completely.

I openly look him over too. Harrison in a dinner suit is much more than I ever imagined. "You look very dapper tonight." I smile at him. It isn't a lie. I have seen him in suits almost every day. But there is something about seeing him in this black tuxedo, with the fancy lapels and the clean, impressive, shiny black shoes, that not only exudes money and power, but a self-assured confidence he seems to pass on to me.

"You look exquisite," he murmurs quietly, and I am at a loss for words. His face is serious, and I can't move my eyes from his as my breathing temporarily stops. No one has ever called me that before, and I know he means it. Whenever he talks, people listen, and it is because he is always in the moment. His focus never wavers, so you know whatever he is saying is genuine. It is one of the things that attracts me to him the most. His eyes sparkle as his lips curve upward, and I feel my cheeks heat.

"Your team did an amazing job. Thank you," I say to him. I feel like a princess going to the ball.

"Let's talk strategy," Oscar pipes up, breaking our attention. It is a short drive to the venue, and we fill the time talking about how to play out the evening. My role tonight is to meet and greet guests with Harrison and the boys and to spend time with Arthur—neither of which could ever be classed as work for me. So even though I will see Mrs. Langford again, I am quietly optimistic that it will be a good night.

As we enter the room, my body is electric. I am on edge. When Harrison stepped out of the car and turned to give me his hand, my nerves skyrocketed and haven't yet settled. In unison, we step into the ballroom, our bodies humming in anticipation, the two of us aware that it is not just the event itself that is causing it.

I look in awe at the space; it is beautiful and must have cost a fortune. I feel Harrison's fingers twitch, gripping around mine at our sides, the hand-holding shielded by my gown. I glance up him and catch him looking down at me. It is like we are the only two people in the room, despite the flashes of light.

He leans over then, his mouth next to my ear. "Your body looks fantastic in that dress, but I am itching to get it off you..." he murmurs, and my lips part at his confession as I take a sharp intake of breath. Pulling away, his eyes glisten and his smile grows wide, and he gives my hand a quick squeeze. I push the hair back from my face, feeling a little flushed.

"Let's get this party started!" Eddie says, his tone like a college student, loud enough for just us to hear, which breaks any thickening tension. I throw my head back and laugh, and I hear cameras click, bringing me back to reality again with a thud. I look back at Harrison and catch his gaze of admiration on me.

"Work," I say, to remind him of where we are.

"Work," he repeats, and our hands let go just as he is enveloped by a group of men. I take a breath to settle any remaining nerves, straighten my spine, and put my professional suit of armor on. With Harrison on one side of me and Eddie on the other, I am surrounded by men in suits. I listen to the greetings and watch the backslaps as I also take in the trays of champagne, the three-piece band, and then my eyes settle on the floral arrangements... all still with baby's breath.

I grind my teeth, not because I am upset, but because I already know how this night is going to end. People will walk out early with sniffles and headaches; no one will hear the speeches clearly because the acoustics are not right in the room, and by the looks of the trays of champagne and how quickly they are going, most people will be drunk before nine p.m.

Out of the corner of my eye, I see Lillian Harper looking like a supermodel as she walks up to Harrison and latches on to his arm on his other side. I struggle not to roll my eyes. Harrison stiffens slightly beside me, the movement so minute that no one else would notice. But I do. I also notice how her manicured red nails wrap around his elbow as she laughs loudly at something one of the men in the group was saying, injecting herself into their conversation. I turn around and see that Oscar has already wandered off and has started networking and am thankful that Eddie stands firmly beside me, since Harrison is now stuck with a group of men and Lillian, with no chance of escape for a while.

I tried to do some due diligence last night to prepare for tonight, looking through the guest list and trying to put faces to names so I wasn't totally out of my element. My searching led me down a rabbit hole of Harrison, which also led me to investigate Lilly more. So while in bed, wearing my mismatched sleepwear and a dollar store face mask, I succumbed to image after image of the two of them. I have researched her before, but never to this depth, and after seeing so many pictures of her and Harrison together from over the years, I couldn't help but feel inferior to her glamorous looks.

As I look at them together now, my confidence in my appearance tonight begins to wane. Yet another reminder that I am in a world that I have absolutely no right to be in. I am just surprised I haven't spilled a drink yet or caused some other catastrophe. Although the night is still young. Maybe I will be a true Cinderella and last until midnight before it all disappears.

"Are you ready to enter the ring?" Eddie asks, and I smile.

I push my shoulders back. "Yes. I'm ready."

"Remember the plan. Smile, meet and greet, and chat with Arthur."

"Got it."

Leaving Harrison to his chatter, we walk into the room, and Eddie introduces me to a few people. The men eye me up and down, and I don't particularly like it, but I talk with their wives and greet them all warmly, taking on board what each of them say and making mental notes that I can report back to the team on. Eddie grabs my elbow and steers me across the crowded room and introduces me to another two men, who both look almost as attractive as Harrison.

"Beth, these are my other brothers, Tennyson and Ben."

I find out Tennyson runs the family construction company, and Ben is the CFO and new CEO of the law firm now that Harrison is amid his campaign and potential governorship.

"So you are the woman who put our mother in a bad mood all week. Cheers," Tennyson says, raising his glass. My eyes widen as I feel the sarcasm dripping from his lips.

"No drink?" Ben asks, looking around and signaling to a waiter.

"I don't drink," I respond, shaking my head. I have never been a big drinker. I don't even want to think about the type of damage I would cause if I had a few drinks; my clumsiness is not something that needs enhancing.

"You will soon since you are dealing with her. Water?" Tennyson asks as a waiter passes, and I nod quickly before he hands me a glass. He seems to really dislike his mother, and I am glad I am not the only one who appears to not get along with her.

"Thanks. So... does your mother hate me?" I ask, scrunching my face, ready for the slap of truth that is coming.

"Our mother hates most people, so I wouldn't take it to heart," Ben says, and all three boys smirk like it is an inside joke.

"Well, she and Lillian seem to get along," I mention as I see the two of them crowding around Harrison across the room.

"She wants Harrison and Lilly to marry, but that is never going to happen," Tennyson says as the other two half laugh, half snort in agreement, and my stomach drops to the floor. Combating Lilly is one thing, but his mother is an entirely different issue.

"She seems lovely," I offer, taking a sip of water. She certainly looks the part. Jealousy coils in my stomach as I watch her swan around Harrison. She would be a very elegant first lady of Maryland and that thought stabs me in the chest as her hand curls around Harrison's arm again. The move seems natural to her, yet I see Harrison step sideways, away from her a little. Creating distance. A move he doesn't do with me.

"She is like a sister. Our little bratty sister. Harrison

feels nothing but brotherly love toward her," Ben says by way of explanation, and I remain quiet.

"But by the looks of things, he has his eye on someone else," Tennyson says, and I turn to see who Harrison is looking at and find him looking directly at me. My heart stills. The heat in his gaze is evident to everyone in the room. I feel like I need a sip of wine after all.

"Oh no. Looks like the boss man is looking for you," Ben quips with a sly smirk as he sips his glass of whiskey. If only he knew...

"Okay, off to work I go," I say with a well-practiced, plastered smile, ignoring their looks of intrigue. I subtly brush my sweaty palms on my dress and clench and re-clench my clutch.

"Great to meet you both," I offer as I walk over to where Harrison is standing with another man, my knees already feeling like Jell-O.

"Beth," Harrison says with relief and a small smile. "This is Ronald Harper, a long-time friend of my father's and a great supporter of my campaign." Harrison makes the introductions while his hand settles on the small of my back. The move is startling because it is something the whole room can see if they are watching. My eyes flick to his immediately, and he gives me a wink. I don't know why that makes me feel so good, but it does, and work or no work, I don't want him to move it.

"Great to meet you, Mr. Harper," I say, extending my hand to shake as Lillian's father looks at me with a pinched expression. I can already feel his coldness toward me like I am about to touch ice.

"Harrison, I was expecting Lilly to be on your arm

tonight?" he questions, ignoring me and my outstretched hand completely.

I drop my hand and move a little in my high heels, feeling slightly uncomfortable as Harrison's hand curls around me even more, now gripping my hip, keeping me close, his body almost like a protective shield. My heart rate increases and I'm not sure if it is nerves at being so obscene to these people they don't even want to greet me, or the fact that Harrison is being so overt with his actions. Mr. Harper's eyes flick down to Harrison's hand, taking in the movement, and I see his shoulders stiffen. He is not happy.

"This is Beth, my project manager." Harrison finishes the introductions, ignoring the previous comment, and I wonder how anyone in this room gets anything done with the amount of ignoring that happens. If I spoke to everyone here tonight, I bet I would find so many elephants in this room, it would be suffocating.

I feel Harrison's hand continue to caress my lower back and warm tingles ignite my body. I know he is trying to ensure I am okay, so I straighten my spine. I have dealt with worse men in my life, and I can hold my own, but I need to be professional. This is a work event, regardless of the fact that my temporary boss moves his hand, firmly placing it on my lower back, making me feel like I am a princess at his ball.

Before either of us can talk further, the emcee comes onto the microphone and asks us all to take a seat.

"Remember, you're sitting with Eddie and me at our family table." Harrison words coast across my ear as he leans down to whisper. Mr. Harper has already walked away, and I take a deep breath, hoping I don't do something stupid like trip over my dress. We make our way to the table, where we are both meant to be sitting, but there is only one spare seat.

"Harrison, you are over here, next to me," Lilly says, sitting up straight in her chair, smiling like a Cheshire cat. I look up at Harrison to see him fuming and eyeing his mother, who remains quiet.

"I can move," Eddie offers, going to stand as he and Oscar both look between me and Harrison. This is Harrison's family table, but he added Oscar and me as his key staff. Clearly, I was moved at the last moment, yet no one bothered to tell me of the switch.

"No!" I say quickly, putting up both my hands to stop him from moving, my wide smile as fake as my lashes tonight. "I am sure I can find my seat elsewhere. It is no trouble."

Growing up, I was often teased at school because I never had a mom come to the special Mother's Day events. The one thing my father always said was to kill the bullies with kindness. So I make the decision to slaughter Mrs. Langford and Lilly with my smile.

"Beth," Harrison murmurs, his hand still not leaving my back, where it has been for the last five minutes, the warmth the only comfort I have from the cold eyes staring at me from the table.

"Harrison, sit, please. I will find a spot," I say, stepping away from him, pulling on all my inner strength, yet feeling like I am back at school and the popular crowd doesn't want me to sit with them at the lunch table.

"Mother, I..." Harrison starts to say, about to walk

toward her, and I grab his hand, stopping him mid-stride. He looks at me, and I shake my head, feeling his grip on mine get tighter. He is not happy, and I give him a small smile, trying to reassure him I am fine, when really, I feel anything but. Glancing around the room, I notice that most people have taken their seats and all eyes are on us.

"Let me get you another seat," Harrison says, looking up and around the room.

"It's fine, I promise. I spot Arthur over by the bar. Let me chat with him." I pull away from him quickly to avoid any scene being caused.

Nodding to everyone, I flash my bright smile even wider, stepping away quickly and quietly as the emcee starts to officially welcome everyone. As if my fairy godmother appears, I spot Arthur standing by the bar, watching the interaction, and breathe out a sigh of relief. I go to him without a second thought.

"That family are assholes, Bethy," he mutters so only I can hear, before handing me a glass of cold water.

I take it and throw back half of it immediately.

"Thanks, I needed that," I whisper.

"You hold your head high. Harrison has seen something in you. Don't let his mother or anyone else bully you around."

"I'm used to it. Happens all the time in events. Besides, it is a work event. I need to remain professional."

"Seeing how Harrison behaves around you, I would say it may not be all about work with him, my dear," he says as the emcee announces entrees are being served, and the crowd starts to chatter as their food is brought out. Arthur is perceptive, but I didn't think he, of all people, would bother looking at Harrison's and my interaction. Maybe we weren't as subtle earlier as I had thought we were.

"Let's go and hide around the back, away from these pompous assholes," Arthur says, pointing to a private space at the end of the bar.

"Don't you have a seat?" I ask, starting to panic that they didn't include him either and wanting to ensure he eats.

"Oh, I have a seat, Bethy, but they are not serving my meal. They are serving some raw Kingfish crap that I don't eat. So I want to get your thoughts on something, then I am leaving," he says matter-of-factly

I look over to where Oscar is, having already gotten up from the table and now in deep conversation with another businessman sitting on the other side of the room who we are trying to secure support from. When my eyes find Harrison, I see him stand from the table, his gaze already on mine, and I shake my head a little and give him another smile of reassurance.

We both seem to understand the other without even talking. The two of us are in tune; it is like nothing else I have ever experienced with another person.

I don't want him to be worried about the seating arrangements, but rather focused on his speech tonight. I turn and walk around the corner and sit with Arthur, where we hide for the next hour, skipping the entrees and mains.

"Tell me, why should I be supporting Harrison? Give me your thoughts. You were quiet at our meeting. I want to know what you think." Arthur goes straight into business mode, and I appreciate it.

"To be honest, it is a big decision. I don't know half of your history with him or his family. What I do know is that I have known him for merely a few weeks. I have been part of his campaign team for only a short amount of time, yet there is something about him. I don't know what it is, but he is not like his mother. I never knew his father, so I can't compare him, but he is solid, dependable. I challenged him in relation to the development of my community center, and he held strongly to his redevelopment idea, but showed flexibility in the approach to it, ensuring that community consultation would happen. I can't tell you what to do, Arthur, and I am still learning all about this political game. But he has my vote, and I am excited to see what he can achieve once he is named governor," I say, the honesty flowing from my lips. I love Arthur and I would never just give him a sales pitch. His friendship means more to me than all the money in this room. He is also smart enough to make his own decisions on this, more informed than me on the topic, I am sure.

"Well, if he has your support, Bethy, he will have mine," Arthur says, taking a sip of his whiskey.

"You are doing this because you want to, right? Not because of me?"

"I am doing this because Harrison will make a great leader. I believe, despite his awful parents, that he will do good for the community, and if what you say about his investment in infrastructure is correct, then he will be good for the local economy too. Besides, he will win,

Bethy. Make no mistake, your world is going to change a lot in a few months when he becomes governor."

"I am with him for three months for his campaign, then I am back in DC," I state in a rush, feeling the need to clear up any confusion.

"We'll see. Baltimore looks good on you," he says cheekily, and I smile. I tend to agree with him. I am so excited, I want to hug him. So I do. With big smiles on our faces, we step away from our quiet corner at the bar and, together, we watch just in time to see Harrison take the stage to give his speech.

He doesn't miss a beat. The same speech I have heard fifty times over the past forty-eight hours rolls off his tongue with precision, and his eyes look over the crowd, ensuring everyone feels connected.

"Your boy is good, I'll give him that," Arthur murmurs as the crowd erupts into cheers for him, and I am still on cloud nine from getting Arthur's support.

Then it starts.

Arthur sneezes. Grabbing his handkerchief, he rubs his nose.

"Damn baby's breath. Didn't you tell them to leave that out?" Arthur asks, my previous tales of events over the years firmly scorched into his brain.

I sigh. "I did."

He sneezes again.

"I will leave you to it. I can't stand these allergies. Chess this week?" he asks, already stepping to the door.

"Maybe. Let's talk," I say with a smile, and he waves his arm at me as he walks out the door, not looking back.

I turn and survey the room. I see a few men wiping

their noses with their pristine white handkerchiefs, while the black uniformed staff members scurry around them.

"So, you must be starving?" Eddie says as he comes up beside me.

"Hey! No, actually, I'm doing fine." I am so excited about Arthur that I couldn't possibly eat now.

"I apologize. That was not the table seating that Harrison approved. My mother..."

"It's not a problem, Eddie, really. No harm." Even though it made me feel stupid, he doesn't need to feel bad about his mother's actions.

"It won't happen again. Harrison was pissed." My heart fills a little at knowing that Harrison was just as upset as I was that we couldn't be together tonight. Our distance was not something of our own doing.

"So, I got Warner," Oscar says as he joins us, his smile small but there just the same. I listen to his tale of how he got one of the leading physicians over the line to support our healthcare policies while my eyes roam the room. People are leaving already, and the event looks like it is wrapping up. Much earlier than I was anticipating.

"So he is supporting Harrison and donating twenty-five thousand to the campaign as well, which is great," Oscar says, and I want to share my news with them, but I want to tell Harrison first.

"I see people leaving; is it over already?" I ask. In DC, these parties go for hours, but the staff have only just finished serving dessert.

"Everyone has allergies," Eddie says.

"You've got to be kidding?" Oscar says, bewildered, looking around the room, his voice tense.

I remain quiet, even though I want to say *I told you so*. I look at the people remaining. I notice Harrison shaking hands and chatting with some men near the bar. The media have all packed up and no doubt have gone to file their stories for tomorrow.

"Beth, you're still here?" Mrs. Langford says from the side as she joins our conversation.

"Oh, yes. It is a great event, Mrs. Langford. The room looks lovely," I comment, wanting to try and be nice, when I only want to tell her what I really think.

"I am so sorry for the seating. We must have missed you on the seating chart!" she says in a fake apology.

"It's fine. I actually had a very productive meeting while everyone was eating so it all worked out well." She pays little attention to me as she slips on her coat.

"Well, I'm off for the night. Good night, boys," she says, ignoring me as she sashays out the door, along with most of the guests. Shocked, I look around the room, wondering who is responsible for cleanup. I notice Lillian over by Harrison, trying hard to push into the conversation he is having with one of the key funders I met earlier tonight. Harrison's body language tells me everything I need to know about that situation, not including her at all.

"Excuse me for a minute," I say to Eddie and Oscar, walking out to the kitchen to speak to the venue crew. As expected, they have no idea what is going on. They have trays of coffee and petit fours lined up to be served, but with over half the guests now gone or sneezing their way through dessert, no coffee will be needed.

I decide to take charge of this event and get it sorted. I

tell them to stop serving and start cleaning up instead. I head out into the main room and grab the waiters into a small group over in the corner and brief them of the new plan. They look relieved at finally having some direction and they inconspicuously start cleaning tables and ushering guests. I position more staff at the cloakroom to push through the departing crowd quicker, and I help the bar team close down the tab and get the final paperwork sorted. Nothing has been paid, so I grab all the invoices and find Oscar, and together, we finish everything off.

"There you are." Harrison's warm voice soothes me from behind. I have been so busy the last hour with the event logistics, I hadn't even seen where he went.

"Oh, sorry, were you looking for me?" I ask, turning to see his deep eyes locked on to me. He looks stressed, his hair a little messy, like he has been pulling at it all night.

"Are you alright?" I ask, concerned something bad has happened.

"No. I hated not being with you tonight, and I have been looking for you for the last hour," he grits out as he stalks straight up to me and grabs my hand. He doesn't stop as he begins to pull me toward a small darkened alcove off to the side of the bar.

"Harrison?" My steps quicken in my heels, trying to keep pace, my heart thumping at the thought of what he's up to.

We reach the secluded spot, and he stops us. As he turns to face me, I see everything in his eyes.

"Fuck, Beth, I have wanted my lips on yours all night," he growls, and he slowly steps closer, like he is stalking his prey. Heat flames my insides as I watch him unravel in front of me.

"Really?" I tease, making his smile turn into a sexy smirk.

"God, yes." He sighs before closing the distance between us and grabbing my jaw with one hand as the other curls around my waist. I meet him halfway, my hands fisting the lapels on his tux jacket and pulling him to me as our lips smash together, needing each other more than the air we breathe. The feeling of his lips on mine is everything I've been yearning for.

He growls deep and low in his chest as he pushes me backward, my body hitting the wall behind me with a gasp as he deepens the kiss even more.

My heart races as my grip remains white-knuckled, pulling at his jacket, almost mauling him. The night ended mere moments ago, and we're on each other like wildfire.

"You feel so fucking good," he whispers between kisses, his hand traveling up my hips and waist and back down again, feeling my curves. I moan into his mouth at the feel of his touch, arching a little, craving so much more. His tongue sweeps out, running across my lower lip, then sliding against mine in a dance that has my mind whirling.

I can't remember the last kiss I had. I don't date; I don't have one-night stands. I work and look after my dad. That's it. I lost my virginity awkwardly in college, and had a few other boyfriends afterward, but nobody has ever made me feel this way. Like a kiss could be the end of my sanity. I clutch on to Harrison in the hope I don't lose the feeling in my legs and fall because he is all-encompassing.

"I don't want to stop. I need you," I whisper against his lips, throwing all my good judgment out the window, probably along with my job, as my body presses against his, almost to the point of begging.

I feel his grip on my waist tightening as he growls, our bare raw need thrumming in both of us, to the point that I am surprised we are even still clothed. My heart beats rapidly, and I'm feeling almost drunk with sensation.

"Fuck, I need to get you home," he says, tugging on my bottom lip with his teeth before kissing me again, both his hands now encasing my waist, as mine curl up around the back of his neck, playing with his hair.

I whimper, having never felt so safe and secure. I feel like I am floating.

"Yes, you do," a voice says from close by, and we pull apart suddenly to find Eddie standing in the hallway a few feet away with a wicked smirk on his face.

I gasp in surprise and Harrison growls in warning, the sound traveling up my chest and making my nipples peak.

"I thought you left already?" he grumbles, his hold on me loosening, and I want to bury my head in my hands, knowing that I have embarrassment written all over my cheeks. I look around, not seeing anyone else, then I look at Eddie eyeing us both, his gaze dancing in delight before he says his goodbyes and struts away.

The realization of what we just did now filters in my mind. There was a line. We both knew it and we crossed it. There is no going back now. The understanding of what my life is now going to be like sits heavy. It is going to be increasingly hard to try to remain strictly professional around him until the elections. It might be the hardest job I have ever had to do. But I will. I made my choice, and I don't regret it.

Harrison's hands drop from my body, the two of us aware that if the gossip websites got wind of Harrison being romantic with one of his staff members, it would not only make headline news, but could jeopardize his chances of becoming governor, regardless if I am a temporary secondment or not.

Were we stupid to kiss? Absolutely. Would I do it again? Without hesitation.

"You ready?" he asks, looking down at me like he wants to devour me whole, his gaze making me feel giddy with excitement.

"I'm ready," I say, smiling, and his own lips quirk as his eyes glisten in delight.

My heart skips as his hand takes position at my lower back, and we walk out of the venue behind Eddie through a back entrance, where no one can see us.

16

HARRISON

Holding her hand in the elevator is pure torture. But I remind myself that I am a fucking gentleman, despite the desire swirling in my body that makes me want to rip her clothes off right here, right now.

My commitment for no distractions during this campaign flew out the window weeks ago, because my mind has been consumed by the beautiful woman whose hand I am holding for almost every minute of every day since I saw her again in DC I clench and unclench my other hand, pulling on my restraint like never before to ensure I do this right with her. When, really, all I want to do is push her up against the elevator wall, get on my knees, lift her dress, and put my face between her fucking outstanding legs. I crack my neck to keep myself standing still, as I see the lights in the elevator move up to my penthouse at what feels like a snail's pace.

If I am honest with myself, bringing her on my team was an impulse. I saw her, I wanted her, and I had to have her. But seeing how well we work together, it is like she is an extension of me, and when I saw her tonight, all bets were off. There was no way I could keep my hands to myself any longer. PH lights up on the wall, and when the elevator opens to my penthouse floor, I barely have her inside my private residence before my lips find hers again.

"Harrison," she says breathily as I capture her lips with mine, tasting her, my tongue swirling with hers. I can't get enough.

"You look fucking incredible in this dress," I groan against her lips, my hands running up and down her perfect body, wanting to memorize her curves.

"All thanks to you," she murmurs, as my lips leave hers momentarily, and I dive into the crook of her neck, licking and savoring her skin, her signature rose aroma now my favorite scent. Her head falls back, opening herself to me, as her hands reach up and dive into my hair, gripping and pulling, massaging my scalp, and I fucking love it.

"I feel like I have been waiting forever for you," I say honestly. The last few weeks have felt like years, waiting for the moment I'd finally get to kiss her. Oscar was right. She has been a distraction, and now I am diving headfirst into her.

"But what about the campaign..." she says, bringing it back to reality. "I don't want us to be an issue." My lips find hers again, and she whimpers against me, kissing me back with just as much passion. Pulling away, I take a breath and try to ease her worries.

"We will keep us private, until we know what this is.

But to be honest, Beth, I don't know how I am going to work with you and not touch you. I already need a medal for my self-control up to this point." I huff a laugh and smile, which she returns.

"Okay, we will keep it between us..." she says as she lifts on her tippy-toes and puts her lips on mine again, and that is all the invitation I need.

"I want to rip this dress from your body," I groan. I have waited so long to make her mine. I still remember that first time I saw her, mopping up the spilled champagne from my shoes. I must have looked like a total asshole watching her do it, but I was mesmerized. Trying to erase the memories of her eyes has been a daily activity for me since then, and now that I have her in my arms, I am not going to let her go.

"Don't you dare!" she scolds me. "The zipper is at the back; it is too beautiful to rip." And I don't hesitate. My hands move around to the back of her dress and I find the zipper and pull it down, feeling the soft skin of her back and her ass as much as I can with the action.

I step back and see her swallow, and I don't know how, but I wait, patiently, for her to do the rest.

"Let me look at you," I say, my voice pained. I am rock hard and still fully clothed, but I want to see what is underneath this dress more than anything else. She is a little tentative at first, but slowly, she shows me. She lowers the dress from her shoulders and lets it fall from her voluptuous figure, the material skimming her skin before falling to the floor, puddling at her feet.

"Fucking beautiful." Her cheeks pinken at my compliment, and I step forward and pick her up.

"Harrison!" she squeals in my arms as I carry her bridal style and walk down the hall to my bedroom, leaving her dress on the floor near my front door.

"Harrison! Put me down!" She laughs, wriggling in my arms.

"Fine!" I say as I throw her onto my bed before I rip my tie off and pull my jacket from my shoulders.

I watch her breasts bounce, before her body sinks into my silky sheets, and I am pulling at my shirt at a pace that is sure to tear buttons. She looks around the room before her gaze lands back on me, and she drinks in my now naked torso. The last time she saw me half-naked, she couldn't stand to look at me, but now she can't stop.

"You are carved from stone," she murmurs as she admires my body, her eyes on me doing wonders for my ego as I undo my belt and pull down my suit pants. Now in nothing but my boxers, I stalk toward her. My gaze is hot on hers, and I watch her swallow roughly.

"Your body is fucking amazing." I get closer and run my hands up her body. Feeling her curves, watching her breasts fill her strapless bra, her breaths making them quiver as she shivers beneath me. She has black lace underwear, the kind I really want to peel from her body with my teeth.

I lean over her, taking her lips again, as I join her on the bed and sink my body onto hers. Pushing my hips into her, my cock brushes her core, making her moan, wanting her to feel what she does to me.

"See what you do to me, Beth. See how hard I am for

you," I grit out as my nose trails a pattern from her cheeks down her neck and back again.

"It's been a long time..." she says, looking up at me, vulnerability showing in her eyes.

"I will take care of you," I whisper, and I must say the right thing, because her hand cups the back of my head and she pulls me to her lips again.

As we unravel, her hands run up my body, exploring my ridges as I move lower and pull her bra cup down, taking one of her ample breasts into my mouth, sucking on her nipple and wondering how long I can last because I already want to explode.

She whimpers, arching her back and thrusting her chest out farther and I pull the other cup down, before moving my mouth to the other side. She has fantastic breasts, and I mold them with my hands, pinching her nipples, which enlists another whimper from her.

"Goddamn, I could kiss your lips and this beautiful body all fucking day," I groan against her skin. My hands flex and clench, grabbing her, massaging her. She is all woman, and I love it. I discard her bra completely, throwing it across the room, and I make my way down her body with my lips and tongue, tasting, exploring, wanting to mark her skin as mine.

"Harrison, you feel like you are everywhere..." she murmurs as her back arches, her hands running through my hair as my lips skirt around the hem of her underwear.

I run my hands up her thick thighs, pushing them open and settling myself firmly between them, and I hear her gasp. My fingers trail up her warm, wet center on the outside of her pretty black underwear, and see her hips relax as she spreads her legs even wider. I groan at the fact that she is wanting me to touch her.

"You're so wet for me... These need to go." My hands move around her hips and grab the delicate fabric, pulling it down her legs. Now lying underneath me completely naked, she looks up at me, her eyes almost begging me to take care of her, and the feeling thrums strongly through my body that this woman is different. Very different.

I lean over her and kiss her again, the feeling of her tongue against mine addictive as my hand travels down her curves, wanting to feel all of her, wanting to touch every inch. I circle her clit with my fingers, and at the contact, she gasps. And her warm, wet center shows me exactly what she thinks of me. Her hips automatically move in rhythm to my fingers, grinding up into my hand. Our kiss becomes ferocious as my hand goes a little lower, and I push one finger inside her before taking it out and circling her clit again. I repeat the action slowly, teasingly so, over and over as she moans in my mouth, and I capture the sound.

Her body starts to squirm, her hips move a little more, and her grip is tight around my neck, keeping me close to her as her moans flow from her lungs.

"I want you to come on my fingers, baby. Then I want to feed you my cock," I murmur, and the dirty talk is obviously something she likes because, in that moment, her orgasm rushes from her, her fingers white-knuckled against my skin, her breath hitching before she lets out a high-pitched moan and I feel her body shaking beneath me as her hips gyrate against my hand even faster.

"I'm coming, oh God!" she moans, her head falling back onto the bed, and I watch her release transform her expression into one of euphoria.

"Fucking beautiful," I murmur as I watch her catch her breath and open her eyes to look at me. I am so fucking hard, I'm struggling to be a gentleman, and then I see her sly smile appear on her face as I run my hands up her body.

"Harrison, that was... amazing," she says on a breath as I lean over and take one of her nipples into my mouth again and suck on it slowly. Lifting away, my gaze remains on her as I bring my fingers to my mouth and suck. Her eyes widen and her pupils dilate, looking at me tasting her, and she tastes as good as she looks.

17

BETH

My body sinks into the bed underneath the man who has totally swept me off my feet tonight, the one who has my heart racing like never before.

I can't believe this is happening. I am panting, my muscles in my legs quivering, my heart beating so fast. But it has already been one of the best nights of my life.

"That was fucking fantastic," he says, kissing my skin, which is now coated in a light sheen, and lazily sucking on my nipple, which he has quickly caught on is my kryptonite as are his filthy words.

I moan as my hand falls into his hair, massaging his scalp, and I hear his chest rumble in pleasure. Lifting up, he looks into my eyes intently before capturing my lips with his again. Damn, he is a good kisser. He kisses like he really means it. He is passionate, wanting me like I am the last female on Earth.

I match his energy, gripping his hair hard as my tongue dances with his, and I can feel his hot and heavy cock as it rests against my thigh. I trail my hand down his torso, lightly skimming my fingers against his skin, until I feel his boxer briefs, the only piece of clothing left on either of us, and I slip my hand inside.

I grip him, eliciting a groan as his lips pause on mine, then I start to massage and pump his length, reveling in the way he shivers in response.

"Fuck, keep doing that, and I won't last long at all," he growls before he jumps up off me, and I sit up and lean on my elbows to watch him.

Standing on the floor at the side of the bed, he takes off his boxer briefs, and I get my first full glimpse of the man I already know is going to be the next governor. My eyes roam over him, taking in his extremely fit body, his chiseled muscles, which trail into a V at his pelvis. Then my attention drifts down as I see him gripping his perfect cock, pumping it, his eyes watching me looking at him.

Without taking his eyes from me, Harrison walks to the nightstand and opens the drawer, grabbing a box of condoms, fishing one out and leaving the others nearby. My stomach flutters in anticipation.

He is a man who is in control, knows exactly what he wants, and what he wants is me.

He sheaths himself before coming back to the bed and grabbing my hand, helping me off the mattress and walking me over to the large armchair that sits to the side of his bedroom suite.

"I want you to control our first time, Beth," he says, keeping our hands intertwined as he takes a seat like a king in a castle on the large chair and leans his head back, his eyes running up and down my naked body. "Now be a good girl and come and sit on my cock."

Good girl... Those two words light a fire under my skin. Out of the bedroom, if a man said that to me, I would probably slap him. But right here, right now, I feel my insides melt even more.

Harrison's eyes light up as I step closer. His nostrils flare and his grip on my hand tightens as he pulls me on top of him.

"You like me praising you just as much as you like my dirty talk, don't you, baby?" Harrison comments just before his warm, wet mouth encases my nipple, sucking it.

"I do," I admit breathlessly as I straddle him, getting into position on my knees. I should feel awkward, but I don't. I feel wanted.

"Well, then be a good girl and slide your wet pussy onto my cock until I make you scream."

I slowly lower myself, as his hand grips his length and he pulls me into position. I feel his tip pushing at my entrance, stretching me. He is huge, and I hold my breath, waiting for all of him.

"Breathe, Beth. You can take me, I got you." His mouth closes in on my nipple again as my hands grip the back of the armchair behind his head. I lower myself more, feeling all of him, and my head falls back as I take him in completely, letting out a long moan.

"Fuck, you are tight. Move your hips for me... Show me what I do to you," he grits out as both his hands grip my ass cheeks and his head falls back to the chair again, admiring me openly. His eyes are lust drunk, and he bites his lower lip as I begin to move. My hips grind and bounce like a dancer, even though I am one of the most uncoordinated people I know.

"That's my girl. Fucking beautiful dirty girl jumping up and down on my cock," he moans, sparking desire throughout my body, and every time I move, I feel like I am going to explode.

"Harrison, this feels..." I pant, becoming breathless, my breasts heaving in time with my body.

"Fucking amazing," Harrison finishes for me, and I feel his hand slide up my bare back, and grab my hair before he fists it, pulling it back.

My head falls back with it, my body arching, my hips now moving differently, the pressure on my clit intoxicating. I feel like I am having an out-of-body experience.

"Harrison, I can't, I'm going to..." I pant out, our bodies slapping, our deep need for each other evident as his fingers grip my skin with one hand as the other pulls my hair even tighter.

"Come for me, Beth, come all over my cock like the good girl you are." My hands remain white-knuckled as I buckle and gyrate on Harrison, letting my release overtake me.

"Harrison!" I yell his name out into the room, thankful we are on our own because I hear the echo as pure ecstasy consumes me.

"Fuck, Beth!" Harrison shouts almost in sync with me, his grip tight, his ab muscles clenching as he thrusts deeper, his orgasm as intense as my own.

I'm hot and breathless, my hair a mess of waves

around my head, and as I come down from my high, I loosen my grip on the back of the chair and slump against him. Harrison's hands massage my body, moving up and down my back, drawing soft moans from my chest.

I'm spent. Never before have I experienced the level of arousal I have in the last few hours with Harrison.

We are quiet for a few minutes, both sated and perfectly content.

"Let's get in the shower. I want you on your knees for me with that pretty little mouth of yours wrapped around my cock." His dirty talk continues, and I lick my lips, already knowing that my knees will buckle for him gladly.

I pull back to look at him, giving him a lazy smile.

"Yes, sir." I smirk, already looking forward to what else Harrison has in store for us.

WE MAKE it back to his bedroom, showered, with wet hair and weak muscles, ready for sleep. As I lie on top of his enormous bed, I watch him as he walks toward me from the bathroom.

"I like you in my bed," he says as his eyes glide over my naked body, taking in my long red hair that I grew up hating, which now makes me feel invincible. The confidence I now have in my body compared to only weeks ago is surprising, but I trail my fingers up over my hips, tracing my curves, and lowering them again. He watches with interest.

He turns off the light, leaving us in the light glow of the moon from his windows as he crawls in next to me.

"How do you feel?" he asks, looking at me, the wrinkle between his brows showing me he is somewhat concerned.

I lift my hand and rub the small dent between his brows like I have wanted to since the moment I met him, the tension in his head leaving immediately.

"Perfect," I say quietly, because it's the truth. I have never felt this good naked ever. I have never felt this good before, during, or after sex, period. As Harrison's eyes sweep across my face, I give him a small smile, one which he returns.

"Good. Me too. Are you sure you are okay after what happened with the table seating?" Harrison asks, referring to his mother and her antics.

"It wasn't ideal, but it's fine," I say, putting up my hand in front of my chest in surrender, wanting to just brush it off and forget about it.

"It is not fine, and it won't happen again," he grits out, clearly still angry over the incident, and he grabs my hand from in front of me.

"Seriously, it is no problem." I again try to brush it off as he intertwines our fingers down by our sides. The touch soothes me, any stress or tension I felt now drifting away.

"It is for me. Tell me, why did I see you chatting with the waiters and walking in the kitchen tonight? Did something go wrong?" he asks, his eyebrows crinkling once more. I take in a deep breath and sigh, the hectic night now catching up with me. His thumb strums across my hand and tingles shoot up my arm.

"No. Just finalizing the event. Your mom left early, and I couldn't find Lillian, so I just did it," I say with a shrug, starting to feel exhausted. Yet his touch is giving me his strength.

"What a mess..." he murmurs, rubbing his head and remaining quiet.

"Oscar got the doctor," he says with a smile, his blue eyes dancing with happiness.

"Yes, I know. That's great," I say, my smile automatically matching his.

"It is. How was your night? Where did you go?" His question leaves me warm. It is nice to know he was looking for me. That I wasn't out of sight, out of mind.

"I was chatting with Arthur for most of it," I state coyly. I am so happy about what I'm about to share, and I know he will be too.

He pauses, his brow rising at the look on my face. "And? Any luck?" His eyes are wide, waiting for my answer. I chew on my bottom lip, trying unsuccessfully to hide my grin.

"He is donating one hundred thousand and will be writing a public letter of support tomorrow, which he is going to publish in the newspaper," I say, not able to help the broad smile that stretches across my face.

"What?" Harrison sits up, shocked, his eyes now wide as his smile turns into his watermelon trademark grin.

"Yep! He can see the good work you will do and is happy to support your campaign."

"Yes!" he says, grabbing my face and pulling it up to

meet his, catching me in a panty-melting kiss. The movement catches me off guard and I squeal, gripping his shoulders for support.

"Beth, that is amazing!" He stops and lowers me back to the bed, and his hand lazily skirts down my neck, over my shoulders, and down my bare body. His face stays mere inches from mine, and I feel his hot breath on my lips.

"You're amazing," he murmurs, and my pulse speeds up from the way he's looking into my eyes. I momentarily lose the ability to breathe.

"So are you," I say honestly, trying to remain calm, but feeling the total opposite.

Lying side by side, we stay quiet for a while, sharing sweet kisses, caressing each other's bodies, his eyes rarely leaving mine for more than a second.

All is exactly as I could ever dream it to be until my mind starts spinning.

"How are we ever going to hide this, Harrison?" I ask, not wanting this moment to end.

He looks serious for a moment, deep in thought. "I don't know. But what I do know is, now that I have had a taste, I have no idea how the hell I am supposed to work with you and not want to bend you over my desk every chance I get," he grumbles, his fingers pressing into my hip.

"But we can't. We have months of campaigning ahead of us. One small slipup could mean the end of it all. I don't want to be the reason you don't win."

Harrison looks at me, his wrinkle now back. "I don't want the media to hound you or your father, to interrupt your life. I don't want you to become a pawn in their game. Because if they get wind of this, then that is what will happen," he says seriously, his hand moving up to cup my cheek.

"Then we are professional at work..." I say, hoping this means I still get to have him in some way.

"And I have you all to myself behind closed doors..." he finishes, then leans forward and takes my lips again.

The night is still young, and our poorly thought-out plan is moved to the back of our minds. Our thoughts are now only on each other.

18

HARRISON

As I tee off on the third hole of the day, my body is weary, but my mind is racing. I have been having a shit round of golf with my brothers so far and just to prove that I am consistent, my ball now soars over the lush green of the fairway and lands with precision into the bunker.

"Shit," I mumble, yet not at all disappointed. My smile is a mile wide because I can still smell her scent on my skin.

"That is a shit shot, asshole. Why the hell are you still smiling?" Tennyson says, looking at me dumbfounded. I would say he is grumpy this morning, but he is always like this, so I just shrug and walk back to my bag.

"Did you get laid last night?" Ben asks, and Eddie laughs.

"None of your business," I say to them as I walk away from their glaring stares, throwing my club back into my golf bag and standing near the cart, waiting for the rest of them to take their shots. My emotions are a mix of delight at having Beth in my bed and tasting every inch of her body, to confusion at waking up to her gone.

She left me a note, telling me she had to get home, but I wish she had woken me. Clearly, all the exercise we did had me out cold, and I was looking forward to more of her this morning. But I know that one night is not the end, and a woman like Beth needs to have space to think through our decision.

I want her, in every way. But I also want to be governor and if I could win both, then that would be amazing. But since I am just starting my campaign, I can't be seen publicly romanticizing a new woman, especially one who is on my team, no matter how much I want to be with her. She knows it, and I know it. So we will be professional out in the open, and I hope to repeat our activities from last night each and every night to come. I just hope she still feels the same.

Ignoring my brothers, I answer my vibrating cell, seeing it is Oscar. I have been waiting all day for his call. The first approval poll results of the governor campaign are being released today, and I need to know how I am positioned so early on in the campaign.

"The poll results are in," Oscar says, and I am trying to interpret his tone.

"And?" I ask as Eddie comes to stand next to me, while my other two brothers are chatting with each other over near the golf tee. About work, no doubt.

"You're in the lead by a small margin. Your current approval rating sits at fifty-two percent, which is good.

The opposition is sitting at forty-eight percent, though, so it is close."

"That's good. Are you happy with that?" I ask him as Eddie nods at me with a small but proud grin.

"It's great, but we still have a bit of work to do. Have you seen the *Baltimore Business* afternoon edition?" he asks hesitantly.

"No. Why?" I ask him as Eddie gets busy bringing up the news outlet on his cell.

"They have a small story about you. About the event last night. It is fine, no issue, but you may want to look at the image they ran with. I've got to run. Talk later," he says before he ends the call, and I look over Eddie's shoulder.

Up on his cell screen is a picture of Beth and me on the front page. She looks stunning, throwing her head back in laughter, me looking at her adoringly. I remember the moment clearly. It must have been taken mid-conversation when we first arrived last night—before I got bombarded with people and dragged away from her. Eddie and Oscar were right next to us, but have been conveniently cropped out of the image.

Ben walks up, looking over Eddie's other shoulder. "So, Beth, huh? You couldn't keep your eyes off her last night."

"Beth is great. Just don't fuck it up," Eddie says to me as he pockets his phone, and I wonder if he is talking about my campaign or Beth. I file it away to ask him later.

"She is hot. I wish I had spotted her first!" Tennyson adds, stepping into the conversation. Like a true blood-hound, his reputation as a ladies' man is almost as big as my father's was. Now *he* is a playboy. My eyes thin at him, while I try hard not to grind my teeth.

"Shit, you really like her? Does she mean something to you?" Tennyson prods, knowing he hit a nerve.

"The last thing I needed was her. The last thing I was looking for was a woman. You know that. But she flew into me and now she is all I can think about," I say, running my hand down my face.

I grab a golf ball and my driver to take another shot. I might as well; my game can't get any worse.

My three brothers watch me as I position myself at the tee and hit the ball strongly down the fairway again, but this time, it lands in the scrub at the side.

"Shit," I say again, walking back to where they are standing.

"Get your head in the game and off your dick," Tennyson jibes.

"What's wrong with my dick?"

"Nothing, you have a great fucking dick, almost as big and beautiful as mine," Tennyson says with a smirk.

"Can we just leave your dicks out of this?" Eddie chimes in from behind me.

"You leave your dick out of it," Tennyson pushes. "What happened to 'I'm staying away from women and focusing on my governorship campaign'?" he continues, and he is right, of course. I told them all I was swearing off women for the length of my campaign, and I have done the complete opposite.

"He's not marrying her." Ben sticks up for me as the four of us get into the golf cart to go and find our balls.

"Stop talking about her like that," I snap, hating them

for talking about her like she is just a random woman I met. She is so much more than that.

All three look at me, gobsmacked.

"Holy shit. You like her, like her. Like *really* like her?" Ben says in awe.

"Oscar is going to be pissed," says Eddie, shaking his head with a smile.

"I don't give a shit what Oscar thinks. She is different. I can't explain it. She isn't interested in my money, my family, or my business. Her head is not stuck in her phone or taking selfies. She is independent, strong, resilient, intelligent, kind, fucking beautiful..." I trail off. My brothers are quiet as I watch them all gaping at me.

"But we need to keep it quiet. At least until the end of the campaign," I say, dropping the truth bomb like it hurts. My brothers are still for another beat.

"So she will be your dirty little secret? You know how that is going to look if it gets out?" Eddie says, clearly not happy with the situation, already being a big fan of Beth's.

"It won't. Only you three and Beth know. And I am keeping it that way," I grumble, not liking it at all, but knowing this is how it has to be.

"So what are you going to do about Lilly?" Eddie asks.

"Lilly is deaf to anything I say. I have spoken to her already. I have spoken to Mom as well. They don't seem to understand that being with Lilly is not something I want. She is a great girl, we all know that, but she is like our sister."

"Her father wasn't happy last night. He didn't like

your hand on Beth when you introduced her to him, and so don't be surprised if he ends his support for your campaign," Eddie says as we drive down the freeway to our balls.

"Doesn't matter, I got Arthur," I state, having not told anyone yet about the fantastic news Beth delivered to me last night.

"What?" Eddie stops the cart sharply, and we all fall forward.

"Arthur Stratten?" Ben asks in shock, the man no one thought would ever support a Langford publicly now doing exactly that.

"How the hell did that happen?" Tennyson asks, looking dumbfounded.

"Beth."

"Beth?" Ben asks, his eyes widening.

"No wonder you fucked her," Tennyson says, and I lean over and punch him in the arm. He is the second youngest of us four boys, younger than me by only a few years, but he is just as tall and broad, so I feel like I hit cement.

"Not that I have to explain anything to you three single assholes, but she is good with people, excellent in the community, loves talking and helping. She is gold for me and for my campaign."

"Is that all she is gold for?" Ben asks, trying to gauge where my feelings are with it all. Perceptive, as always.

"No. She is fucking ingrained in me. Now, let's get back to the game," I say as I jump out of the cart to my ball in the scrub. Standing tall, my brothers are silent as I take my shot. I hit again and watch my ball fly through the air, soaring close to the putting green before leaning left and landing right in the bunker.

This is going to be a long fucking game.

19

BETH

I could not feel any further from how I did last night. Literally less than twenty-four hours ago, I was being primped and polished by the team of magicians that Harrison sent to my hotel for the event his mother planned. Before the billionaire himself made a meal out of me for the remainder of the night. Today, however, I am on my roof, in the oldest clothes I have so I don't get anything decent from my wardrobe ruined by the muddy slush I am combing from the gutters. As the gray clouds that were in the distance this morning now close in on me in the late afternoon, I rush to try to find the hole in the roof that is causing the leak into our ceiling.

Usually, this is something a landlord would fix, but Dad and I made a deal with him that for a lower rent, we would do all the maintenance ourselves. At the time, we thought that nothing would need fixing, and for a few years, we were right. But as the house gets older, it is not as nice as it once was, and after almost fifteen years in this place, it is starting to get even more run-down.

"Dammit!" I curse under my breath, hoping to find the hole and plug it all before Dad gets home from the center and yells at me for being on the roof. I dig my hand under the gutters and feel if I can find the area where the rain tumbles. The damp ceiling looks worse today than it did last week. So I know that if I don't find it and try to plug it in, the maintenance and repairs required to fix it will skyrocket.

I yawn slightly, tired from my night. My body is sore in places it hasn't been for a very long time. I smile at myself. Last night was magical. Like my own Cinderella dream ball. Except my Prince Charming did ungodly things to me that already has my core thrumming for him to do it all again.

I bite my lip as I think about his lips on my skin. My cheeks heat and my body feels warm, even though the wind is whipping up and the sun is now behind a dark cloud. I continue to feel around the roof cavity, my arm elbow deep in sludge, hoping I don't get bitten by a spider or worse as I continue to daydream.

"Yes!" I shout aloud to the empty garden below as my hand lands on a small hole. It is big enough for my hand to fit in, and I feel pride in myself for finding it. Quickly, I turn to grab the tools I brought up on the roof with me, some that I borrowed from my neighbor earlier in the week in preparation, and I think about how I will close it up. But as I try to wriggle my hand out of the hole to grab the spare materials, my hand doesn't move. I twist and pull, and as I do, my feet slip slightly on the tin, my body jolting to keep balance. The force of my movement rips my hand out from the hole in the tin roof and it slices my palm, straight down the middle.

"Ahhh!" I scream, grabbing my hand, losing my balance, and falling from the roof. Panic fills my bones as the air leaves my lungs, and I throw out my good hand to grip on to something. Anything!

I manage to hold on to the gutter as my body flings over the edge of my house, and I hang limply, my body dangling for exactly two seconds before my weight is too much for my grip and I let go. I thank my lucky stars for the large flower bush that catches me, softening my fall before I hit the ground hard and my butt lands in the muddy grass. No doubt my skin will be bruised for days if the pain radiating through my hip is any indication.

I sit for a moment to gather myself, the shock causing me to fill with adrenaline, but I know that I need to keep a level head. There is no one home but me. I take some deep breaths and will the tears to stay away, because that could have ended much worse. I wiggle my toes and bend my knees, finding that nothing is sore or broken until I look at my hand, covered in red, the blood freely flowing down my wrist.

With Dad at the center with Larry, I have no idea who to call. It doesn't feel like an emergency for the paramedics, but I don't have a car and the buses only run every hour on Sundays. I sit and think as the blood starts to coat my forearm and I wiggle my toes again to ensure that I can stand. With my hand feeling numb and mentally blocking out any pain I feel in my body, I get up and walk a few steps toward the front door before my vision starts to go blurry and I need to sit again.

My heart rate is increasing because I can feel raindrops start to fall. I limit my risk of any more injuries by shuffling on my knees and slowly make my way across the lawn to the footpath to the front door, where I left my keys and cell phone.

My clothes are filthy, my knees now hurt, my hip is throbbing, and the pain in my palm is so intense that I feel like it is on fire. It looks like it is with the blood that is pouring from it, so I hold it upright, praying for the bleeding to stop. It slows a little, and I thank the heavens. Looking up to the clouds, I think of my mother, who I know would be scolding me from above.

Gritting my teeth, I lean over awkwardly and pick up my cell, calling the only person I know who has a car and may be available.

Tom, my driver.

With luck, he is nearby, and within twenty minutes, I see him pulling onto my street. I watch as the car comes to a stop at the front of my house and he dashes out as quick as a flash, running down the path toward me.

"Beth! What happened?" he asks in a rush, his face panic-stricken, and I look down at myself, realizing how much of a mess I am.

"Nothing. Just a little accident. Do you think you can run me to the hospital? It is just fifteen minutes away." I feel foolish, but I slap on my wide smile, gritting my teeth behind the facade.

"Come on. Let's go," Tom says as he leans over and helps me up, grabbing my good elbow and escorting me slowly to the car. He holds the door open as I slide onto the soft black leather seat and let out the breath I was holding. Keeping my hand elevated and wrapped in my sweater, the trip takes no time at all because Tom drives like a madman, and as we pull up to the ER department, I get myself out.

"Thanks, Tom. I really appreciate it. Sorry for calling you on the weekend."

"Wait, let me take you in." He's out of the car in the next second, running around to help me walk in.

"No, no, I'm fine. I'm practically a regular here. Please go back to your family, enjoy the rest of the day," I say, brushing his help away, feeling guilty that I had to call him at all, even though the black dots continue blocking my vision as I try to walk into the ER. Tom doesn't listen to me. He walks me all the way in until I get to the counter, and then steps back, giving me privacy.

"Oh, Beth, what have you done now?" Mary, the ER nurse, says to me, because whether he believed me or not, I am a regular here and have been for years. If they had a loyalty program, then I would be their number one ticket holder.

"Just a little cut, Mary, nothing too serious, but I might need some stitches," I reply, not wanting her to worry either, even though my palm is burning, and I feel light-headed. I know they deal with a lot here, and I feel bad for being yet another person on their very long list today.

"Here, let me wrap it a little to keep it clean because it will be a wait until the doctors are free today, I'm afraid," Mary says, and I am glad to have a friendly face.

"Thanks, Mary." I sigh, exhausted from the entire ordeal already.

"How did you do this?" she asks as she wraps it quickly, noticing the line of people now behind me.

"I cut it on the roof."

"Do I even want to know?" she asks, eyeing me suspiciously.

"I was just trying to fix a leak."

"A leak? Beth, you can't do everything. Haven't we told you this before? There are some things that professionals need to do, and I would suggest that getting on top of a house is one of them!" she scolds me and I silently nod.

"Have a seat, sweetheart. We will be with you when we can. Do you want some water? A blanket?"

"No. I'm fine. Really, it's just a scratch." I offer her a small, reassuring smile. Even though I am parched and cold, I don't want them wasting their resources on me. Mary pats my hand knowingly, and I move out of the way so she can attend other patients.

Turning around, I notice Tom still here, and he watches me as he pockets his cell phone.

"It's going to be a long wait, Tom. I'm fine here. You go. The nurses will look after me."

He eyes me suspiciously, but nods. "Fine. Call me if you need anything," he says, and I watch him leave reluctantly as I take a few steps and collapse into the white plastic chair in the waiting room. Mary was right; they are busy, but I guess this is normal for a late Sunday afternoon.

I pull my legs up to my chest and wrap my arms around them, curling my body in tight as the noises and the smell of disinfectant take me back to a time that I don't want to relive. A time when I was being rushed through the doors by paramedics.

I bury my head into my knees, wanting to forget it all, yet the visions come back in full force, and I squeeze my eyes shut to push through the throbbing pain in my hand. Keeping myself small, just like I did here when I was a kid, the memories of my mother pull me under.

And like back then, all I see is darkness.

20

HARRISON

As I finish up on the eighteenth hole, my cell phone buzzes in my pocket. I have ignored it for the last ten minutes as I try to finish this awful game, not made any better by the relentless teasing my brothers continue to give me about Beth. I can't help but smile and laugh, though. I haven't felt this light-hearted in... well, forever.

I pull my cell from my pocket as we are driving our cart back to the clubhouse, surprised to see that it is Tom.

"Tom?" I answer in question, because it is Sunday, our one and only true day off for the week.

"It's Beth. She's in the hospital," he spits out quickly.

"What? Where?" My heart rate increases, and concern fills my veins. Tom reels off the address and what he knows, and as soon as the cart stops, I am already running to my car.

"What happened?" Eddie asks as all my brothers look at me, ready to jump into action.

"It's Beth. She is at the hospital."

"Wait. We will come!" Eddie says.

"No. I will call you later." I close the door of my car and start the engine, leaving all three of them standing in the parking lot, watching me leave.

The hospital is an hour away, but I make it in forty minutes, and I see Tom standing next to his car outside, exactly where he told me he would be.

"She is still waiting in the ER. They haven't seen her yet," he says as I run past him and head inside. It is bedlam. People and nurses are everywhere, nothing like the private hospital in Baltimore City where our family goes.

People are yelling, machines are being pushed around from room to room, and the phones are ringing off the hook. There is a line of people waiting to be seen, and the staff all look exhausted. My eyes wander over everyone until I spot her vibrant red hair.

"Beth!" I say, relieved that I can see her, but panicked that she looks like she is out cold.

"Beth," I say again as I get to her, her body curled up on a cheap plastic chair, her eyes closed, and I see dried blood on her cheek.

"Beth," I say again, a little louder, and I shake her shoulder gently.

"Hmmmm," I hear her moan, her eyes squeezing shut as she wakes.

"Beth, are you alright?" Pulling her shoulders back, I brush the hair off her face. Her beautiful skin is stained with blood, her face pale and cold, and she doesn't have much strength.

"Ouch, ouch, ouch!" she says as her eyes open slowly,

squinting at the bright lights, and she pulls her hand up to block the brightness. All I see is red. Blood coats her hand and arm, the poorly wrapped bandage soaked, and now I am angry.

"Nurse! Nurse!" I yell at the older lady at the counter who looks up. Her eyes widen in recognition before she rushes around to where we are sitting.

"Beth, how are you feeling, darlin'?" she asks like she knows her.

"How do you think she is feeling? She needs a doctor, now!" I state, barely containing my anger.

"Exam room one has just cleared. Let me get a wheel-chair," she says, her eyes full of concern as she starts to waddle down the hall.

"It's fine. I've got her," I grit out as I lift Beth up bridal style, her body limp in my arms, her beautiful head falling to my shoulders. I stand up strong, holding her close, wishing she would look a little more lively. She's making me nervous.

"Harrison?" she murmurs. "What are you doing here?" Her eyes are barely open, and I realize that she has probably lost a pint of blood by the look of her clothes.

"I'm taking care of you, Beth. Taking you to see a doctor down the hall here," I try to explain simply, not sure how lucid she is.

"You smell good," she whispers against me, burying her head into my neck, and I chuckle, glad she is still talking and awake. I try to ignore the tug in my chest that happens every time I am near this woman.

People stare at me as I maneuver my way through the

waiting room and down the hallway, following the nurse. I know I have been recognized as some of them have their cell phones out and are now recording my movement. I pull Beth tighter, shielding her from the cameras. I look straight ahead and breathe a sigh of relief when we step inside exam room one where a doctor is waiting.

"Ahh, Beth, did you miss me?" the older doctor asks with a small chuckle as I lay her on the exam table, and he smiles warmly at her. Even though I place her gently, I see her grimace as she tries to move her body into a more comfortable position.

"Hey, Doc. Sorry it has been a little while since my last visit," she says, groaning softly.

"So what happened today?" he asks with an air of familiarity. Between him and the nurse, they both seem to know Beth well.

"I fell off the roof," she states, and I almost fall over myself.

"The roof? What the hell were you doing on the roof?" I ask, shocked.

"Fixing a leak. I cut my hand on the tin," she says, lifting her hand and placing it on her chest, giving us all a view of the bloody mess it has created.

"Okay, I will get this cleaned up, and then we can assess the damage," the doctor says.

"I'm Doctor Standford. Will you be waiting in here or in the hallway, Mr. Langford?" he asks me, and I look down at Beth and notice her eyes closed, a small puff of air leaving her lips.

"I'll step out. Give you some privacy," I say. I slowly

walk out the door, closing it behind me. Finding a white plastic chair at the front of the room, I take a seat, exhaustion nipping at my heels. I lean my elbows on my knees and keep my head down, trying to get my heart rate under control.

"Don't worry about Beth; she will be right as rain. Always is. She just lost a little too much blood, is all. Now are you calling her father or am I?" the nurse says from beside me.

"I'll take care of it, thank you."

"You're welcome, Mr. Langford," she says, her smile small, and I watch her waddle back down to the nurses' station to attend to the long line. I watch, having never seen anything like it before in my life. I have been to hospitals, many in fact, but only for ribbon cuttings and seeing my father before he passed, all of which are state-of-the-art private facilities that are spotless, with lots of staff and up-to-date equipment.

Here, it is like a war zone. The floor tiles are cracked; the walls need new paint; a light flickers constantly down the hall, and the equipment looks to be decades old as they're being passed from room to room. I grab my cell and pull up my contacts, looking for Beth's emergency contact details and finding her father's number.

After a brief rundown and him not sounding at all surprised or shocked at Beth being in the hospital, I arrange to send Tom over to the community center to collect him and take him home, which he only agreed to if I promised to bring Beth straight home as soon as Doctor Standford has finished up with her. After I hang up, I look at my phone. I don't think her father likes me very much, if the one and only time of meeting at the community center is anything to go by, and my call today will no doubt make him like me even less.

I call my brothers, and then Oscar, also asking him for a rundown on our healthcare policy. This hospital needs to be the first place we invest in—something we will do immediately.

As I finish up all the phone calls, Doctor Standford comes out of the room.

"She is good as gold. A few stitches in her hand, and she should take it easy for the next day or so. There's a large bruise on her hip, but otherwise, she is tough as nails, that one," he says with a smile before the head nurse scurries over and drags the weary older doctor down the hall to the next room with another patient.

I open the door and walk into the silent room. Beth is sitting up and looking straight at me.

"What are you doing here? Don't you have a golf day?" she asks, surprised but tired.

"I came from the course. Tom called me."

"You didn't have to come. It is just a little cut."

"A little cut? You fell off the damn roof!" I'm trying to remain calm, but my voice increases in decibels with every word I say. I run my hand through my hair and start to pace the room.

"I'm totally fine. I don't want you worrying about me," she says, and I can't believe that she is the calm one.

"You are *not* fine. And I will worry about you." She purses her lips at that, and I already know whatever comes out of her mouth will be something stubborn.

"Harrison. I. Am. Fine," she says slowly, and I release

the breath I was holding, seeing the truth in her eyes. Even if I'm still upset, I believe her.

"I didn't like waking up alone this morning," I murmur, feeling the stress in my shoulders. I should probably wait to bring this up, but I can't.

"I didn't want to wake you," she offers with a small smile. Only, I'm not buying it.

"Why did you leave so early?" My question is a simple one. But I see her take a deep breath like it pains her and she is resigned to tell me her answer.

"Last night... I felt like Cinderella. I felt beautiful, carefree, and being with you was amazing. But my life is not that, Harrison. It's none of that. I haven't felt carefree in forever; I never wear pretty clothes; I never feel beautiful. I needed to get home to my reality, which is far different than your luxury penthouse with its perfectly curated art and luxurious amenities," she says quietly, and I don't like it. Not one bit.

"You are beautiful. You are beautiful every damn minute of every day. And if I have to show you that, I will," I growl, wrapping my hand around hers, where she remains sitting on the hospital bed.

"I feel like your dirty little secret, Harrison. I want to be with you, more than anything, but I guess it will just take a little getting used to." She leans into me, where I stand in front of her, her body relaxed from the painkillers, no doubt.

"Beth, I know you have responsibilities. You have your dad to take care of, and that can be overwhelming. Let me help you. Let me be there for you; let me lighten your load. I want to be with you, every second. I want to touch you more than I should, and I know the next few months will be tough, but you are not my dirty secret, Beth; you are my hidden treasure," I tell her, putting my feelings on the line, wanting to drum it in, wanting her to know that she means way more to me than that.

I look down at her and notice her eyes getting glassy. My tough, beautiful woman is vulnerable in my arms right now. That's not something I have seen from her before, and my heart clenches in my chest, the pain of seeing her upset almost suffocating me.

"Just promise me no more getting onto the roof?" I say to her in warning, because I still can't believe she did that. She remains suspiciously silent.

"I will call Eddie to organize a building maintenance team to come to your place tomorrow to fix it."

"No! I don't need charity, Harrison. I can do it myself," she says with a huff, her stubborn self now back in action.

"It is not charity. It is me looking after you."

"I don't need looking after and I don't need your money." Even in her tired state, she slides off the bed, coming to stand right in front of me.

"You listen to me, Beth. Last night was not a one-night deal for me, and I thought I made that clear, but I will once more. I want you. All of you. I want you in my bed. I want you working by my side. I want you in my life. So I will fix your goddamn roof, and I will do it with my money, whether you like it or not."

I am panting. I am so angry. We hold each other's eyes, and if looks could kill, I would be the one lying on the bed right about now. But something switches, and before any more words can be spoken, I take her in my arms and kiss her.

21

BETH

I grip his shirt with my good hand as his lips devour mine. His hands cup my face, pulling me toward him, holding me like he never wants to let me go. Our lips mesh as our tongues explore, and I whimper a little at his touch. The pain I feel in my hand and my hip is now long forgotten. All I can feel is him.

There is no hesitation, no feeling of uneasiness, just pure want, need, and demand, as he keeps my lips against his. He is warm, his body covering mine, cocooning me in a warm blanket of security I want to wrap myself in and never leave. I never thought I was the type of girl who would find the dependability of a man comforting. I have always managed to look after myself and my dad. I am independent, strong, and used to doing things on my own. But my body melts in his arms, and when he holds me, it is like everything is going to be alright. He smells of a mixture of sunscreen and summer breeze, and I want to lie in his arms forever.

We pull back slowly, looking at each other. Our

breaths labored, my grip on him remaining. His hands stay on my face, cupping my cheeks as his eyes search my face. I see the concern etched in his brow, that deep line telling me he is worried, and any annoyance or anger I had earlier has now dissipated.

"You're stubborn. Has anyone told you that before?" he says, resting his forehead on mine, looking right into my eyes.

"You're bossy. Has anyone told you that before?" I counter before we both smile softly at each other.

"You seemed to like it last night..." he murmurs, and I start thinking about the filthy things he said to me, and my body betrays me instantly at the memory.

"I liked it very much last night..." My voice is breathy, and I see Harrison grit his teeth. Our hunger for each other is still very much alive.

"If anything like this happens again, you call me straightaway."

"Absolutely not. This kind of thing happens all the time." I almost laugh at the look on his face, but refrain.

"What do you mean, it happens all the time?"

"Harrison, I fall, I tumble, I spill drinks, I fall off roofs. I am clumsy, a clutz, a catastrophe."

"One. You are none of those things. Two. I am calling Eddie to organize someone to fix your roof tomorrow, and I am not taking no for an answer. And three..." He pauses, looking into my eyes.

"And three?"

"And three, you call me the minute anything like this happens again," he repeats, just to drum it into me.

I huff and look at him staring at me, daring me not to

agree, but I give him a stiff nod, displeased that he talked me into depending on him. I don't depend on anyone, yet he whirls his magic around me, and I agree to anything.

I felt bad leaving him a note this morning, and I still feel vulnerable laying my cards out to him just now. But I feel a little lighter for sharing my life and knowing he didn't run.

"Why did you have to wait for hours in the waiting room? Why didn't they see you straightaway?"

"Because this is one of the most underfunded hospitals in the entire county. Because there are not enough trained doctors and nurses to help all the people that need help. Harrison, I am so clumsy, I am here nearly every month with some ailment or another. I wait my turn. I don't want to be more of a burden on the hospital system; they have enough to deal with without having someone like me in here all the time," I say, sighing, suddenly feeling really exhausted from the day.

He looks around, and I see his eyes assessing the room. The threadbare curtains against the window and the thin sheets on the bed. The white plastic chair at the side of the room that has more marks and scratches on it than not and the chipped floor tiles that have seen better days. But it is all we have. It is all I have ever known.

"Are you ready to go? I called your dad and told him that I will bring you home," he offers, and I nod silently. I know I will get the third degree as soon as I walk in the door, even though I am a twenty-five-year-old woman. More than capable of fixing a hole in the roof. Or not, it appears.

"Don't you have somewhere to be?" I ask, trying to

think about his schedule and what he had on it today. He holds me close as I shuffle to the door, and I grip his arm so I don't do something like trip and fall, which is a very real possibility. Especially since I still feel light-headed.

"I'm right where I need to be," he says, and I feel like I am basking in the sun due to the warmth that spreads through my body at his words. He watches me as his hand rests on the door handle, waiting for me to process what he just said. His words are so simple, but the meaning is so committed. He is making me a priority, again something I have had very little of in my life.

When I look up at him, he gives me a smile of understanding, just as he opens the door and we are greeted with the sounds of a busy hospital.

WE PULL up to my small, worn weatherboard home in Harrison's sports car, which glitters and shines against my very middle-class street. *At least our garden is nice*, I think to myself as he opens my car door and I get out and stand next to him, admiring the home and the pretty red roses in the front yard, albeit with one bush that looks a little squashed.

I have never brought a man home before. There was never a boyfriend in college who lasted the distance. I feel almost nervous as I stand next to his car, which in all likeliness is worth more than some of the houses on this street. Including our own.

"So that is the scene of the crime?" he asks, pointing

to the side of the house where the gutter hangs from the roof a little.

"Yep," I say, popping the *P*, looking at the mess I left behind. The gutter hangs in a way it didn't before. The ladder is still leaning against the house, my small simple tools scattered around the lawn below, and a trail of blood follows my journey to the front doorstep.

"Go inside, and see your father. I will be there in a minute," he says, and I watch him roll up his sleeves.

"Harrison? Really, you don't need to..." I start to say, because he is not dressed for yard work.

"Beth?" My father's voice rings out from the side, and I see him at the open front door. He looks at me before side-eyeing Harrison.

"Go. I'll be in in a few minutes," Harrison says. I watch him walk to the side of the house, pick up the tools, and pull down the ladder.

"What the hell did you think you were doing on the roof?" my father starts in on me as I turn and walk to meet him at the front door. He is not happy.

"I needed to fix the leak!" My defense is weak, but at least I am honest.

"You could have broken your back!" he nearly roars, his own ailment coming into our conversation. My heart beats fast at his tone.

"You should have called someone in to fix it," he says, quieter this time.

"Dad, we don't have the money... The heating bill was a big one, and I knew that calling a team in would cost too much!" I say, pleading at him for his understanding.

I'm not telling him that I am secretly stashing away cash to buy him a new chair.

His jaw ticks, and he gives me a quick nod in understanding.

"Is there something going on here that I need to be worried about?" Dad asks, looking at Harrison fixing up our small yard before his eyes land on me.

"No. But we do enjoy spending time together, Dad. Is it okay that he is here?" I ask tentatively because we have never had the talk about me bringing anyone home. There was never anyone in my life to bring home.

"Out of all the men in town, you bring home the one who is running for governor... Any blind man can see there is something going on, Beth. Just be careful," my dad murmurs as we both watch Harrison tidy the last few things, check the security of the gutter, and fix my mess.

"Okay, I have put everything away," Harrison says, coming up to us, and Dad looks at him with narrowed eyes.

"Well, you might as well come in for a drink and watch the first half of the football game. I owe you that, at least," my dad grumbles as he turns his chair to go inside.

"Sorry, he is usually a little more hospitable," I lie as I turn to Harrison and relax when greeted with his warm, comforting smile. My nerves at having him in my simple home have spiked now that we are standing at the door. Harrison is so tall, he almost hits the top of the doorframe, something Dad and I have never had to combat before.

"It's fine. He was worried. I imagine that if I ever had a

daughter and found out she fell off the roof and was at the hospital, I would be pretty upset too."

I sigh, letting my shoulders slump.

"C'mon, I think the Ravens are playing," he says as his hand connects with my waist, giving me a reassuring squeeze. I raise my eyebrows in surprise.

"You're a football fan?" He doesn't look like a football fan standing here on my front porch with his golf attire on.

"Everyone is a football fan," he says, grinning, and I smile as he leans down, pecking a kiss to my nose before we walk in and I lose him to my father, the two of them bonding over the Ravens' win against Tampa Bay.

22

HARRISON

"How's your hand?" I ask her the minute she steps into my penthouse. She has been here almost every night since her accident. But I gave her the day off today to spend it with her dad. They both had medical appointments at the hospital. Her stitches needed to be removed, and her father had some special physiotherapy he is trialing. I wanted to go with her. But I couldn't. I had hands to shake and people to network with and we can't take those risks. If I take a day off and am spotted spending it with her and her father, then the gossip mill will go into overdrive.

"It's fine. Don't worry. See, all better?" she says as she dumps her overnight bag on the floor and walks over to me in the living room, waving her hand. A well-worn path is now ingrained in my carpet from where I have paced waiting for her.

I grab her hand, pulling it closer to my eyes to inspect it.

"Why are you so worried?" she asks me, and I look at her like she is crazy.

"Because you are mine, and I worry about you when you get injured. I worry about you when you are stressed in the office. I worry about you and your dad living out in that house all alone. I hate it when you are not here with me." Her beautiful eyes stare up at me, and every time I look into them, I weaken even more for her.

"I worry about you too. You work too hard; you need more downtime. You have a lot of pressure on your shoulders. Let me look after you too," she says, concern etched in her brow.

"You missed a bit," I state, wanting her to say it.

"What bit?" she asks, raising her eyebrows.

"That I am yours," I murmur, really wanting her to say it out loud.

"Oh, yes, I forgot that bit. Harrison, *you* are all *mine*," she says sweetly, smiling, and my shoulders relax, not realizing how much I needed to hear it. I look at her hand again, at the thin red line tracing her skin, bringing it to my mouth and kissing her palm.

"Hmmmm... much better..." She toys with me as she bites her lower lip.

"I have been waiting all day to touch you," I confess as my lips trail down the inside of her arm, peppering her soft skin with kisses. "Fuck, I am struggling not being able to touch you whenever I want," I say to her, the honesty whipping out from me, wanting her to know.

"I can't say that the sneaking around is great for me either." She huffs and starts to sulk. I know it is hard for her. Leaving her dad night after night, sneaking into the basement parking garage via Tony, packing and repacking her clothes for our sleepovers, so she has something different to wear in the office the next day.

"It will be over soon... then I will show you to the world," I murmur, already thinking about election night, taking the governorship, all with her by my side.

"I know..." she whispers as my lips meet hers, and I kiss her like it is my last dying wish.

"How's your hip?" I ask her as I move my lips down to her neck, soaking her in, tasting her like I haven't seen her for days rather than the hours it has been.

"It is fine. Doctor said there are no issues," she says, her voice becoming breathy as my hands roam over her curves.

"Good," I say before I bend and pick her up. Holding her ass in my hands, she wraps her legs around my waist.

"Where are you taking me?" she asks, her eyes full of lust.

"I'm hungry." I walk her over to the dining room and perch her ass onto my large table.

"Maybe I can help with that," she murmurs as my lips trace down her neck. I feel her nipples peak almost instantaneously through her shirt.

"Maybe you can," I moan as her hands run up my back. She pushes her chest out, and I trace my hands up the curve of her back as I grind my already painfully hard cock against her.

"I am going to get you naked before putting my mouth on you, and then I am going to make you scream my name so loud the whole city knows you are mine," I growl, my fingers getting busy unbuttoning her blouse.

"You will blow our cover..." she moans as I pull down the cup of her bra and my mouth finds her nipple, sucking it and lapping it with my tongue.

"Fuck our cover," I say before throwing her shirt across the room and removing her bra. I know we need to be careful, but I cannot wait until this sneaking around ends.

"I want you naked too..." she says, her hands on my jeans, lowering my zipper and pushing them down as I tear my shirt off from behind my head.

"You first." I unzip her skirt, leaving it to slip down her body, puddling on the floor before I push her underwear down, letting her step out of both.

"Sit," I demand as I pick her up and put her back on my table, watching her eyes alight. Placing my palm on her chest, I push her backward and she slowly lowers until she is fully naked and splayed out for me.

"Touch your perfect breasts, baby," I grit out, not sure how long I can last, but knowing I want her to come first. I am being demanding, but she responds so well to me in the bedroom.

I watch as her hands seductively skim up her sides until they grab her breasts, and she molds them, her fingers tweaking her nipples.

"Good girl," I murmur as I take a seat and spread her legs, seeing her already dripping with arousal, more than ready for me.

"Fuck, you are glistening." I admire her, my hands grabbing her knees and running my palms up the inside of her legs, pushing her even wider. Her hips move a little, hungry for me, and I can't wait anymore.

I lower myself and lick her. When I hear her breath catch, I do it again.

"Harrison…" she murmurs, her body squirming, but her hands have stopped.

"Keep touching your breasts, baby. Play with your nipples while I taste you with my tongue," I grit out before I delve back into her center. I lick her, savoring every inch of her as she pants and moans, her body reacting immediately to my touch.

"Your tongue is magic," she says on a breath, her back lifting off the table as I suck on her clit. I do it again, getting into a fast rhythm, moving my tongue, tasting, and licking, before sucking on her clit again and again. I continue my assault. Not resting, not letting up, hungry for as much as she will give me. My hands grip her legs, spreading her as wide as she'll go, and her hips begin to buckle.

"Harrison, oh my… Harrison…" she pants over and over, my name on her lips egging me on.

She screams my name so loud that it vibrates through the room. Her hands come to the back of my head, pulling me closer and gripping my hair, the whole scene so hot that I almost come on the spot as well.

She falls back onto the table, panting, and I slowly kiss my way down her leg before standing, looking over the beauty she is.

"How do you feel?" I ask her, my hands running up and down her legs. I can't stop touching her. I would do it all day every day if I could.

"Famished," she says, eyeing me seductively, laying down her intentions, and my nostrils flare.

"Be a good girl and turn around. Put your head here at the edge of the table for me so I can watch your pretty breasts bounce as I feed you my cock."

I watch as she sits up on her fantastic ass, before spinning and lying back down. Exactly how I want her. My hands on the table are white-knuckled as I take her in. Her confidence in the bedroom grows by the day. As she shimmers closer to me, I grab her hair, pulling it out from under her, and watch the long red waves fall from the edge of my dining table down toward the floor.

"Good girl," I groan as my hand cups her jaw, my fingers running across it. She is already licking her lips as her head hangs over the edge a little, waiting for me.

Her hands move over her body, and I watch as they strum up and down her curves, circling her nipples and back down her stomach again.

"You are so fucking sexy," I grit out, my dick feeling hot and heavy in my hand. I step forward, touching my tip against her lips. She is quick, her tongue slipping out and circling, before sucking a little, and I edge it in farther.

She moans as her hands reach back, grabbing my ass and pulling me even closer.

"Fuck, you are perfect," I groan as I pull out completely, and then push back in even deeper this time. Her head drops a little more, opening her throat as I start to pump into her mouth. Her hands remain on my ass, nails digging in, and I watch her breasts jiggle up and down in rhythm with my thrusts.

"God, I can't get enough of you. You look so fucking

beautiful right now," I say in awe, and she moans, the vibrations strumming to my balls.

I lean over and pinch her nipple before grabbing it in my hand and molding it. Her back arches, and she moves one of her hands from my ass, down her curves, over her stomach, to her warm, wet center.

"That's my girl. Part those legs, baby. Show me how you fuck your fingers." I'm panting now at the sight of her. My dirty words cause her to moan again, and I push in deeper as her legs part even wider, and I watch her finger circle her clit before disappearing inside of her.

"Fuck, Beth... are you going to come again, baby? Come again for me while you're fucking your fingers and I am fucking your face." I'm barely hanging on, but forcing myself to, wanting her to find her release again.

Within moments, her body quivers and her jaw relaxes. I pull back and she takes a deep breath before she screams as she comes.

"Fuck, baby, you are so beautiful when you come." At that, she looks at me and grabs my ass again, forcing me forward and back into her warm, wet mouth. I don't hesitate then, moving faster, chasing my release, and I hold on to her jaw and let go.

"Fuck!" I roar as I touch the back of her throat and shoot my release into her mouth. She swallows, and I grip the table to remain upright, then I ease out of her and look down at her. Her eyes are sex drunk, her lips red and glossy, and she smiles. Right then, as I look at her smiling face, a thought enters my mind. One that never has before.

I am going to marry this girl.

23

HARRISON

It feels like a lifetime ago since I was here. But the memory of Beth in her tight yoga pants is still ingrained in my mind, a memory I pull forward almost every night when I am in the shower without her. Now, knowing that she is just down the hall doing that very class, I need to force myself to sit with her father and his friend Larry to watch them play chess.

"So, you're here on your own on a Sunday?" her father asks me as he eyes me suspiciously.

"Well, I never really stop working, and I wanted to come to the center to see how it operates. Get a feel for the community," I say by way of explanation. I clear my throat. *Is it hot in here?* How do I tell him the truth? How much has Beth told him about us, since we're keeping this a secret?

"Mm-hmm..." I hear Larry mumble under his breath, his eyes glued to the chessboard as he takes his turn.

"Wouldn't have anything to do with the fact my daughter is here doing yoga today, would it?" Beth's father spears me with a look that tells me he knows exactly why I am here, and it is not to win votes.

"Beth and I have been spending some time together. I enjoy her company," I say, trying to be honest without spilling too much. I quickly look around me to ensure no one else is listening.

"Beth is many great things, but let me tell you, she is my one and only, so tread very carefully, Harrison." We have a good rapport, built solely on the fact that we are both die-hard Ravens fans, and I had a wonderful afternoon on his sofa screaming at the football game on TV alongside him after the hospital visit. We bonded much to Beth's dismay, and even though I hear his warning loud and clear, he follows it with a small nod and a brief smile that tells me he also approves.

"Mr. Langford!" a man's voice exclaims beside me, and I turn in time to see the center's manager, Jeff something-or-other, walking up to me.

"I didn't know we were to expect you today," he says as I stand and shake his hand in greeting.

"Just a casual visit with the community to talk and to listen."

"Oh, well, Larry and George are in an excellent position to tell you all about the center and everyone in it, as they are here almost every day," Jeff says as he moves a little to stand next to Beth's father's chair. It is an odd move I don't really understand.

I hear Larry murmur again, this time his eyes flicking quickly to meet mine before they lower just as fast back down to the chess game in front of him.

"Harrison?" I hear Beth's breathy voice from behind

me, and I turn.

"Hey, ba... Beth," I say, catching myself before I call her baby in front of everyone who has gathered.

"What are you doing here?" she asks as her eyes light up upon seeing me, and the fact that I can do that to her makes me feel like a king. But I don't miss Jeff as his eyes roam over her. I don't like the way he looks at her. Not one bit.

"He was just popping in to talk to the local people," Jeff answers for me, and when I look at him, my eyebrows crease. *Did he just talk for me?*

"Of course," Beth says, waving her hand around like there is no other possible reason that I would be here. Yet the image of the woman standing in front of me all sweaty in her gym clothes is another memory I can now pull on and the sole reason for me being here on my one day off a week. Her hair is up in a messy bun; her body has a light sheen of sweat; her breasts look fucking fantastic, and I really, really want to peel her clothes off her right now.

"I was just chatting with your dad and Larry here for the last hour or so. They are serious chess players," I say with a smile, one that she matches, and her father clears his throat behind me, bringing our attention back to the situation and not solely focusing on each other.

"Beth, why don't you give Harrison a tour of the vegetable garden out back," her father mumbles, and I raise my eyebrows. The old man is giving me an opportunity. Seems like he knows the score.

"Of course, let's go," she says, her smile beaming, and I follow her out the door.

"What are you really doing here?" she whispers to me as we step through the back garden, where large tomato plants are blooming and competing with the peppers.

"I had some free time and wanted to see you," I say honestly. Because seeing her is all I can think about outside the campaign trail. We continue walking farther down the path, into the bushy garden and away from prying eyes.

"You saw me yesterday and last night! Anyone can see us here... It probably isn't smart..." Her look of concern guts me, because I know deep down that I am the cause of it. We pause, standing behind a large lemon tree, and I see her eyes darting all around the yard, ensuring no one else is here.

"Will you calm down? No one is here." I grab both her hands in mine and caress her palms with my thumbs.

"Harrison, I don't want to be responsible for ruining your chance of becoming governor," she says, her face looking pained.

"You won't. We won't. We are being careful, although have you told your father? Because he seems to know exactly why I am here." She groans, the noise hitting me straight in the groin.

"No. Not exactly. I haven't said anything to anybody. But he is smart, so I think perhaps the fact that a Langford who is running for governor was sitting on his small sofa all afternoon watching football with him probably gave it away." She is getting sassy with me, and I fucking love it. I love her challenging me, pushing me, screaming my name in my bed, all of it. I love all of her.

"I liked your sofa; it was comfy," I say, grinning with a

shrug.

"Harrison!" She groans again, and I step closer to her, too close for it to be professional.

"You know what else I like..." I whisper to her, and I immediately see her pupils dilate, and my heart starts beating faster knowing that she likes my dirty talk. The swift rise and fall of her chest encased in her tight crop top gives her away.

"What?" she whispers, her eyes now locked on mine, and I grin.

"I fucking love making you scream my name," I grit out, memories of our previous encounters with each other filtering through my mind, her on top, her on all fours, her in the shower. Any way I can have her.

"Mr. Langford! Would you like to come back inside and see the ladies in the kitchen? They are currently preparing weekend meals for the homeless," Jeff yells from the back door, and I step away from Beth and turn toward him. He is standing, looking directly at us, his line of sight clear as day. I don't know anything about him, but after his interruption and the way he looks at Beth, I can't say I like him very much.

"Thank you, Jeff, it would be my pleasure," I grit out.

"You want to come and introduce me to the kitchen ladies?" I ask Beth, who smiles as her cheeks flush, and she clears her throat, telling me that I flustered her.

"Of course. They make the best tasting food ever!" she exclaims as she starts toward the building.

"Not as good as your pussy, I bet," I murmur to myself as I follow her back to the center, where a furious Jeff stands waiting for us.

24

HARRISON

"Are you sure you know what you are doing?" Oscar asks me for the tenth time this week. I side-eye him as we walk around the pristine top-notch private hospital in Baltimore, visiting the patients and talking with doctors about the new treatment funding they are hoping to secure from me if I become governor.

I told Oscar about Beth and me this morning. I had to. It is getting harder for me to keep my distance. The need to constantly be around her is almost suffocating. I don't think I have ever had the urge to be around a woman as much as I do with her.

But my father left a legacy, one that seeps into me time and time again. Introducing a new girlfriend at the time of campaigning for governorship is not the smartest move, even if the people seem to love her.

Oscar has been giving me nothing but frustrated smiles and barraging me with the same question over and over again all morning. I am frustrated by his constant need to meddle in my life. But I pay him handsomely to do so. To make sure I am focused, to ensure that I give the public what they want so I can win this election and govern their state.

"Fine. I won't ask again. I mean, the polls are going well. I would just hate for anything to jeopardize that. We have done so much good work, and you are so far in the lead you will be almost impossible to stop. Almost..." he says, looking at me with his eyebrows pinched, a warning in his tone. I ignore him and instead, I look over at the woman who has stolen everyone's heart, including mine, as she sits at an older man's bedside, holding his hand as he explains to her about his treatment.

There is no press here today, and I am thankful. We all need some space. The cell phones that captured me carrying her at the hospital over a month ago when she fell from the roof all sold their photos to the society and business news outlets and me and my staff members were front-page stories. Now I am seen as a fantastic, caring boss, looking after his staff on the weekends and Beth is the wonderful staffer who is just like one of the people. Living in the suburbs, getting treated at the local hospital. It was great for my approval rating and brought Beth and me even closer.

"So, we can see up to seventy patients here in the ward, with special chemotherapy rooms down the hall, but we really need additional nurses and ward staff and an injection of funds to help us look into complementary medicine, which is proven to help patients on their cancer recoveries," Doctor Warner says. He's one of the leading physicians in Baltimore and the biggest health-care supporter of my campaign.

"What kind of complementary medicines are you looking into?" I ask, genuinely interested, because I haven't really heard a lot about mixing Western medicine with alternative therapies, but it makes sense.

As he answers, a loud clap of thunder roars overhead and startles everyone, including Beth, who I watch as she jumps up from her chair and is now fidgeting next to the man who looks more concerned about her than he is about himself.

"We hope to include aromatherapy, acupuncture, and massage to begin with. We might also introduce chiro-practic care and other things as we progress. I really want to have a multidisciplinary team who are committed to ensuring our patients are cared for physically, psycholog-ically, emotionally, and spiritually. It's about caring for the medical needs, but also their well-being. I think we could really become a state-of-the-art specialist hospital here." I admire his passion and commitment.

I nod to him and look around; it is a far cry from where Beth and I were at her local hospital. Here, every-thing is new, freshly painted, clean, and looks to be running professionally and systematically. Yet, on the other side of the city, it is a different story. I can under-stand the need for medical advancement here. But other hospitals need a bigger injection of funds just to bring them up to this standard. There is certainly a lot of work to do in the healthcare space, that is for certain.

I leave Doctor Warner talking with Oscar, and I make my way over to Beth.

"Hi there, I am Harrison Langford." I introduce myself to the man lying in the bed who is holding Beth's hand. I stand behind her, my other hand on her back, the movement natural and one that the old man doesn't miss. I give him a wide, genuine smile as she sinks back into me a little. I like being close to her at all times lately.

"Hi, Harrison, I'm Tony," he says with a nod.

"Tony here is in today for his last round of chemo, isn't that fantastic!" Beth says, her smile bright and filled with joy, and I can't help but notice her body shaking a little as more rumbles of thunder roll around outside. Absentmindedly, I rub her back in comfort.

"Great to hear that it is working well for you. What do you think of the hospital here?" I ask, keen to get his perspective.

"They are great, really professional, and offer a lot of different options depending on your diagnosis. They offer an individual approach." I nod.

"Sorry to interrupt, but we need to be making a move," Oscar says, coming to the bed, giving Tony a small smile and a nod.

"Thanks for visiting, Harrison. And Beth, it was lovely chatting with you. I wish you both the best of luck in a few weeks' time at the polls. I will be voting for you."

"I appreciate it," I say, shaking his hand again, before Beth leans over, giving him a small hug, which brings an even bigger smile to his face. And although no words fall from his lips, I know exactly how he feels.

~

THE STORM HASN'T LET up all day. I lean back in my office chair and watch Beth at her desk. She is on the phone, confirming our meetings for later in the week, and I admire her openly with no one else around. Something I catch myself doing more and more, especially when we work late, which is often. Another loud clap of thunder comes from outside and I see her jump in her chair, which she has been doing all day.

Out the window, there is nothing but miserable gray clouds, and I think about my weekend schedule. We have been busy this week, and Beth, Oscar, Eddie, and I have been working long days, pulling together information on our policies and working with our finance team on our budgets. Constantly refining and adjusting as new information comes in. As promised, I got a public letter of support from Arthur. Things weren't bad before Beth came on board, but they are certainly better than they have ever been. If only I could stop looking at her and concentrate on the policy paperwork in front of me, but the itch to have her hums through my body, it being too long since I saw her fabulous naked body.

We haven't had a lot of alone time this week... and she is all I have been thinking about. Now, as I watch her in her office, her desk only a few feet away from me, her rose scent wafts into my space and the urge I have to bend her over my desk is at the forefront of my mind.

"Am I interrupting?" Eddie asks me as he stands in front of my desk. I didn't hear him come in and he is looking at me like the cat who has caught the canary.

"What do you want?"

"Sorry to interrupt your viewing pleasure..." he says, raising one eyebrow at me.

"Watch it..." I warn him.

"The dinner event you had scheduled tonight at the outdoor atrium in the city has been canceled. Obviously," he says, waving his hand to the window, as we both watch the rain teem down outside.

"So now, dear brother, you have a rare Friday night off to do as you please. I wonder what the hell you will do?" he asks sarcastically as we both turn and look at Beth.

"Just know the media are camped out below the building. Obviously, news has been light this week, and they are waiting for you to do something, so I suggest that the two of you keep a low profile," Eddie says to me with a small smile. All my brothers know about Beth and me, and I appreciate the heads-up from Eddie.

"Thanks," I murmur, my eyes homing back in on the beautiful woman across the room.

"What? What did I miss?" she asks as she hangs up the call she was on and looks at us both in question.

"Harrison will explain. I'm off. See you Monday," he says with a beaming smile.

"Oh, okay. Have a good weekend," she says, stepping into my office as Eddie leaves, and I jump up from my chair as my office door closes, giving me the privacy I want.

"So what happened?" she asks me as I walk to meet her halfway.

"My event tonight has been canceled. So I'm taking you home." I reach out and take her hand, bringing it to my lips.

"Harrison," she hisses quietly in warning, her eyes darting to the door.

"No one is here; they have all left for the weekend," I murmur to her as I bend down, putting my lips to her neck. I hear her gasp, the sound shooting me directly in my cock, which is already tenting in my pants.

"We can't get caught," she moans as her head tilts back slightly, offering me more of her. I move my hands around her waist and hold her to me firmly as I ease toward her lips, peppering kisses along her jaw, wanting to taste her. Before I can, a loud clap of thunder bursts from outside and she jumps feet into the air, screaming.

"Beth?"

"Sorry, I just got a little startled..." she says as her hands rest on her chest and I notice her breathing rapidly as her eyes dart around outside the window.

"I'm taking you home," I say, a little more sternly to try to jolt her out of her fright.

"The weather is shocking. We can't drive in this!" she says, looking at me as though I am crazy.

"We are not driving anywhere. I'm taking you upstairs to my penthouse..." I say as I slowly walk back toward her, like I am approaching a frightened animal.

"And then I am going to undress you and do ungodly things to your beautiful body, starting with having you come all over my cock," I say, my face mere inches from hers, and her eyes light up.

"Really?" she asks, a small smile gracing her lips, and I pull her tight against me again, wanting my hands on her body.

"Tell me what else you have in mind," she says, her

hands moving to my chest, then down my front, one traveling farther south and cupping my rock-hard cock. I growl as she massages my length through my trousers.

"Well, right now, I think I will lock my office door, before I put you on my desk, spread your beautiful legs, and fuck your pussy with my tongue," I grit out, almost ready to pick her up and walk out of here with her over my shoulder. I know we are in extremely dangerous territory standing here like this in my office. I should not even be talking to her like this... Anyone could walk in.

"Well, Mr. Langford, that does sound like an offer I can't refuse. Let me lock the door for you," she says in her professional tone, and I am not sure if it is the fact she called me by my full name or the fact that she wants to play out my fantasy, but I'm more turned on than I thought possible. I watch her sway her hips in her tight black pencil dress and hear the click of the lock on my door, before she does the same on hers. I take a seat at my desk, leaning back in my office chair, admiring her as she walks back to me. Her curves are highlighted today in her fitted black attire, her flaming-red hair is loose, running down her back. I'm a fucking lucky bastard.

"Come here," I say to her, and I watch her slide her body between me and my desk and stand right in front of me. Leaning forward, I skim my hands up her legs, pushing her dress up her thighs, going higher until it is bunched up around her hips. I get rewarded by the view of my favorite thin black lace underwear, the ones that make me groan on sight.

I lean in, nuzzling her, trailing my nose over the lace. The pain underneath my own zipper almost pushes me to my breaking point. I stand then, my hands firmly under her ass, and lift her so she is sitting on the edge of my desk.

"Lean back and lie down," I growl into her mouth as I plunge my tongue inside and push her body gently back. I can feel her breasts against my chest, her hands gripping my shirt, and her little moans that are barely audible are like flickering flames on my skin, making me want to get her naked and quickly.

"That's it. You look beautiful lying on my desk..." I murmur to her as I stand back up, looking down at her. She is perfection, her hair splayed out, her back arching slightly, pushing her fucking fantastic tits out even more. I have no idea how I got her, but I'm fucking glad I did. Before I take a seat back in my chair, I pick up each of her feet and place them on each arm of my chair. I run my hands up and down her bare legs, her body already shivering under my touch, before my fingers skirt across the thin black lace between her thighs.

"You are already so wet for me, baby..." I groan, feeling her damp underwear as I pull aside the black lace and gently rub her with my fingers, finding her clit and circling it, teasing her perfect pussy that is waiting just for me.

"Harrison..." Her hands run up and down her thighs in need before she puts them by her sides and her fingers grip around the edge of my desk.

"Shhhh. Lie quietly, baby. I need to have you," I whisper as I lean forward and brush my tongue along her folds. Her taste spreads on my tongue, and I do it again and again, because the first time wasn't enough.

"Oh... my..." She whimpers as her hands delve into my hair, and she starts massaging my scalp, which she knows I fucking love.

I trail my hands up the insides of her legs, stopping on either side of her hips, and I spread her legs wider, so she is completely open for me to dive in. I circle her clit with my tongue, over and over, before I delve inside, repeating the motion until I feel her hips rocking against my face.

"Harrison..." I hear her whisper faintly as her hands leave my hair and grip my desk again.

"Mmmm... baby?" I murmur the question, not wanting to move my mouth, enjoying her too much.

"You are so good at that," she pants, and I see her bite her lower lip as her hips slowly rock against my face.

"Give it to me, baby. Come on my tongue for me." I'm trying to be quiet, even though my office is soundproof.

"I'm going to..." is all she gets out as I suck hard on her clit and her body arches off my desk, her hands gripping back into my hair, pulling it taut, but I don't let up. I suck her as her body jolts and little moans seep out, then she falls back onto the desk in a heap. I lick her gently, not wanting to stop, before I pull away, replace her lace underwear, and shimmy her dress back down.

"God, I love the taste of you," I say as I pull her up and into my arms.

"Is this what they call Friday night happy hour?" she jokes, a wide smile coming to her face.

"Well, I am pretty happy, baby," I say with a grin, and her eyes dance in delight.

"Me too..." she says as she slides from the desk and fixes her hair.

"Let me take you home for round two," I growl into her ear, then I kiss her neck, nipping her skin.

"Lead the way."

I don't wait a minute longer. I grab my bag, and we make our way to my private elevator, discreetly leaving the office for the weekend.

25

BETH

I have been on edge all day. The storm started this morning and is showing no signs of disappearing. But after Harrison had me on his desk, the fright left my body a little bit, the stress of the thunderstorm still there, but less so.

We are getting closer and closer, almost to the point that I don't remember what life was like before him. He has kept to his word. He supports me, looks after me, and in private, he makes my body come alive like it never has before.

We're serious about each other. How it all happened is like a blur in my mind, but I am happy. The happiest I have been in forever. Our relationship is still just for us, and while I know Harrison wants to make us public, it has been nice to get to know him privately first. There is less pressure, less expectation. We can be just ourselves around each other. I think that is why we have bloomed so quickly together.

His apartment is quiet and dark with no lights on,

and being so high in the clouds, we are surrounded by gray. I stand near his large floor-to-ceiling windows, looking out at nothing. Just the gray abyss, my mind somewhere else as Harrison takes a call in his den down the hall. I practically live here now, the switch from being an Event Manager in DC to being Harrison's everything, both professionally and personally, was swift. But it feels like I finally belong.

I reach out, putting my hand flat against the window, feeling like I am touching the storm.

"Sorry, baby," Harrison says, coming up behind me, interrupting my thoughts. His tender nickname for me is something he has gone to say a few times in public, something we need to be more careful with. But I love hearing it.

His phone wouldn't stop as we arrived in his private elevator, so I have been standing here for fifteen minutes, waiting for him to return.

"Everything okay?" I ask as he stands flush with my back, his hands circling around my waist as his head dips, kissing my neck. I open to him like a flower, resting my head against his shoulder as his hands move up my body and cup my breasts, squeezing them. I moan a little under my breath. I love him touching my breasts.

"Fine. But I have a problem," he murmurs against my skin, and I feel like I am losing the ability to stand as he hits a spot right between my ear and shoulder and my nipples immediately peak.

"What's that?" I ask in a breathy tone. His hands and lips feel like they are all over me. My body turns to mush whenever he touches me.

"You have too many clothes on. Come on, let's take a shower," he says as he swoops down and picks me up, walking me down to his room. This is an act that I realize he likes. Manhandling me. As a bigger girl, it was something I always balked at. I'm too heavy to be picked up and carried. I feel self-conscious. But Harrison's hold on me is firm, his walk confident. There is no wavering, no pinched expression. It is like holding me is easy and he welcomes it.

"You will break your back carrying me all the time." The quip leaves my lips before I even realize I have said it. Excuses for my heavy frame are so ingrained in me through years of apologizing for myself that I automatically offer everyone a way out of treating me normally. I'm a big girl; there is no denying it.

"If I break my back, that just means you have to sit on my face more while I am recuperating... so I don't mind one bit." Harrison being funny and cheeky is something new, and I laugh, feeling lighter again already.

Walking into the bathroom, he sets me down on my feet as he leans in and turns on the shower. It is massive. In fact, the entire bathroom is as big as my home. A large bathtub, large enough for at least five people, sits along one wall, the double shower next to it, and a double vanity across the other wall. All framed with another large floor-to-ceiling window, with no view today, because of the thick gray clouds outside.

I watch as Harrison rips open his tie and the top buttons of his shirt, before he skillfully and quickly opens each button, ripping his shirt off his shoulders and throwing it across the floor. My eyes are glued to him. I have seen him before, but it is a sight I will never tire of, and my hands automatically go to his chest.

"I like your hands on me," he says as his hands cup my face, and he pulls me to him. Our lips smash together, melding and moving as our tongues explore, neither of us able to get enough. I feel his hands lower and move around to my back as he skillfully lowers my zipper and pushes my dress from my shoulders.

He pulls back and looks at me, standing in his bathroom, surrounded by steam, in nothing but my matching black lace bra and underwear, and my black patent leather high heels. I should feel awkward, embarrassed, but I don't. The way Harrison looks at me fills me with confidence I didn't know I had.

"You had this on under your dress all day and didn't tell me?" Harrison questions, shaking his head as his hand comes to my chest, brushing against my nipple.

"You need to concentrate at work. You don't need distractions," I say with a wink.

"You were a distraction from the moment I met you a year ago. Now that I have you, there is no way in hell that you are disappearing on me again." Every day I spend with him, I fall more and more. I never thought I would find my person. I never thought I was worthy enough. But Harrison makes me feel desired and like I am everything to him. After years of feeling like a disappointment and never being enough, it fills me with so much power to be myself.

His hands trace up my skin, and he grabs my bra straps and pulls them down each shoulder, then tugs the cups of my bra. He openly admires me.

"You are such a breast man," I say with a giggle as I reach around my back and unclasp my bra, letting it fall to the floor at my feet.

"Oh no, I'm not... I am a Beth man. Your breasts, your ass, your curves, your hair, your fucking eyes every time you look at me. The way you walk, the way you talk, the way you make those little moans every time I touch you, the way you pant before you come. The way you are such a good girl when I slide my cock down your throat... Fucking everything about you I like. So I am a Beth man through and through..." he says, and for the second time in under five minutes, I am rendered speechless.

He moves quickly then, undoing his belt and pulling his pants and underwear down in one swoop. His cock is large, throbbing and ready, as he hooks his thumbs in my underwear and slowly pulls them down my legs, letting me step out of them, then throwing them to the side to join our other clothes.

"Let's take a shower before I get you dirty again," he says as we step into the steaming water.

"Dirty?" I ask, admiring the water as it skims over his pecs and shoulders, needing to pinch myself that I am actually with such a man.

"Fucking filthy," he grits out, pulling me to him, our naked bodies pushed together, him holding me tight. I feel him throbbing at my belly and I pull my lips off his, looking him in the eyes and slowly lowering to my knees. Our eyes don't leave each other's, but I see his jaw tick slightly and his chest rise and fall a little quicker.

"How filthy?" I question as I lean forward and skirt my tongue around his tip, and I see his grip on the shower frame above my head tighten, his knuckles almost white.

"Are you teasing me, baby?" he says, barely able to get the words out, his eyes homed in on where my mouth is currently taking him in.

"Mmmmmm," is all I can say around him. He is large, thick, and heavy on my tongue, and delicious.

"Fuck, baby, that feels so good," he groans, his hips moving slightly as I continue to take him deeper and faster.

His eyes never leaving mine, he cups my jaw, his thumb caressing it for a moment.

"You're greedy today. Your hungry mouth looks beautiful wrapped around my cock." He bites his bottom lip, his eyes still glued to mine. "Touch yourself. Touch your pussy and tell me if you are wet for me."

I don't hesitate, and as my hand skirts down my stomach and into my center, I moan when my fingers find my clit.

"Good girl. Good fucking girl..." he moans, my pace on him steady, his hips in rhythm. "But I want you to come on my cock," he says, bending down, grabbing me under the arms, and lifting me to my feet. Then he quickly grabs my ass and hoists me up his body, pushing my back against the tiled wall. He is agile and moves me around like I weigh nothing.

Our hunger for each other overtakes any ideas we had of slow and steady tonight. I hook my legs around his waist just as he enters me, and the air momentarily leaves my body. I feel completely full.

"Fuck, you are tight, baby. So fucking tight." His lips

find mine, and we kiss as I adjust to his size. One of his hands massages my breast, needing and pinching until I am whimpering into our kiss. His other holds my butt, gripping it so hard that I know I will bruise. But I love every touch he gives me.

He starts to grind his hips into mine slowly, his pelvic bone hitting my clit in a new way, and I almost combust on the spot.

"Oh, Harrison... faster," I moan as my head rolls back against the tiles and my fingers dig into his flesh at the back of his neck, no doubt leaving half-moons dented on his skin.

He starts moving faster, filling me completely on each thrust, our bodies fitting well together with each slap. His thrusts are hard and fast, and I tighten my legs around his waist, pulling him harder, wanting more, needing more.

"Fuck, Beth." He thrusts into me so hard, my breasts bounce around against his chest, our skin slapping under the steaming hot water, both of us clawing at each other, wanting to completely devour the other.

"I'm going to..." I pant out, never having experienced anything like this before. My mind is a whirlwind, my heart about to explode from my chest, and Harrison's grip on me gets even tighter, as one hand moves to my clit where he massages for a second before I absolutely explode.

"Harrison!" I scream his name to the ceiling and hear it bounce around the tiled room as I throw my head back, my body arching against him, grinding on him, my muscles shaking, my hips jolting, and my body quivering as he leans forward and sucks on my nipple before I hear him growl.

"Fuck!! Beth, baby. Fuck, Fuck!" he yells as his orgasm rushes through him. Our movements slow as the steam whirls around us and he slowly lowers my feet to the floor.

His lips remain on my body, the two of us still panting.

"Let me clean you, baby," he says, grabbing the soap and sponge, and he slowly rubs my back as I lean into him, bone-tired.

"You don't have to," I say only half-heartedly, because his hands on my body feel so good.

"Yes, I do, but don't worry, baby, my thoughts are still dirty. You will be filthy again by morning…"

I smile at his chest as his hand comes to my chin, lifting it so I look up at him.

"All mine," he says, before sealing it like a pledge with his kiss.

26

HARRISON

I have been lying here watching her for the better part of three hours. I find myself doing this more and more. In the quiet of the early morning, before the hectic life I have starts. I lie in silence, propped up on one elbow, watching her sleep. Her face is completely relaxed, her lips pouting, her chest moving up and down rhythmically. She is my meditation, and I wonder how I ever survived without her.

The rain hasn't stopped outside, and low rumbles of thunder continue to get louder as the storm gets closer again. The morning light shines dimly across her body, highlighting her curves that are wrapped in my sheets. She has a faint scar that runs across her body. It is long, but so thin and faded you would not even know it was there unless you were inspecting her as closely as I am. The small peak of her nipple comes into view from under the sheet with every breath she takes. It is like it is taunting me, playing peek-a-boo, and I finally give in. Not wanting to wake her, but needing her more.

Leaning over, I wrap my tongue around it, suck and nibble it, feeling her delicate flesh in my mouth, not sure how I will ever not want her. I hear her rouse a little. Now that I have started, I can't stop as I climb over her, positioning myself between her legs. Her eyes are still closed as she continues to doze. I pepper small kisses over her stomach and hips, tracing the small scar that runs down her side. She rouses a little more, so I continue, my lips finding her warm center where I position myself, my tongue tracing her folds slowly, my dick already hard and pressing against the mattress.

"Harrison?" she utters quietly as she wakes.

"Hmmmmm?" I reply as my tongue twirls around her clit, massaging slowly, teasingly, before I suck gently on her. I love women, their bodies, their moans, their taste, but Beth, she is something else entirely. I close my eyes, getting lost to her; the feeling of ease and wanting mix together when I am with her. It is easy with her, yet my body thrums for her. She makes me breathe and hold my breath, the pull of protection and desire pool in my stomach, calling to my heart and mind.

"Oh God, that feels so good..." she moans as her hips move against my mouth, and her hands find my scalp. I'm in heaven. This right here, with her in my bed, I could die happy.

I increase my assault, my hands moving up her body, capturing her breast, and I know she is close as her legs edge wider and her movements get rapid. I suck hard then, my need for her becoming demanding, and I twist her nipple a little and she lets go.

"Oh my God..." she gasps, her head lifting from the

bed, her eyes finding mine. Her hair is tousled across her face, her lips parted, and her eyes scrunched up. She is fucking beautiful.

Her body slumps back down, and I trail my lips back up her body. She giggles as I pass her tickle spots on her waist, my smile the widest it has ever been.

"Hmmmm... good morning," she murmurs, and my lips capture hers.

"Morning."

"What time is it?" she asks, stretching as she wakes, her naked body on full display.

"It's about nine a.m.," I mumble as I play with her breasts. They are one of my favorite things about her. I should feel bad about waking her. She has only had a few hours of sleep because we were busy all night.

"Go back to sleep..." I murmur as my tongue sweeps around her other nipple.

"Unlikely..." she says, and my eyes flick to her, seeing her grin.

I am about to talk dirty to her when a loud clap of thunder steals my voice, and Beth jumps about ten feet in the air.

"Oh my God!" she shrieks, her voice full of fear, her hands gripping the bedsheet to her chest, white-knuckled.

"It's alright, it's just a storm," I say, watching her, grabbing her hand to pull her back down to me. She grips it tight. Her eyes look around the room frantically, and she draws her legs to her chest. Her breathing has escalated, and I notice her hands start to shake.

"Hey, come here," I say, sitting up against the headboard, pulling her into my side. I drape my arm around her, and she snuggles in tight.

"Sorry, I just hate storms." I can feel her beating heart on my skin. Concerned, I rub her back and pull her even closer.

"I've got you."

Another rumble breaks through the calm bedroom, and she jumps again, although this time clinging to me even more. I pull the sheets up and cover her.

"Have you always been scared of thunderstorms?" I ask, curious to learn more about her.

"Since I was about five..." she answers as she looks at my large window. I see nothing but dark-gray clouds, still thick like the night before.

"What happened when you were five?" I ask, my breathing becoming rapid, matching hers.

"I was in a car accident. That was the night my father lost the use of his legs and the night my mother died," she says, and my heart stops. I pull her even closer. My heart grows heavy for her and all she has endured.

"I'm sorry. That must have been tough," I say, my voice low, as I wait to hear more about her history. I rub her arm with my hand for comfort.

"Yeah. It was," she says, not giving me much, but I notice her staring out the window, watching the gray clouds as they skirt across the sky. I don't push her. I am grateful she is opening up to me. I want to know it all; I want to know everything about her, but in her own time.

"I think your mom would be really proud of the woman you have become," I offer, because she would be.

Any parent would be honored to have someone like Beth as their daughter.

"Do you think so?" she asks, her big blue eyes looking at me now. My heart thuds in my chest, and I drink her in. She continues looking innocently at me, like I can give her the world. And I will.

"I know so," I confirm, and she gives me a small smile. I sense that this is a topic she doesn't want to talk about in depth, so I steer the conversation in a different direction.

"I had a pet dog when I was five called Ralph. A golden retriever."

"Lucky boy."

"He was my best friend... We went everywhere together. My mother hated him. He was always in trouble and had a special liking for digging up her rosebushes... I still miss that slobbery, hairy friend of mine," I say, a small smile of remembrance gracing my lips.

"Good to know it isn't just me your mother doesn't like, then. I think I would have liked Ralph," she says, looking up at me.

"Ralph would have loved you. And my mother hates everyone, but she will come around once she knows how important you are to me," I state honestly as I entwine my fingers with hers, seeing the other scar on her palm from that roof fall a few weeks ago. She looks like she wants to say something else, but my small declaration hangs in the air for a bit until she speaks.

"You've got to be downtown this morning, don't you?" she asks, changing the subject, always attuned to my schedule.

"Yeah, I have to meet with the Baltimore Business

Bureau for lunch with my mother, then I need to go meet Ben to talk through the law firm quarterly financials," I say as I rub my head, already hesitant to leave my bed and start the day.

"Well, why don't I go and make you coffee while you take a shower?"

"I would rather you take a shower with me," I say, running my hands across her body.

"Yes, but then you will be late, and some people will see that as disrespectful, and I don't want to be the reason your approval rating starts to slip..." I know she is right. I know that I need to keep my eye on the prize. But I find it increasingly hard to take my eyes off her.

"We have only a few weeks to go..." I say, leaving the timeframe out there, because once I win governor, I plan on making our relationship public.

"I know..." she whispers, the weight of time heavy on our minds. "Go!" she says, playfully shoving me while smiling, and I need to make a conscious effort to get out of bed, rather than pull her up with me. Begrudgingly, I sulk to the bathroom, and start the shower, watching her naked body walk around my bedroom before she sheaths it in my white shirt, looking like every man's wet dream.

27

BETH

I walk around naked and slip on Harrison's white shirt, the material feeling like the warm protective hug I need, his scent wrapping me up tight, but I am still jumpy with every rumble I hear. This storm has been active for hours, and I need to call and check in with Dad to let him know I am okay. He stayed with Larry last night, so at least he is with people.

He is aware I am spending time with Harrison. No doubt he became suspicious due to my constant smile and daydreamy eyes. Dad doesn't say much, but I know that the two of them are growing closer as well, as Harrison's trip to the community center did wonders for their relationship.

I quickly tidy Harrison's room, because with our clothes strewn everywhere and the bed unmade, it looks like a bomb went off, then I pad down to his kitchen and come to a halt.

It is like nothing I have encountered before and takes my breath away every time I see it. Large, with streamlined cabinetry, black and glossy without even a finger-print anywhere. The black marble countertops are free of clutter. He has about five different appliances that all look like ovens and a massive refrigerator that looks like it is from the movies.

Stepping inside, I walk quickly into his butler's pantry, which really is just another kitchen but hidden. Setting up the coffee machine, I get busy putting together a coffee for each of us, and even though it looks highly technical, it is relatively easy to use.

As I froth the milk, I think I hear a bell chime. My eyes flick to the oven, then the dishwasher, but both are off, and seeing nothing else, I turn my attention back to the job at hand. Smiling to myself, feeling the post sex flush, I finish the cups and walk back into the main kitchen, my dreamlike state at being with a man like Harrison firmly planted on my face.

"What the hell are you doing?" I hear a high-pitched shriek, and I jump, the coffee cups splashing the boiling hot coffee onto my hands and pain shoots up my arms. The cups fall from my grip, smashing all over the clean polished floors. Harrison's pristine kitchen is now totally in shambles. Because of me.

You can't have nice things. You ruin everything.

"What the hell are you doing here?" the screech of Mrs. Langford hits me from across the breakfast bar. She is dressed in her signature matching Chanel tweed suit. Her designer handbag and shoes match, and her hair is blow-dried and quaffed. Even though her makeup is perfectly done, her bright-red lips shining, her eyes are squinting at me like I am the devil. In contrast, I am naked except for her son's business shirt, my hair a mess, and I am pretty sure Harrison left love bites on my neck last night.

"Mrs. Langford!" I exclaim in shock, trying to push the pain in my hands out of my mind because now I can't move my legs. Shattered porcelain is scattered around my bare feet, so I can't make it to the sink without tearing them up. I breathe through the pain, hoping like hell I don't get blisters on my hands.

"I knew you were trouble the moment I laid eyes on you. And here you are, the latest tramp in my son's quest to bed all the women in the city. I guess he flashed his smile at you, and you just lay down and opened your legs like the little slut you are!" Her words are like venom, and I am taken aback by her ferocity.

"Mrs. Langford, it isn't like that..." I stutter, feeling like a lamb headed to the slaughter.

"You fuck my son, expecting to get his millions, is that it? You are nothing but a piece of shit on his shoes. He is going to be governor. You are nothing. A nobody."

"But, Mrs. Langford, I am not..." I again try to explain that I am not just some one-night stand, but she cuts me off.

"Do not talk to me. Clean up this disgusting mess and put on some goddamn clothes. And a word of advice before I go..." she says, taking a step toward me, and I can hardly breathe as I wait.

"Make no mistake, Beth, the event planner..." she spits out my name like it is poison. "You are not good enough for my son and never will be. So get your fat ass out of here and don't come back," she seethes, and I look at her, wide-eyed, shocked at her display of hatred toward me when she doesn't know anything about me.

I stand still, watching her as she throws her shoulders back and walks into the elevator. I remain frozen until the doors close and she is gone.

My heart is racing from the confrontation, almost breaking at the situation. My feelings for Harrison are unlike I have ever felt before, and the bubble I have been living in with him was just popped by her words. The pain from the hot coffee sears into my hands, bringing me back to reality. With no other option, I step toward the sink, cursing under my breath as the sharp shards of porcelain penetrate my feet. I make it within a few steps and hurriedly turn on the cold tap and immediately push my hands underneath. I sigh as the water takes away some of the pain.

"Beth? Shit, what happened?" Harrison says as he steps around the corner in nothing but a towel wrapped around his waist, water running down his torso.

"I just dropped the coffee. I'm so sorry, Harrison," I say on a whisper, the events of the morning now making my eyes water.

"I don't care about the mess, baby. Are you okay?" he says as he walks toward me with concern etched into his face.

"Stop!" I say, putting up my hand. "You will get the shards in your feet. Do you have a broom?" I ask, and I see him look down, then look at my feet, then flick his gaze to my hands that are currently still underneath the cold rushing water from his tap.

"Did you burn your hands?" he asks, looking panicked.

"I'm fine. You need to go and get ready because you will be late," I say firmly, pushing my emotions back down deep and pulling my shoulders back.

"Beth, I am not leaving you like this," Harrison says as he looks around, assessing all the damage.

"Harrison. I'm fine. You need to go and get ready. I will clean this mess up and head home." I just need him to go away, because otherwise, I won't be able to hold these tears back for much longer.

"Beth, are you in pain? What's wrong, baby?" he asks like he can sense it is more than a broken cup.

"Harrison. You need to stick to your commitments. No distractions, remember?" I pull on Oscar's terminology and see his lips thin in disagreement. He walks to a cupboard and grabs a broom, quickly sweeping the broken shards into a small pile and removing them from around my feet.

He then walks toward me and pulls my hands from the water, inspecting every inch of them closely. My chest tightens, my emotions running rampant. He picks me up then, sitting me on the counter, and checks under my feet. My heart is heavy, equal parts about to burst at his affection for me, while about to break because I know his mother is right. He is going to be governor. I am a nobody.

"Your feet are okay; your hands are too. Are you okay, though?" he asks as his look of concern drills into me.

"I told you... I am clumsy," I murmur with a shrug,

because there is no way I am telling him about his mother's visit.

"You are not clumsy, you are beautiful," he states before pulling me from the counter and carrying me back to his bedroom. He helps me get dressed and calls Tom to take me home. All the while my insides turn, and it isn't until I get home that I walk straight to my bathroom and vomit, the stress of this morning overtaking any sense of normalcy I have, knowing that I have fallen in love with the one man I could ruin.

28

HARRISON

BREAKING NEWS

We have one week to go until election night and the polls have a clear winner so far in Harrison Langford. Harrison and his team have been busy campaigning endlessly these past few weeks, securing the votes he needs, his popularity skyrocketing in the outer suburbs where he needed to make up the numbers.

However, Harrison cannot rest yet, as the final week of the campaign is traditionally the most fraught, with elections being won or lost this week as both parties kick up their campaigning, and those sleepless nights start to emerge.

More to come.

It has been a hectic time and the campaign trail has been brutal. I have meetings from sunup to sundown, and a few nights a week, I get to have Beth in my bed. I would prefer to have her every night and be the kind of couple that is out and about together either for dinner, having brunch, or just simply being. But we remain purely platonic in the eyes of the world outside. With the election approaching, everything is getting busier, my stress levels have increased, and more than anything, I wish we could be open about our relationship, but we can't rock the boat. Not now.

I see Beth as an asset to me in every way. But Oscar is firm that any big news, of which being in a relationship with Beth would constitute, will affect the polls. I think it would be positive, but Oscar is not sure and doesn't want to risk it. Beth remains quiet about it all.

In fact, she has been quieter than usual since the weekend she stayed during the storm, where she spilled the coffee in the kitchen. At first, I thought it was due to her opening up about the car accident and her mother. I know how history can creep up on a person and change their viewpoints on things. But as the weeks have gone on, even though we are still just as close, the light in her eyes has dimmed. I watch her like a hawk at work, ensuring she has everything she needs. Likewise, she does the same with me. The two of us dote on each other like we are scared the other will break.

I am beginning to think that the sneaking around is what is making her more reserved. I don't like to keep her hidden, but we spoke about it early on. She knew the reasons for it and still supported me all the way. Now I am too scared to broach the subject with her, because a week out, if she wants to go public, then I have no idea what I will do. I don't want to lose her or the election. So I have remained tight-lipped, moving through the motions. This last week is going to be the hardest and the slowest week of my entire life.

My team and I now all sit in the conference room at the Baltimore Police Headquarters, meeting with the chief of police and his team. We are receiving a police briefing on the safety procedures that will be introduced on election night. The possibility of me becoming governor is real. It is a tight race, and it isn't over by a long shot. But I have a chance, and a chance is all I need.

"So what we usually see and what we are expecting is an enhanced police presence across the city. There will need to be an increase to your security detail, both in the days prior to the election and after," the police chief says, and this is all to be expected, so I am not worried.

"So, we will increase our personal security team, and there will be more police on the street?" Eddie asks, wanting the details.

"Yes. With large events like an election of this size, we do require additional resources, the safety of the public and all participants our primary concern. I would also advise if you have the means to increase your personal security of your family and close contacts as well."

"Is there a security threat to us?" Beth asks, and I can hear the nervousness in her voice, and my eyes flick to her face, seeing concern in her eyes.

"I would hope not, but we need to be prepared." The police chief does very little to give her any assurance. I watch her as she reaches for her glass of water, her hands shaking slightly. As if my body knows, I lean toward her a little, and as she tries to grab the glass, she misses it, swiping it to the side, pushing it along the desk, before it reaches the edge and starts to fall.

But my hand is there. My body moves on its own, and I catch the water before it falls, her gasp falling from her lips as all eyes look at me.

"You okay?" I ask her quietly, my question not necessarily about the glass, and she knows it. She gives me a small nod as I pass the glass to her, and I watch her take a slow, steady sip before placing it back on the table.

"So what numbers for security do you suggest?" Oscar talks specifics, getting everyone back on track as I continue to watch Beth. I know I shouldn't, but I reach out under the table and grab her hand, giving it a squeeze in support. Her head whips around to me, and her eyes widen. It is the first time in a professional setting we have touched like this. She is shocked, yet I want more. I settle for rubbing my thumb across the top of her hand and watch her come to terms with the fact that I am here for her. Always.

"Road closures will also need to occur on election night. We will map your route. At this stage, we have you positioned at the Four Seasons Hotel from late afternoon until the announcement. Upon leaving the hotel, you will have a police escort down President Street, through the city, to home."

"That all sounds fine. Eddie will increase our personal security, making sure that everyone here and our close friends and families are managed. We will fall into line with whatever you suggest in terms of enhanced police presence and any access you need to me or the team or our venue prior will be granted as you need it.

Safety of everyone is most important," I say. The police chief looks relieved to have all his suggestions approved, but I am not taking any risks. Everyone's safety is paramount. I stand, shaking his hand, and the team and I leave, needing to get to our luncheon, the final one before the elections.

WE ARRIVE AT THE RESTAURANT, and I am immediately swept up in backslaps and handshakes as Beth chats with the venue manager to ensure the luncheon is on track. People are laughing and smiling, and although the election has not happened, everyone is feeling confident. Including me.

"Harrison darling, how are you feeling? There are only days to go!" My mother's voice sweeps across the room, positioning her as a loving, doting mother. Out of the corner of my eye, I see Tennyson roll his eyes before heading to the bar, while Ben and Eddie watch her flow across the room to me, commanding everyone's attention as her gold bracelets jingle on her arms and her tweed Chanel suit fits her to perfection.

"Mother," I say in acknowledgement and kiss the air near her cheek. As I do, I look around for Beth and see her talking to Arthur across the room.

"Come, everyone, let's take our seats," my mother says, sweeping her gaze around the room, and everyone finds their spot. My mother sits next to me, with Eddie on my other side. Lilly is sitting directly across from me, gazing at me with a smile of longing that I wish she would erase. Beth sits with Arthur and Tennyson down on one end, the three of them laughing and carrying on, making everyone else jealous at the fun they are obviously having. But I smile as I watch them. She looks so good when she's happy.

After everyone has enjoyed their meal, I stand and clink my glass to get their attention.

"Everyone, I would like to take this opportunity to thank each and every one of you for your ongoing support, your pledges, your guidance, your counsel, your time, your connections. With the election fast approaching, my team and I will be busy, seeing more and more of the people and promoting our campaign, ready for Saturday," I say, and a few cheers go up in the crowd.

"I am confident, with all of you at my side, that I will walk away with a new job on Saturday, with new responsibilities, and I know I can count on all your support then as well. It means the world to have you here and..." I stop as I look at Doctor Warner. His face is red, and he is struggling to breathe.

"Dr. Warner?" I ask, and everyone looks at him.

"Oh my God!" my mother exclaims, clutching her pearls, and I see Beth push her chair back and run to him.

"Doctor Warner. Do you have an EpiPen?" she asks, seemingly already knowing what is going on and what needs to be done as the rest of us sit back, watching her, some still sipping their champagne like this is their entertainment.

He pulls it from his pocket as he slumps down in the chair.

"Shit," I say, finally springing into action as I run over

and grab him under the arms as he begins to slide off the chair, laying him on the floor as Beth grabs the EpiPen.

"Okay, here it goes," she says before she stabs him hard in the thigh. I hear my mother gasp again, Lilly standing behind her, comforting her as the rest of the crowd looks on. My eyes meet with Beth's over the top of Doctor Warner, and I know we are thinking the same thing.

"Oscar, call 9-1-1," I bark, knowing he needs the paramedics.

"Already done; they are here now," he says.

"Let's clear the room, people. Paramedics are here," the venue manager says, pushing the doors wide and moving people out of the way as a team of paramedics walks in with a stretcher. Beth and I step back as they take his vitals. I watch with concern, but he is already looking better, sitting up gradually and talking to them coherently. He is breathing well, and I see Beth talking to one of the paramedics, giving him a rundown as is the venue manager. Then he's loaded onto the stretcher and taken away.

My guests are gathering their things—some have already left—and I look at Beth, trying to understand from her what happened.

"What meal did you serve him?" my mother demands from beside me, looking at Beth with venom, and everyone stops talking and watches the exchange.

"His dietary requirements were noted upon confirmation of the event. I will need to investigate..." Beth says, still looking like she is in shock.

But my mother won't let her finish.

"Obviously, you are totally incompetent! You nearly killed the man! And with only days to go until the election. You have probably ruined any chance of Harrison becoming governor, you stupid, stupid girl," my mother spits.

"Mother. That is enough!" I grit out to her, not liking where she is going with this and not liking how public it is.

"Okay, everyone, I think we will wrap it up now. Thanks for your support, and we look forward to seeing you at the election party on Saturday night," Oscar says as he and Eddie start corralling our guests out the door. The luncheon is now dead in the water. My nerves are frayed. I'm concerned that this will affect the polls, and as I look to Oscar for reassurance, I don't get it. His pursed lips and side-eye tell me all I need to know.

"Harrison, I knew the moment you hired this girl, she was trouble. Now she has ruined everything," my mother pushes, agitating me even more.

"Mother, I said enough!" I bark as I try to gather my thoughts. I run my hands through my hair and watch as the last guests leave, shaking their hands and plastering a fake smile on my face to reassure them that everything is fine when I don't even believe it myself. Beth is a professional; I know this is not something she simply missed. She hasn't been herself for a few weeks, but still, there has to be another explanation.

"Harrison, I checked the dietaries twice; his meal was correct," she says, looking at me, her eyes pleading with me to believe her. And I do.

"Harrison, don't be a fool. She is probably working

for your competition. Did they pay you to create a spectacle so they would win? You need the money, right? You live in Riverside, don't you?" my mother seethes, like being working class is the devil's work.

Beth's eyes widen, and she takes a step back at the cruel words. I go to move toward Beth, but she shakes her head, stopping me in my tracks. I swallow my anger and look around the room. There are many eyes watching this exchange, and I look back to Beth who remains stoic, giving me a look to make me stay right where I am.

"Jesus Christ," Tennyson murmurs, and I see him throw back the rest of his whiskey as Arthur Stratten steps up behind Beth in support. My feet won't move as I stand between the two most important women in my life, wondering what the hell is going on.

"We should go," Oscar says from beside me, the only clear head in this shitstorm.

"Yes, we should," my mother huffs, giving Beth another horrid look.

I rub my hand over my face, wondering how something as simple as a thank-you lunch has pushed me into very dangerous territory of losing the election for nearly killing one of my main supporters. I am sure the media are circling already. Paparazzi are probably following the paramedics and lined up at the hospital. I can already see the headline: *Baltimore Boy's fall from grace after attempted murder.*

"News crew just pulled up outside." Eddie cringes.

"We have a back exit," the venue manager pipes up. My eyes remain on Beth. I see her swallow and take a deep breath.

"Beth, you should come with us," I state, because I really need to have her in my arms.

"You go with Eddie and Oscar. I will fix up the situation here," Beth says, and I watch her push her shoulders back, putting on her professional armor. I know she didn't do this on purpose. I know it must have been some terrible accident. But I have been focused on becoming governor of Maryland for years. It has been a lifelong dream. And it may now all go down the toilet, because of one dietary requirement at an event she managed for me. My emotions and feelings are running rampant.

I swallow as I look at her. Her body is stiff.

"Go," she whispers, her eyes glassy, and I want to grab her, tell her it will all be okay. Tell her I love her. Because I do, and in this moment, I want her to know it.

"Harrison, for God's sake, let's go," my mother says, huffing out before walking toward the back door.

"Ten will look after her. I will call him to make sure everything is okay," Eddie whispers in my ear, and I look at Beth, with Arthur and Tennyson at her side. I give Tennyson a look to make sure he stays here with her, and he nods. That is the only thing that makes my legs move. Knowing that he will watch her for me.

Because I can't have distractions. I need to focus.

29

BETH

I watch him as he steps out the back door, and as the door closes on his silhouette, I lean on the chair in front of me so I don't collapse. My palms sweat and my heart is racing as fear, stress, and foreboding sweep through my body, making me nearly faint. Event management is in the top ten most stressful jobs in the world, and this is why.

"Bethy, it will be okay," Arthur says.

"How did he get the wrong meal? It was clear as day on the paperwork!" I ask no one in particular. The panic is coming up my spine and settling in my chest, the place it is always most comfortable.

"Let's look through the restaurant paperwork. We will need to gather all the information anyway in case the doctor sues the restaurant or Harrison," Tennyson says, and my body stills. That thought didn't even cross my mind. I was so worried about Doctor Warner's health, I didn't think of the possibility that he would sue Harrison. My mind is a whirlwind, my body tired, and the adrenaline of stabbing the doctor with his EpiPen slowly flows out of my body as the three of us wait for the venue manager to come back before we ask her our questions.

"You should both go," I say, not wanting to keep them any longer. Who knows how long the venue manager will be. I can see her rushing other patrons, wanting to close the restaurant.

"We can stay with you," Arthur says, and my heart warms a little. He has been such a great friend to me.

"It is fine, Arthur. I'm a big girl. Besides, there is probably going to be a lot of media here soon, so I think you both should go before you get snapped and make front page of *Society News*," I state, and they both think through what I said.

"Fine, I will go. But call me if you need anything," Arthur says before giving me a small hug and walking quietly out the door. He likes his quiet life now and I don't want him dragged into this mess.

"Harrison wants me to stay with you," Tennyson says.

"It really isn't necessary."

"Maybe not, but I appreciate my life, and if my brother found out that I left you here to deal with this on your own, then I am pretty sure he would kill me." He makes a joke, but I don't laugh. Deep down, I know Harrison cares about me, but the fact remains that I may have just ruined his chance of becoming governor. I knew seeing his mother today was not going to be easy. I haven't seen her since that morning when she berated me in his kitchen. Since then, I have felt off, not myself. Never in a million years did I ever think she would hate me so much. All for loving her son. I know Harrison didn't want to leave me, and that is the only reason I was able to push him out the door. I know he trusts me and believes in me. He knows I didn't do this, but I do need to figure out how it happened.

"Okay, they are gone. Let me get the paperwork and interview the chef, and then we can chat about what happened, Beth," the venue manager says as she sweeps in and out of the room. I know these things take time. I see Tennyson look at his watch.

"Go. Please. You must have a million things to do and sitting around here for the next few hours reviewing paperwork and babysitting me is not going to be fun," I say to him, trying to get him to leave. I don't need to be responsible for another Langford as well.

"Fine. But give me your phone so I can put in my number." I do as I am told because I don't have any energy to argue.

"Call me for anything," he says, and it is a lovely gesture but one I won't take him up on. I am a professional; I can deal with it alone. Just like everything else in my life.

"Sure, now go!" I say, giving him a brief smile of reassurance, and then he does something that startles me. He pulls me in for a hug. His large arms wrap around my shoulders and my eyes start to water.

"My mother is evil, but Harrison only has eyes for you. Please just be patient with him. He has a lot on his plate," Tennyson says, and I nod, having lost the ability to speak at his kindness.

"Call me," he says, stepping back slowly, and I watch him leave and wait for a few moments before I sink onto the chair and hang my head, wondering how to fix the mess I have made. *Stupid, stupid, stupid,* I berate myself. I have never messed up this badly before. The man could have died! I think about calling Kelly for advice, but knowing she is in her newborn baby phase, I decide to leave her out of it.

I sit with my head in my hands for thirty minutes as I wait for the venue manager to come back, which she does, with her head chef in tow.

"Okay, I have all the paperwork here," she says in a light tone with a small smile, which indicates to me that the restaurant didn't make a mistake and their conscience is clear. My heart sinks.

"So I have your emails and final paperwork here all signed, both outlining the dietary requirements of the man in question," she continues, and I am confused.

"So what happened, then?" I ask, looking between her and the chef and back to the paperwork.

"We had a late change," she says, looking at me.

"What do you mean by a late change?"

"Well, an hour before the event began, we got a call to make changes to the dietary requirements."

"From whom?" I ask, surprised because I didn't call, and I am pretty sure Oscar didn't either.

"From you. You called and spoke to the head chef here, requesting the change."

I look at her, bewildered at what I am hearing.

"I didn't make any such call."

"I spoke to you. You explained the change you needed. The specific requirement was that the man in question be served seafood sauce on his steak instead of the red wine jus. I told you that such a late change would result in a fifty-dollar fee, to which you approved."

"Do we have any proof of this phone call?" I ask because I know I didn't call him.

"I have been caught out before, at a restaurant I used to manage in DC, where someone called to make these changes and left the guests with a large bill they didn't approve, so I record all my work phone calls now," he says as he hits play on his cell phone and I hear Mrs. Langford's voice come through the speaker, requesting the meal for Doctor Warner to include seafood sauce on his steak and agreeing to the additional fee. Doctor Warner is allergic to seafood. Clearly, the sauce was what made him go into anaphylactic shock.

The caller confirms her name is Beth, but it is clearly Mrs. Langford's voice. I am so shocked, I can barely breathe. This woman hates me so much that she would risk a man's life to get rid of me.

"We will be providing all the paperwork to our lawyers, so please note that if you or the doctor plan to sue, we have full documentation and the copy of the voice memo," the venue manager says, laying out her cards. I nod in understanding. It isn't their fault someone nearly died.

"I think the three of us here know that the person on the end of that phone is not me. It doesn't sound anything like me. And an hour before lunch, I was in a meeting with the chief of police, so I have a full alibi," I state and they both nod. They know as well as I do whose voice it is. None of us want to say the name out loud.

"We understand." The venue manager offers with a

small smile of pity. She already must know Mrs. Langford is a handful.

"Can you please print those out and put them with the final files, so my team is aware of the additional cost and the situation. I would also like a copy of the voice memo emailed and texted to me if possible?" I need to cover my back.

"I will have them sent over with the full incident report and final invoice now before I close for the night." I look out the window, seeing it is black outside. I have been here for hours, and the fight has all but left me. I was feeling fragile since Mrs. Langford said those poisonous words to me in Harrison's kitchen weeks ago, but now I can't believe the extent she will go to keep Harrison and me apart.

I say my goodbyes and leave, stepping into the dark, cool night, wondering how best to get home. Tom is not around, having had to shuttle Mrs. Langford and the others this afternoon, and I didn't bother calling him back. Instead, I wrap my coat around me and walk to the bus stop with my head down. I continually tell myself that I am shivering because of the cool night air, and not because of the small rumbles that are starting to break through the sky. It is only eight p.m., but I already know with Dad away at Larry's, this is going to be a long night for me.

30

HARRISON

I left her. I know I shouldn't have, deep down I know that, but with Oscar and my mother all but pushing me out the door, I knew I needed to escape before the media got wind of what happened today. So I left her.

"I just called the hospital again, and Doctor Warner is fine. I have told him we will visit him early in the morning," Oscar says, coming into the living room and sitting on the sofa next to Eddie. My team is all here in my penthouse, minus one.

"God, how did it all go so wrong?" Eddie says, leaning back, saying the same words we have been saying to ourselves over and over all evening. We have been over it a dozen times. Paperwork from the restaurant has come through that his dietary requirements were changed, but I left Ben and my legal team to sort through it. My eyes can't look at any more contracts or policies, my mind almost numb from it all.

"I am sure it was a simple error..." I say mindlessly,

my eyes still stuck on the window, looking at the dark clouds. Because there is no other explanation. Someone missed something accidentally. It happens. The doctor is fine.

"A simple error that could have literally had you embroiled in a murder investigation," Oscar mumbles, blowing the entire event up into something it isn't. Accidental manslaughter maybe...

"Thank God Beth knew what to do," Eddie says, and he is right. The rest of us just stood around watching Doctor Warner go into shock and struggling to breathe. Like useless statues, we all were rooted to the spot, and Beth was the only one to jump into action. My lucky charm. She always comes to my rescue.

"Beth always knows what to do..." I murmur, frustrated that she isn't picking up my calls and hoping that she is alright. I have thought of nothing but her all night. I want to see her. I have to see her. My brother Tennyson is also strangely quiet and not taking my calls. Although I know he often works late on our international construction projects, often in conference calls with China.

"I can't say your mother was any help with the entire situation. Are we going to have a problem there? Any more fires that may pop up in the next few days that I might need to manage?" Oscar is sitting, flicking through his cell phone, no doubt running defense on the high number of media inquiries we are now getting.

Eddie snorts. "Wherever our mother is, be assured that there is always trouble that follows her."

"She was totally out of line today. Her tone with Beth will not be tolerated again. If anything like that happens in public again, you need to remove her immediately because I will stand up for Beth. I won't be walking away again like today," I say, my stomach feeling heavy, angry that Beth didn't want me to stand by her today and angry that my mother put us in that position at all. But mostly angry at myself for listening to either of them. I should have grabbed Beth and gotten us both out of there, and the fact that I didn't makes me feel sick to my stomach.

"We have the photo shoot tomorrow, for her friend at that women's magazine, and then I will tell her to stay home and lay low until election night," Eddie says almost on autopilot, as my eyes continue to roam the dark sky.

"Tell me why we are doing a photo shoot for a women's magazine again," I ask, confused about seeing that on the schedule.

"I wish I knew the answer. It was something Mom raised early on in the campaign, needing you to do the shoot to help her friend who runs the magazine publishing company. At the time, we thought it may help garner the votes of older females in the outer suburbs," Eddie relays, the whole conversation now coming back to me.

"It will help us promote a positive picture of Harrison. It might be the thing we need to lift his profile in these last few days. Hopefully, it covers any negative media attention that may come out from the luncheon today," Oscar contributes, making sense as usual.

"Oscar, we all know that Harrison doesn't have a problem winning the female vote." Eddie's snide remark does little to lighten the mood in the room.

"Getting back to your mother. She doesn't seem to

like Beth at all... Did they have some type of disagreement that I don't know about?" Oscar asks, and I see his eyes lift to me in the reflection of the window.

"No. It is just Mom and her rich, pretentious way of trying to control Harrison, her firstborn favorite child." Eddie has malice in his tone.

I leave them to continue their conversation with each other behind me. My eyes remain focused on the clouds as their banter is blocked from my mind, and I watch the dark-gray sky continue to darken and swirl, almost hypnotically in motion. I sip my whiskey slowly, feeling the burn in my chest, and I rub my eyes, willing the headache and tension to disappear.

I think about the election. Polls are positive, but these last few days matter. I need to get things right and back on track for the campaign. But I also need to get things back on track with Beth. I feel like I am being pulled in two directions. I was expecting the final week of campaigning to be long and stressful. Meeting lots of people, shaking hands more and more. I just need to get through the next few days, and win both the polls and the girl.

Startling me from my thoughts, I hear the deep rumble of thunder, and a sharp flash cuts across the sky, lighting up the thick, voluminous clouds that now shroud the city, and I know that there is only one place I need to be.

"I need to go," I say suddenly, sliding my empty whiskey glass onto the kitchen counter and grabbing my keys and jacket as I walk to my elevator and call it up.

"Where are you going?" Eddie asks, concerned as both he and Oscar stand up from the sofa, looking at me.

"It's a storm," I say as I fix my collar while waiting for the elevator.

"And?" Oscar asks, his eyebrows rising as if I have lost my mind.

"And Beth needs me," I state, just before I step in and hit the button for my basement. The elevator doors close on both of them looking at me as though I am crazy and perhaps they are right. I am crazy.

Crazy about Beth.

31

BETH

The house is dark, cold, and quiet when I step in the door. My hair and clothes are wet, the rain teeming down around me, soaking me as I was walking home from the bus stop. My cell phone has been vibrating nonstop in my bag, but I was so focused on getting home safely, I have ignored it all evening. Stepping inside, the house doesn't give me the automatic warm reprieve I was expecting. It is empty, silent, and makes me shiver.

I immediately switch on every light in the house and get undressed, putting on my warm sweater and my baggy track pants, ready for a night of curling into myself. I check each room, ensuring the windows are locked and the back door is secure. As I retrace my footsteps along the small hallway to the front living room, my body stills as all the lights go out.

"Shit," I curse under my breath as my hand instinctively shoots out to my side, and I find the wall and take a few more tentative steps toward the living room. I am almost to the sofa, where my blanket is waiting, and then it hits.

The largest roll of thunder claps right over my house. The windows rattle and my knees give way. I fall to the floor and curl up into a ball, making myself small as I shuffle my body to the wall until I feel it at my back.

My breathing is fast, my heart rate explosive, and a quiet tear slips from my eye. I hate being like this. It happens every time there is a storm. My general good sense flies out the window and I feel like I am that small young girl again, stuck in the back seat of the car, with the storm raging around me.

"You are fine. You can do this. It's just a little storm," I tell myself as my pulse punctuates my skin at my wrist and my mouth becomes dry. I hear the rain and see the bright flashes of lightning through our thin curtains, and I know that the storm will be sticking around for a while. I need to try and pull myself together. At least until I get to the sofa and curl up into the blanket.

I clear my throat and slowly start to uncurl my body. Staying on all fours, I slowly crawl my way to the living room. The roof rattles with another thunderous bang, and I immediately cower, my hands covering my head as I squeeze my eyes shut. But it isn't as loud as the first clap of thunder. I hear it again, and I look up, trying to see in the blackened house.

"Beth!" I hear a shout at the front door and immediately scramble on all fours toward it.

"Beth!" I hear my name again, barely over the loud rain, and I pull away the flimsy curtain at the side of the front door and look through.

Standing tall, in his designer suit, soaked from the rain, is Harrison. His hair is wet and falling down his forehead, and my eyes quickly flick to see his car at the front on the street before I look back at him. His eyes find mine, and I swallow. I am still sitting on the floor, my hands shaking, my heart racing. But I pull myself up and open the door.

"What are you doing here?" I ask, shocked to see it's really him and not some figment of my crazy imagination.

"It's storming!" he yells, the water dripping from his face, running down his cheeks as he stands there looking at me.

"Harrison, I didn't..." I start to tell him that it wasn't my fault today. But I also don't want to tell him that it was his mother. How heartbreaking it is going to be for him to know his mother would do that. The words get lodged in my throat.

"I don't care about today. I don't care about anything else. Just you. I just care about you." I see his eyes pleading with me as the light display from the sky highlights his face.

I watch him, the rain running down his clothes, soaking him through. Another loud clap of thunder vibrates through the house and in an instant, he is right in front of me. His large frame envelops me, and I bury my head in his chest. He picks me up and kicks the door closed, then takes me into the living room and sits me on the sofa.

"No lights?" he asks, looking around, and I can make

out the wrinkle between his eyebrows in the dull light from outside.

"Power went out," I say quietly as I pull my knees to my chest. My body shakes almost uncontrollably, cold mixed with fear, mixed with anxiety. I pull at my weighted blanket to cover me somewhat, feeling my body giving in to the fear right in front of him.

He takes off his wet jacket and throws it over the back of the sofa and sits with me, pulling me to him tightly.

"It's okay, Beth. Everything will be okay," he whispers in my ear, hugging me tight. He leans over, grabbing the blanket and throwing it over both of us, and I curl into him. My hand grips his shirt as his runs up and down my back. My body continues to shake, but I try to control my breathing.

As the thunder and lightning continue their assault, Harrison keeps whispering in my ear, sweet things, the way he cares for me, how glad he is he found me, all the words a girl like me always wanted to hear. He talks for over an hour, through the entire storm, and doesn't stop until the storm does.

We are quiet, the only sounds in the room now the light pattering of rain on my tin roof and our breathing. I can hear his heart beating, strong and rhythmically through his chest, the steadiness filling me with his strength.

"We weren't meant to be in the car the night of the accident..." I say quietly, the words flowing out of me. Harrison remains silent, listening and letting me tell my story.

"It had been sunny all day, warm even. Mom had met

some new friends through work, and they invited us to their house for dinner. Mom was very social, always making new friends, and Dad and I would tag along, happy to explore and meet new people too." I swallow, my mouth dry but I continue.

"They were a wealthy family who lived close to DC, much wealthier than us. I remember their house was big, majestic, like a castle. It was beautiful, nothing like I had ever seen before. They didn't have children, and I don't think they liked having me in their home. I remember being scared of them, timid and staying close to my dad," I whisper, my voice tentative. I haven't told anyone this story before. I have always kept it close.

Harrison rubs my back, holding me tight, and kisses the top of my head.

"We were there for about an hour. My dad was having a few drinks with the husband; my mom was chatting and laughing with the wife, and I sat quietly on their sofa, too scared to move. I remember they had a long dining table, and as dinner got closer, the table started filling up. Not an inch was free. Plates and plates of food were put out, too much for just us. It was a feast." I hear my voice change a little, the memories of that night now vivid in my mind as I pull on my recol-lection.

"I stood up and walked over to the table. I just wanted a closer look. All this food, a real-life feast, not one just in my Cinderella books. I wanted to see it with my own eyes. But I shouldn't have. I should have stayed sitting by myself in the living room."

I pause, my heart rate increasing, my palms sweating

and my head starting to pound as the recollections thump inside of me.

"What happened?" Harrison whispers, prompting me to continue.

"I stood next to the large table, just looking. I never touched any of it. As I was about to turn and go back to my seat on the sofa, the door from the hallway opened and a large Labrador came bolting through. He took one look at me and ran straight toward me. I never had a dog, so I didn't know he was friendly. I was scared. I thought he was going to eat me for dinner," I say, my words starting to come out faster.

"The dog pounced on me, and I screamed. I fell backward and grabbed the only thing I could so I didn't fall. The tablecloth. I fell down screaming in fright and the dog jumped on me and started licking my face, but my fist was still curled up tight with the tablecloth and the entire feast came tumbling down on us.

"My mother was so embarrassed. I was always so clumsy. Always ruining things. She and my father wrapped me up in my coat and shuffled me out the door quicker than the lightning strikes that had started happening that night.

"I remember there was lots of yelling when we got into the car. My dad had a few drinks, so my mother drove us home. The weather had turned as nighttime came and it was dark and stormy. The thunder and lightning were both frequent and persistent. The roads were full of water. It wasn't a long drive, but it seemed like it took forever because she was driving so slow since she couldn't really see through the thick rain. I remember the windshield wipers swishing back and forth so quickly it was almost comical. My mother was angry, though. Yelling at me, screaming at me for ruining their night and embarrassing her in front of her new friends. She had warned me before going that I wasn't to do anything to ruin the night. I tried. I tried so hard to be good. I sat quietly. I used my manners. My mother was furious and berated me all the way home. You know, I can still hear her voice. *'You ruined everything! I can't take you anywhere. You embarrassed me and your father.'*

"She was really worked up. She was driving, yelling, the rain was pelting down, and the thunder and lightning were scaring me. My dad was trying to talk with her, to get her to calm down and concentrate on the road. It all happened so fast. One minute, I heard her yelling at me, then the next, all I could hear were my screams."

"You were just a child. It was not your fault," Harrison says, his words ricocheting off the metal shell I imagine that is protecting me at the moment.

"She ran a red light, hit another car, and our car rolled. My mother wasn't wearing a seat belt and died on impact. My father broke his back and lost the ability to walk, and I have metal rods in my shoulder from where the seat belt saved my life but shattered my bones.

"There was a family in the other car. Both parents died and the little boy became an orphan.

"I killed my mother that night. It is my fault that my father can't walk. I made a little boy an orphan. It is my fault, all of it. I ruin everything, Harrison, and I am so scared that I am going to ruin you too." I can't stop the tears as they run freely down my cheeks. Harrison pulls my face up to look at his, cupping my jaw, and catches each and every tear, brushing them away with his thumb.

"That accident was not your fault. Your mother was driving. The weather was bad; people weren't wearing seat belts; there were so many factors," Harrison says the words that every counselor has said to me before.

"But I was the reason we were driving at that time in the first place."

"You were a child. This is not your fault. It was a horrible, terrible accident. The pain of it is not yours to carry like this. You need to let it go. You need to let me carry you. I've got you, Beth. I will carry your load. I will carry you forever. Let me," Harrison whispers to me, his breath touching my lips.

"I'm so scared..." I whisper, feeling like that little girl again.

"I've got you. I won't let you fall," he says as his lips touch mine, and he seals his promise to my lips.

I just hope he can keep it.

32

HARRISON

BREAKING NEWS

We are mere days away from the state of Maryland elections for governor and clear favorite Harrison Langford's campaign has hit a speedbump. Our sources say that at a thank-you luncheon for funders yesterday, key medical supporter Doctor Robert Warner almost died due to an allergic reaction.

Harrison was seen out and about this morning, visiting the local hospital where Doctor Warner spent the night, and this reporter couldn't help but notice his team was one short today, with the absence of his project manager Beth Longmere noticeable.

Is Beth to blame for the close call at the restaurant yesterday, or is Maryland's sweetheart somewhere else?

More to come.

"Maryland's sweetheart, seriously, those reporters have no idea," my mother scoffs from next to me in the back seat of the car as she listens to the radio. We are on our way to a photo shoot in Patterson Park, something my mother set up for me months ago with one of her society friends at *Town and Country Magazine*. We thought it was a great idea at the time. Now, after having only a few hours' sleep with Beth on her sofa last night, I want to be anywhere else but here.

Beth is currently in the car behind us with Oscar and Eddie. She's upholding extreme professionalism, but steering well clear of my mother, and I don't blame her.

"You were out of line yesterday," I say to her, because I was too angry to talk to her yesterday after the situation with Doctor Warner. The protective streak I have for Beth is now wide awake and thumping through my veins after what she shared with me last night. The truth of her history now cements for me that she is stronger than many people give her credit for. But just because she carries it well, doesn't mean it isn't heavy, and I will do what I said. I will carry her. I will carry everything for her.

"Ohh," she scoffs again, waving her hand in the air to brush my words away. "Don't be silly, Harrison." She's not accepting any responsibility for her actions. I go to say something more, but we pull up to the park, and I don't wait for her as I step out of the car, needing to create space. I feel like I am going to explode. My emotions are everywhere and instead of being a nice, supportive parent, my mother is making things worse.

I walk straight to my team. Oscar and Eddie are

talking with Lilly and I wonder what she is doing here. My eyes wander to Beth who is already a few yards away, chatting with the photographer, and I see her smile and I start to relax.

"Okay, so let's get this over with," I mumble to Oscar, who claps his hands.

"Right, where do we start?" he asks the journalist.

"Well, as Mrs. Langford suggested, we were planning to take some photographs down near the lake, of the two of you watching the ducks," the young journalist says.

"Two of whom? My mother and me?" I ask in question because I thought this was a solo shoot, but I could be wrong. Maybe they want a family shoot.

"No, silly," my mother says, her fake smile splashed across her face, and I look at Eddie. She is up to something. He nods in agreement.

"It is with you and Lilly, of course!" my mother exclaims and hugs Lilly's shoulders, then the penny drops.

"I don't think..." Oscar starts, but my mother doesn't let him finish.

"It is merely a piece to show Harrison's life and how he grew up. Lilly here will just take a few shots with him, which they will use in the piece to talk about how you are lifelong friends," my mother continues, and while I am sure it isn't as simple as that, I want to get this over with. I take a deep breath and blow away my frustrations.

"Fine, let's go," I grit out and don't wait for anyone as I stomp toward the lake. The photographer, Lilly, and the journalist follow as Beth and the others stay back at the cars. I notice a few paparazzi pull up, and I assume it is because of what happened yesterday because we don't normally have paparazzi following us around town to insignificant events such as this.

"Fucking great," I mumble to myself, wondering if this day could get any worse.

"Here will be fine. So just stand next to each other and chat among yourselves. I will get the lighting right first," the photographer says, and I sigh, not really wanting to chat with Lilly right now.

"So how are you after yesterday, Harrison?" she asks.

"Fine. Doctor Warner is all better so that is the main thing." I spoke to him this morning and he is fine and holds no grudges, and while he will be sluggish for a while, he is still a staunch supporter.

"Of course, but it was such a horrible mix-up," she says, leaving her accusation out in the air.

"Great. Okay, if you two can look at me and smile," the photographer yells out, and we do. The two of us are well trained.

"It could have been much worse," I offer her, not wanting to get into specifics. The restaurant sent more papers to my law firm earlier. Ben and his team are going through it all this morning.

"Yes, of course, but Beth could have killed a man with her incompetence. That is something you really should distance yourself from, Harrison," Lilly says, and I pull back and look at her, wondering how sweet Lilly, the young girl who used to follow my brothers and me around every summer, became a miniature version of my mother. As I look into her eyes, I can see the evil starting to seep out of her, her smile as fake as her nails.

"Watch your words, Lilly," I growl at her quietly. Because the disrespect people are showing toward Beth, I am starting to take extremely personal.

"So, in a few days you will be governor. Are you excited?" she asks, changing her tone and the topic, looking up at me and beaming. I give her a small nod, because despite the hiccup yesterday, the polls are still strong, and my lead is still present.

"It isn't over yet, Lilly," I say, not wanting to get ahead of myself.

"Oh! Oh no!" she says, quickly looking down.

"What?"

"I dropped my ring," she says in panic.

"What do you mean?"

"My ring, the diamond ring my grandmother left me." I know what ring she is referring to. A large knuckle buster of a thing that looks ostentatious on her hand. I look down and see it sparkling in the grass.

"I see it, let me grab it." I bend down on one knee and retrieve her ring, handing it up to her, and then I hear cheers, the camera clicks, and I look around before realizing what's going on.

My mother and Lilly set this up. I am positioned like I am proposing and handing her the biggest diamond that a camera lens a few yards away could capture. Just right for those few paparazzi who *randomly* turned up right on time. I immediately look up to the cars and spot Beth looking right at me, her mouth agape, but she quickly disappears behind my mother, who steps in front of her, blocking my vision, giving me the biggest smile of all.

Then I realize that, yes, this day can get a lot worse.

33

BETH

I watch from afar as the camera takes photos of Lilly and Harrison down by the lake. They look great. Lilly's hair is shining in the sun, and she is wearing a beautiful floral dress that shifts just right in the breeze. They are picture perfect. My stomach feels heavy at the sight, but I push my shoulders back, burying any jealousy that starts to rise. Harrison was with me last night and has been with me for months. I take him at his word, I know that he feels for me like I do him. *It is just a photo shoot,* I say to myself.

After opening up to him last night, I feel lighter. My secrets and my fears have been buried for so long. The guilt I carried since I was a little girl was eating away at me, and after a very long and frightening night, Harrison managed to help me relieve it a little.

"Oh, they are a perfect couple, wouldn't you agree, Beth?" his mother says to me from the side. The only words she has spoken to me for months, aside from her public accusations of attempted murder she threw at me yesterday.

"They are both professionals in front of the camera. I would expect nothing less of Mr. Langford," I say, giving her a smile, remaining professional as my grip remains white-knuckled on my paperwork. Eddie steps a little closer, looking at me knowingly. I already feel deep sadness at how upset both Harrison and Eddie are going to be at knowing exactly who tried to frame me yesterday and the lengths she will go to. I watch Mrs. Langford, wondering if I peered into her soul what I would find. Sure, she is mean, but I have a feeling that she is also very sad and lonely.

"I cannot wait until they get married and give me grandchildren. It will be the biggest society wedding of the year!" she gleams as she claps her hands together. Oscar squints at her like she is insane, and I hear Eddie growl. My stomach drops again a little, because I know that there is literally nothing that this woman wouldn't do to ensure Harrison is the biggest name in the country, and obviously, she has deep affection for Lilly. I look back at the perfect couple, together they fit, but I notice Harrison's shoulders are stiff, his smile wide but not genuine. The wrinkle between his eyes has been present since he arrived today, and even though I can't see it now, I know it is there.

My cell phone vibrates in my handbag. Pulling it out, I see that it is Jeff. I throw it back in my bag, not wanting to chat with him right now.

"So when did you set this up, Mom?" Eddie asks, clearly fishing for information and making small talk. I listen keenly, although my eyes remain on Harrison. He is tired, stressed, and I hate that I contribute to some of that.

"Oh, Edward, this has been in the works for months. I really wanted to capture the moment Harrison got down on bended knee," she gushes, clapping her hands together in glee. My head swivels in her direction, and Eddie looks at me over her head, the two of us wondering what the hell she is talking about.

My phone vibrates again. Pulling it out, I see Larry's name lighting up my screen. I am about to answer when I hear a lot of shouts from the paparazzi beside me as their cameras click into action and I look up at the commotion.

Harrison is on one knee and passing something to Lilly. I squint to get a closer look and there is no mistake that it is a diamond ring; it is sparkling bigger than the sun. Lilly is smiling and gushing like he is giving her the world, and my stomach drops. I want to run down and rip it from his hand and throw it in the lake. But my feet remain glued to the ground as my heart stops beating. My eyes flick to Harrison, and his face looks confused as he stands and looks around, trying to find me. Our eyes meet as my mind tries to understand what is happening before Mrs. Langford stands right in front of me, blocking my view of him.

"Congratulations, my son! I can't wait for the wedding!" she yells out and cheers, and I stand, stunned.

Was he lying to me? Last night when he said that he wanted me, would always be there for me, was he lying? I look at Eddie and Oscar and they look as shocked as I do.

"Beth," Eddie says, coming toward me. "Take slow,

deep breaths," he whispers to me, and I realize I am almost hyperventilating.

"I'm confused. Did Harrison just propose?" I ask, looking up at him, trying to gauge the look on his face to see if this is real or just my nightmare. Eddie looks back down at the scene before looking back at me. Shock is evident on his face, but there are no words confirming or denying.

I take a step to the side and look over Mrs. Langford's shoulder and see Harrison walking toward the photographer with his hands up, his shoulders near his ears, clearly not happy about something.

My phone vibrates again, and I grab it, seeing it is Marci calling this time, and my body stills for an entirely different reason.

Something is wrong.

"Hello, Marci?" I pick up the call, my voice wavering as I walk away from the crowd who are getting noisy with people now starting to yell. I ignore them all, my heart already in my stomach, knowing something isn't right. The photo shoot at the lake is now all pushed to the back of my mind.

"Beth, honey, you need to come. Your father has had a heart attack." Marci's voice is panicked through the phone, and my legs are already moving faster on their own accord.

"Oh my God, what happened?" I ask her, panicked, and I can hear people yelling my name from behind me, but I can't think about them. I need to get to Dad. I look at the cars and see Tom blocked in by others and I know I can't wait. When I glance up the road, I see a taxi, so I run.

"I'm coming, Marci, I'm coming," I pant out, running like I have never run before. My heart hurts, and I feel like I am going to vomit. I shove my paperwork in my large bag, the contents rattling around as it slams against my body.

"The ambulance has just arrived at the center," she says, keeping me informed.

"Where are they taking him?" I pant at her as I slip into the taxi.

"The General. Where are you?" she asks, and I can hear panic in her voice as well.

I quickly tell the driver where to go and promise him a big tip if he hurries, which he does. His tires squeal as he pulls away from the curb and drives like a madman in and out of traffic to the freeway.

"What happened?" I say as I try to calm my racing heart.

"He was playing chess with Larry, like usual. Said he wasn't feeling well, and Jeff said it may be because of this new juice cleanse they are doing. So we got him something to eat to see if that helped. But it didn't and he started getting a lot of chest pain, so we called the paramedics. I'm sorry, Beth, but he has now lost consciousness," she says, and I can hear her crying.

"Oh my God," I whisper, tears welling. I can't lose him.

I hear my cell beeping, telling me other calls are trying to get through, but I ignore them all.

"I am going with the paramedics, so I will meet you at the hospital," Marci says, and as I hear the sirens in the background, the tears start to fall freely down my cheeks.

"Okay," I whisper, and she ends the call. My phone

lights up immediately, with Harrison's name flashing on the screen. I hit ignore. I can't right now. I need to think of my dad. Harrison and his campaign need to wait.

34

HARRISON

I am fuming. Livid. The blood pushes around my body so viciously I can hear it in my ears. I clench my fists over and over again, trying to get a grip on what exactly is going on, yet I feel like I am in an alternate universe, and my lifeline is not taking my calls.

Lilly is crying; my mother is shrieking at me, and Oscar and Eddie are confiscating every camera we can see, deleting any and all footage. This is yet another thing I don't need right now.

How I can go from soon-to-be governor to this mess with only a few days to go is beyond me. I need Beth. I need to see her, talk to her, touch her.

"She is nothing but trouble, that girl. I am glad we got rid of her." My mother spits out her poisonous words at me as the cameras are given back and the journalists start to leave. I narrow my eyes as I look at her, and I see Eddie squirm a little beside me. Oscar looks on with interest, and Lilly dabs her eyes next to my mother.

"What is it you don't like about Beth, Mom?" I ask her

point-blank, my hands clenching along with my jaw, because I am pissed. Really pissed.

"Oh..." she scoffs and waves her hand in the air like my question is the most ridiculous thing she has heard all day.

"Well?" I ask, pushing her because I want answers.

"Oh, Harrison, you cannot be serious. She is nothing, a nobody. Who the hell are her mother and father? They are not part of society. She is from the poor part of town. A Langford doesn't socialize with those kinds of people. She is what? Eighteen, nineteen? She is a baby! Seriously, Harrison, you know better. If you are not careful, you will turn out just like your father."

And there it is. The hate she has for my father seeping into my life.

And it stops now.

I walk slowly toward her as she stares at me in shock. The look on my face obviously tells her exactly what my feelings are at the moment. My nostrils flare as I crack my neck and stand right in front of her, my face inches from hers.

"I love Beth. She is the woman for me. We have been dating privately for three months, our affair something she kept secret *for me* so the campaign would not be affected and so that we could have some time together to work out if we fit before going public. I love every goddamn thing about her, including her name, where she lives, and her age," I seethe to her quietly, punching my words so she understands the seriousness of them.

My mother stands shocked, her mouth agape.

"There is no one else for me. Beth is it. So I suggest

you get your own feelings in order and stop comparing me to my fucking father!" I roar in her face, and she jumps. I never raise my voice. At her, my brothers, or my staff. No one. I never yell. I am the calm one, the charming one, the original Baltimore boy. But today, I am anything but.

"Harrison, I..." she stutters, but I raise my hand, not letting her finish. She needs to hear this.

"I know how he treated you. I know he was a philandering asshole who had a woman in every city, and I am sorry he hurt you, but if you meddle in my life again, you will lose a son, because I don't want your poisonous attitude anywhere near me or Beth again," I state clearly, and I hear Lilly gasp at her side, but my eyes remain on my mother's. Her face pales, and I watch her swallow.

"C'mon, Mom, let me get you and Lilly in the car and you can go home for a bit," Eddie offers, taking her elbow and leading her away, no other words now able to fall from her lips.

"Having a family disagreement in a public setting is not exactly what I would advise, but... that needed to be done at some point," Oscar says from beside me, the two of us waiting for Eddie to return so we can work out how to put out this fire. Twitter, no doubt, already has my name trending with gossip.

I grab my cell and try Beth again. She looked confused when she saw me down on one knee, but I wasn't expecting her to run. I promised her last night she was it for me, she was the only one, and I hope she still believes that to be true. Max, her paparazzi friend, is still here, and my heart sinks knowing he has just witnessed the situation firsthand. He gives me a small smile as he tentatively walks over.

"Sorry, Mr. Langford. We got a tip to come here today, but we didn't know what for."

"It's fine, Max, you're just doing your job," I say, running my hand through my hair.

"Is Beth okay?" he asks me.

"I don't know; she isn't picking up," I state honestly, not sure why I am sharing so much with a pap. Oscar clears his throat beside me in warning, but says nothing.

"Do you want me to try to find her for you? I know the taxi company she went with, so I can make a few calls," he offers. It feels like spying, but I nod, not knowing what else to do. He makes the calls, speaks to a few people, and looks at me with a brief smile.

"She is at General Hospital. Apparently, there was an accident with her father. The taxi has just left her at the ER there," Max states, and I feel a mix of relief that she didn't run away because of my mother, and panic at what happened to her father.

"Thanks, Max. I appreciate it," I state as I start walking to the cars, meeting Eddie halfway.

"You can't stop fighting for what you believe in, Mr. Langford," Max shouts as I make my way to the car. "I just hope to get the first photos when the two of you finally get what you deserve!" he adds with a broad smile, one I find myself returning.

"Deal!" I say, realizing that I just confirmed our love affair with a paparazzi three days before Election Day, and I don't care. I just want Beth.

35

BETH

I am walking a well-worn path into the already threadbare carpet in the waiting area that Nurse Mary has put us in. Marci is sitting in a chair with her head in her hands, her blue hair still vibrant, her smile now less so. Larry is next to her, remaining stoic, but I watch him as his thumbs roll around each other, something he only does when he is stressed. Jeff is walking like me, in the opposite direction, the two of us looking like soldiers at a palace. Neither of us are able to sit at this point, too nervous for news.

"What is taking them so long?" I whine again. We have been here for close to an hour without any update. My hands won't stop shaking; my heart is almost decimated, and I have been trying to keep the tears at bay all afternoon.

"He's in good hands, sugar," Marci says, her eyes equally wet. I never asked Dad what was going on with the two of them, something I still need to get to the bottom of.

"I wish they would hurry up," Larry mumbles as he rubs his head.

"Beth, what do you need?" Jeff asks, being kind and supportive. The weird vibe I always got from him is surprisingly absent today in this life-or-death situation.

"I just want to see him," I say, stopping the pacing, and Jeff comes over to me.

"He will be fine. I am sure of it." His hand reaches my shoulder, giving it a squeeze. The gesture is friendly, and I appreciate it.

"Beth!" I turn sharply to see Harrison and the boys striding in, making a commotion as everyone looks at them, phones already being pulled out since we are in a very public setting. My heart skips a beat upon seeing him, but my head is a swirl of emotions, none of which I can get a handle on right now.

"What happened?" Harrison asks, looking concerned. I don't have the energy. I want to give him the benefit of the doubt for today, but I haven't had time to process anything. I am at my breaking point, the line so close I can touch it, but I pull on all the strength I have left.

"Her father had a heart attack," Jeff states, talking for me, stepping in front of me slightly. Ordinarily, I would be fuming at his actions, but I can't help but feel relieved to not have to say the words again.

"Beth, baby," Harrison says, walking closer to me, his arms out.

I hear the clicks of cameras, and my eyes skirt around to see everyone's eyes on us.

"Hey, didn't you just propose to some girl in the

park?" a young guy yells out, Harrison now recognized. My eyes catch Harrison's, and I feel the vomit start to rise. Memories of him on his knee, looking up at Lilly, come to mind, and I squint at him in confusion.

"Beth, is there somewhere we can talk?" he asks, looking around.

"Harrison, I can't..." I say in barely a whisper. I feel like I am going to collapse. I have had no sleep and haven't eaten anything. My life took a severe one-eighty this morning, and I can't even think straight.

"Beth, baby, let me hold you." I want to fall into his arms, I do. But I can't move my feet. I know the moment I do that I will collapse, and nurses and doctors will race to me, and I can't do that. They need to be helping my dad.

"She said she can't. Besides, we all saw your proposal online, so why don't you go back to your fiancée!" Jeff spits at him, his words full of anger and I feel Marci and Larry come to stand on either side of me. My mind is whirling... What is happening? I look around at every-one, but I can't really focus. My heart is pumping, and my body feels like it is swaying. *Is this a dream?*

"Beth, baby... I am here for you." Harrison says the words I want to hear, but I can't move. I feel the nausea building in my throat, and I swallow quickly, trying to tamp it down.

"Harrison, we should go," Oscar says, looking around the room, seeing that everyone's attention is now on us.

"Beth. I promised you I've got you. I am not going to break that promise," Harrison croaks, and I feel my eyes close slowly, then open again. I am fighting a battle to keep my body upright, and I can barely hear a thing he says. Black dots dance in my vision, and I try to breathe slowly, willing myself to remain strong, leaning a little against Marci for support.

"Harrison, we need to go," Eddie says, and I see Harrison take a swift look around before I hear him curse under his breath.

"Beth, I will be back, baby. I will be back," he says, before he quickly turns, and I see the back of his well-fitted black suit walk back down the hall and strut straight outside.

He will be back. He promised. I know he will come back.

"Beth?" I hear a man behind me say my name and all four of us turn. Doctor Standford is standing at the edge of the room with Nurse Mary, both looking concerned.

"How is he?" I ask, my body forcing my feet to step toward him, wanting the news.

"We got him stable. He is not out of the woods yet. We have a lot of tests to run, but we have him in ICU so you can come and see him for a few minutes," he says, and I have never seen him look so serious before. Whenever I come in for treatment, he is always so jovial with me. Today, there is not even a hint of a smile.

I nod, wanting nothing more right now than to see my father.

"I'm sorry, folks, just Beth. No other visitors tonight. You can all go home and get some rest and Beth can keep you informed," he states, and they nod. One by one, Marci, Larry, and Jeff all give me warm hugs before they leave me and I follow Doctor Standford into the ICU.

It is quieter back here, and as he leads me into Dad's room. I need to hang onto the doorframe so I don't collapse. He has machines and tubes all connected to him, so much so I can barely see his body from the equipment. I walk tentatively into the room, holding my breath.

"You can sit for a little while. Talk to him; he can hear you. It will do him some good to hear your voice as well. Don't be frightened of all the equipment; it is just monitoring his condition, and we will remove most of it soon," he says as he squeezes my shoulder and then leaves the room, closing the door on us.

I pull a seat closer and sit, glad to get off my feet. I look around, taking it all in.

"Who would have thought it would be you in ICU first?" I whisper to the room, because history would prove that I am the one most likely to be admitted to the hospital.

"Dad. Just be okay, please. I don't want you to leave me too," I say as the tears I have been holding fall freely down my cheeks. I let them fall, coating my face, dropping onto my clothes. It is cathartic in a way, cleansing myself of the stress, the confusion, the pain. I thought after crying with Harrison all night last night, I would have no tears left, but apparently, if the world decides to tear your heart in two, then tears still come.

"So, I am guessing that Larry beat you at chess today and you were a sore loser?" I ask him, trying to lighten the mood.

"It is a bit dramatic having a heart attack, though, Dad. I am sure you could have protested some other way,"

I say, with only the beeping of machines giving me any response.

I sigh and roll my neck. "So Harrison proposed to another woman today. I am not sure what happened, Dad. I thought he was the one. I really, truly did. I told him everything last night. All of it. How the accident was my fault, how I ruin everything, killed innocent people, and he didn't run. He didn't leave me. He held me all night. But then today..." My voice falls away as Mrs. Langford's face comes to my mind.

"I don't know. I just don't know what is going on," I say, shaking my head, the world becoming too much. I squeeze his hand. "Tell me what to do, Dad. I don't know what to do anymore." I lean my head on his bed and rest silently for a while. The steady beeping of his heart machine lulls me to sleep.

"BETH." I hear my name and feel a small touch on my shoulder.

"Beth, wake up," the voice says again, and I open my eyes and sit up, my neck sore from lying uncomfortably.

"Beth, are you okay?" Doctor Standford says from beside me. I look around the room. It is quiet still except for the machines. I look at Dad, and he isn't any different.

"He is still the same, Beth. You have been here for hours. Why don't you go home, get some rest, and come back in the morning. I will call you if anything changes."

"I don't want to leave him," I say honestly, because I

am scared that if I leave him, he won't be here when I come back.

"He is in good hands. I promise I will call you with any changes. We will run some more tests and monitor him closely," Doctor Standford says, and he helps me to stand. I nod, knowing he is right. I need a shower; I need to freshen up.

I look at Dad for another beat before I turn and walk out of the room, the bright lights of the hallway shining and hurting my eyes.

As I look around, I see a man sitting on the hard plastic chairs, and my heart stops.

"Harrison?" I whisper, shocked to see him there. His head flies up at my voice, and he stands. His suit is crumpled, his tie and shirt open at the neck. He is on his own, no Eddie or Oscar, and he looks like he has been here for hours.

"What are you doing here?" I whisper again, tears starting to well in my eyes.

"I'm here for you. I told you last night, Beth, I've got you." he says, standing up tall, his broad shoulders looking prepared to carry the world.

"What about Lilly?" I ask because my mind still can't wrap around the situation.

"My mother set it up. It was all a surprise to me too," he says, taking my hand in his, rubbing his thumb across my palm. We stand like that for a moment before he lifts my hand to his lips and kisses my fingers, one by one each getting a small peck. His other hand scoops around my waist, and he pulls me closer.

"Harrison..." I whisper, looking up at him. The tears

run down my cheeks, and I grab his jacket to steady myself. The relief I have of him coming back for me sweeps through my body.

"Don't cry, baby. I'm here now. I'm not going anywhere. You're not alone anymore." Harrison's words create more tears, and he cups my face, brushing them aside with his thumb, holding me firm, not letting me go.

"I missed you," he says, looking into my eyes. I notice he has the crinkle between his brows as I lean my head against his chest, and he wraps me up in his arms.

"I missed you." My tears wet his shirt, not unlike the champagne all those months ago.

"How is your dad?" he asks, his hand rubbing up and down my back, and I melt into him. I can't talk so I shake my head and bury my head in his chest. The tears come again then. I don't think I have cried as much in my life as I have these past twenty-four hours.

"I've got you," he whispers as we stand there in the hospital hallway late in the evening.

"Come on. Let me take you home. We can have a shower and come back in the morning."

"But the elections?" I question, pulling back from him, looking at him in surprise.

"What about them?"

"You literally have days, Harrison. You can't be with me. You need to be doing your final canvassing, meeting the people, shaking hands..." I say, knowing that Oscar and Eddie must be run ragged at the moment.

"I have a few things I need to do, but that can all wait until tomorrow. Tonight, I am taking my girlfriend home, going to undress her, then put her in a warm shower before I tuck her in tight and sleep with her in my arms. The rest of it will all be here in the morning. I will drop you off here early before I head back to the city."

"Okay..." I whisper, a small smile gracing my lips.

"Okay... Let's go."

And I lean into him as we walk toward the elevator and take it straight to the basement, where Harrison has a car waiting to take us home. Together.

36

HARRISON

I am at yet another senior citizens center, to change the minds of all the older generation who still hate my father, shaking hands and talking. My body is present, but my mind is elsewhere. The media scrum with us is larger than ever, and with no Beth to control them, Oscar is almost bursting a blood vessel.

"Come over here and let me look at ya," an older woman says from across the room as I am smiling and walking through.

"Hello, ma'am, how are you today?" I ask as I offer her my hand to shake.

"Well, aren't you a good-looking boy," she says as her wrinkled old hand comes and rests on my hand.

"Well, I am not sure about that," I say in reply, laughing a little at her brashness.

"Are you married, son?" she asks.

"No. I am not. Are you?"

"Yes, dear. My Gerald is the love of my life. He passed away a few years ago now, and my heart still beats just for him," she says almost wistfully. I pat her hand and remain quiet.

"You know love is a funny thing. I never wanted to get married. I was young, carefree. I was the first of my family to go to school and get a good education. I wanted to be a teacher, have a career. Falling in love was not part of my plan," she continues, smiling.

"What happened?" I ask inquisitively.

"Gerald happened. Showed up out of the blue, almost ran me over in his car one day. Too busy looking at my backside to watch the road, I think..." she answers, and I bark out a laugh. This woman is hilarious.

"Well, I will ensure to always watch the road when I am driving." I nod to her, my mind flashing with memories of Beth's nice ass in those yoga pants at the community center all those months ago.

"You do that, son, but don't forget to look up as well, because you don't want to miss seeing a great ass on your journey." I almost completely lose it in laughter. I have never known an older woman to be so spicy.

"Thank you. It was great chatting with you," I say, smiling, squeezing her hand, which she returns.

"I will vote for you, son. Good luck."

I nod and stand and walk around the room some more, my mind now on Beth and her ass, and not the campaign trail at all. The media continue to take snaps, the clicking sound constant.

"We need to head out the front and take a few questions. The media scrum is almost bursting," Oscar says, and I know the time has come. It has been two days of complete turmoil, and although my political aspirations are still achievable, it is certainly more unpredictable now more so than ever before.

We make our way out of the center and to the front steps, leaving the staff and members to have some peace and quiet after a whirlwind morning. I see a few familiar faces in the paparazzi pack, some journalists I know, and Max. I give him a small nod in acknowledgement.

I wait for a beat for them all to get ready, and when I see everyone looking at me, I start.

"Thanks, everyone, for joining us today. It has certainly been a big week, and with only a day or so remaining, it is wonderful to be here at Willow Bark Senior Citizens Center to hear what advice the older generation can hand down to me and what their needs are moving into the future. I would like to thank all the team at Willow Bark for having us today.

"I will now happily take some questions," I state, squaring my shoulders, ready for the onslaught.

"Harrison, are you engaged to Lillian Harper?" a male journalist from the back of the pack shouts.

"No, I am not," I state clearly before I move to the next question.

"Harrison, is it true that Beth Longmere from your team is responsible for the near-death of Doctor Warner this week?"

"No. My team is still looking into the matter; however, I am pleased to say Doctor Warner is happy and healthy, which is most important."

I look around and take the next question, and the next; they fly in thick and fast, and I answer every one of them skillfully, truthfully, and succinctly.

"Harrison will take one more question before we finish for today," Oscar says, stepping forward, and I nod to take the last question.

"Harrison, is it true that Beth Longmere is no longer a part of your team and that she is to be charged with attempted murder of Doctor Warner?" I should be prepared for this question, but I am not. Who in their right mind would even think this is possible?

"I can assure you that there is no attempted murder case and no case at all. As I said earlier, Doctor Warner is fine, and my team is currently reviewing event protocols to ensure such a mix-up does not occur again."

"That's all the questions for today. Thanks, team. See you on Election Day!" Oscar says quickly, wrapping up the journalists as Eddie and I shake hands, thanking the staff at the senior citizens center.

"We need to go. Ben has called a 9-1-1," Eddie says in my ear. I look at him. We haven't had a 911 since Dad died. He shrugs, not knowing what is going on either. Ever since we were younger, if there was something happening that us brothers needed to discuss urgently, we would text each other 911, and we all knew that we needed to rush to meet.

"Where are we going?" I ask.

"Your apartment. Ben and Tennyson are already there," Eddie says, and my skin starts to crawl. Maybe there is another one of Dad's girlfriends about to ask for more money or something, the timing impeccable since the elections are tomorrow.

"Fine, let's go," I say, already knowing that it is going to be bad news.

"Okay, we are here, what's going on?" I ask as Eddie and I step out of the elevator and into my penthouse to see Ben and Tennyson sitting on the large sofa in my living room.

"You need to sit down," Ben says, looking grim.

"Fuck yeah, you do," Tennyson says, and I see he already has a whiskey, so I know it must be bad.

"Fuck," I murmur, running my hand through my hair as I take a seat and us boys sit on my sofa, all looking at Ben.

"What's going on? Eddie asks, as we are all eager for the news.

"I went through the paperwork from the restaurant," Ben starts, and my heart sinks. Eddie looks at me. We are both convinced that Beth hasn't made a mistake, but maybe we are wrong.

"And?" I ask, impatient as hell.

"You need to listen to something," he says, sliding his cell on the coffee table and pressing play.

We all sit forward, my elbows resting on my knees as we listen to our mother on the phone, requesting a change of meal for Doctor Warner, clearly requesting the very thing he is highly allergic to.

"Fucking hell," Eddie says, sitting back in shock.

"She is the fucking devil. I've been telling you for years!" Tennyson says as he takes another sip of whiskey. Out of all of us, he has the worst relationship with my mother.

"She has really crossed a line here. She almost killed a man!" Ben says, exasperated.

"And pinned it on poor Beth!" Tennyson adds, looking at me.

I'm quiet as I take in all the information and try to sort through the pieces. I think about Beth and the time we have spent together. I look across to the kitchen, remembering the morning she spilled the coffee, the shards of porcelain scattering across the floor.

"Why the hell would she do that?" I ask, looking at Ben, knowing he is the one who will give me the answers. We are both lawyers and have worked together for years. I know he has looked at every angle, assessed the entire situation. I know he will give it to me straight.

"Because she is the fucking deeeevillll," Tennyson says again.

"Well, my guess is that she knew that you and Beth had a thing going and didn't want that to continue. So by making an issue at the event, showing you how incompetent Beth was, it might persuade you to marry Lilly instead," Ben says.

"But she had no idea about Beth and me," I say, looking at Eddie.

"I told no one, so unless Oscar or you idiots did, then she had no way of knowing," Eddie says. My brothers shake their heads, and I know Oscar wouldn't have said anything.

"Unless..." I murmur, my thoughts starting to gather.

"Unless what?" Ben asks, clearly in lawyer mode.

"There was one morning Beth was here and acting a little weird. Wait, let me look at the security cameras," I say, jumping up and grabbing my phone. I take security seriously, all us boys do, so all our penthouses have cameras at the front door, in the elevators, and I have one right here in my living room so I can see exactly who is coming and going. I find the file from the morning Beth spilled the coffee, and watch her as she walks into the kitchen, looking like every man's wet dream in my white business shirt.

"Fucking lucky asshole..." Tennyson says from behind me, and I realize all my brothers now crowd around, looking at my cell.

"There!" Eddie says, pointing to the right side of the screen.

Our mother appears, frightening Beth, causing her to drop the coffee. I turn up the volume, and together, we all listen to their interaction and watch it until I end it when I walk into the kitchen.

"Beth knew and didn't say anything," Eddie murmurs.

"Beth collated all the reports and the recording from the restaurant earlier this week and ensured they were all sent through to us, as per usual. Which means that she already knows Mom tried to set her up as well. She didn't tell you?" Ben asks.

"Fuck, so she tried to save our fucking mother by not saying anything?" Tennyson asks, dismayed.

"No. She tried to save Harrison before the election," Eddie states, looking at me.

"Fuck me. If you don't marry her, I will," Tennyson says, sitting back down and taking another sip. I need to speak to him about his alcohol consumption. I give him the evil eye before I stand.

"Where are you going?" Ben asks, probably wondering if I am going to do something brash.

"I'm going to see Beth. Her dad is in the hospital in the ICU. Heart attack. I can only concentrate on her and the election tomorrow. Mom will have to wait," I state, looking at all of them.

"I will confirm everything with the Four Seasons for election night tomorrow," Eddie says, standing.

"No. I have another idea. I will call you and Oscar from the car." I walk to call the elevator.

"I'm taking your whiskey home," Tennyson says as he stands, grabbing the bottle he opened, looking at the label. It is my best one. A bottle of Sullivans Cove French Oak.

"Just replace it this time, asshole." Tennyson never replaces the whiskey he takes from me.

"Yes, Governor!" he says with a mock salute, and I wonder if he will ever grow up.

37

BETH

I'm sitting next to Dad's bed, holding his hand. I have been here since earlier this morning, my stomach still twisted up with so much anxiety, I can't keep any food down. Not that I have tried. Harrison made me a coffee when I woke up, and I haven't attempted anything since.

I look at his face, his hand, and back to his face again, willing him to wake and to tell me that everything will be alright. Most of the machines have been unclipped and he looks like he is just asleep, with a drip in one arm and a heart monitor connected to his chest.

The only sounds I hear are the constant questions that Harrison is peppered with during his press conference, which is on the TV behind me. Questions about me and my incompetence at the event earlier this week. My reputation is starting to take a hit. I wish I cared more, but I don't. I care about the man lying in this bed next to me and the man on the screen. Everything else at the moment has to take second place. The fact that it was all set up by his mother still sits heavy in my stomach. I know Harrison will see the paperwork from the restaurant, and it will be heartbreaking for him, no doubt.

"Hmm, what does a man need to do to get a drink of water..." my dad croaks and I almost jump out of my skin.

"Dad!"

"Shhhh, Beth..." he says, wincing, and his hand rubs his forehead.

"Dad!" I whisper-yell, "let me get you some water." I rush to the side table and pour a small amount in a plastic cup, which promptly spills all over the small space because my hands are shaking, my body shocked at him suddenly being awake.

I lean over the bed, helping him sit up a little to take a small sip as tears start running down my cheeks.

"No need to cry. I'm alive, aren't I?" Dad says, taking big breaths, slowly getting his bearings from the surrounding hospital room.

"I'm so relieved. I was so afraid to leave you, even for a minute. I didn't want to lose you too, Dad..." I say, weeping uncontrollably.

"Now, now, Beth." He takes another big breath. "You stop that crying. I will be fine."

"I should have been there with you. I shouldn't have taken this job. If I was with you, then I could have gotten you help earlier. I would have seen the signs," I say, berating myself, because I did. I did see the signs. He was pale, tired. I knew something wasn't right, but I ignored it.

"This is not your fault, Beth."

"I should have done more. I need to look after you better... I couldn't be good for Mom, but I promised I would always be good for you," I say, still sobbing, starting to talk gibberish.

"Stop it. Just stop it, Beth. There was nothing you or anyone else could have done. And stop blaming yourself for your mother," he says, his voice breathy but stern. I still. He has never mentioned her name to me before. I could never say her name out loud to him without him walking away. For the first time in almost two decades, he mentions her. I wait for him to continue.

"You didn't kill your mother. She did that all on her own. She was not paying attention to the road; she was overreacting to a kid dropping a few dishes and was driving erratically. We can't live in remorse anymore. For years, we have lived on autopilot. For years, we have blamed ourselves. But it needs to stop. If this heart attack has given me anything, it is the slap in the face I needed to get my life on track, Beth. To start living again. And you should too."

I watch him, his eyes opening and closing, his breathing heavy and strong. My tears have stopped, and I pull my shoulders back. I have never spoken to my dad about the accident, despite numerous counselors telling us that it is exactly what we should be doing. Together, we've become professionals in ignoring the past, burying it deep down and skipping around the outskirts of blame and nightmares that follow such a tragedy. But today, he has said the words that I never thought I would hear. He doesn't blame me. I don't blame him. Slowly, I nod, as the information filters through my brain, my body and mind going through such a whirlwind of emotions these past few days, I am not sure I can even function much longer.

"I love you, Dad," I say, a small smile coming to my face.

"I love you too, pumpkin." He uses the nickname he hasn't in years. His eyes glass over as he squeezes my hand.

"Let me buzz the nurses, see what trouble they can find," I tell him, my smile wider, and he groans because he hates the fuss. As soon as I push the button, the door opens, and three nurses rush in and take over, forcing me to step back and give them some room.

They hover over his bed, taking his blood pressure, asking him questions, refilling his drip, and sitting him up slightly. My fingers and hands twist together as I try to listen to their conversation. My heart is thumping. I want to be excited, but I need to remain calm because I know he isn't out of the woods yet.

Doctor Standford stalks through the doorway, his face serious as he grabs the clipboard to view Dad's chart. Flicking the pages back and forth, he starts asking him questions. My head swings between the two of them, like I am watching a tennis match, my breath almost nonexistent, too scared to say or do anything while I pray to everything and everyone I know that Dad will be alright. I look at Doctor Standford and see him smile. The first smile he has had since we arrived, and I finally take a breath.

"Beth, a word?" he asks me, and the two of us step outside.

"How is he?" I ask the minute we are in the hallway.

"He is strong. Good. He is a fighter, your dad. We will keep him monitored in ICU for a little while, and then if he continually shows signs of improvement, he will be moved to the general ward."

"That's good, right? Great!" At the good news, I begin to feel more alive than I have in days.

"I will check up on him again later, and until then, the nurses are just assessing a few more things. They will come and get you once they have finished," he says before patting my shoulder, giving me another warm smile, and I want to jump for joy.

I watch him leave, walking down the empty corridor, until he steps around the corner and out of sight. I stare at the empty corridor for a minute, until another man in a suit comes into view, and I run. I run the length of the corridor so fast and am met with Harrison's confused look before I leap, and he catches me, just like he said he always will.

"What happened?" he asks as he continues to walk, gripping my butt as I wrap my legs around him, freshly pressed suit be damned. My arms circle his neck, and I bury my head in his shoulder and breathe in his scent, the aroma calming me even more.

"He woke up! He is awake! He is going to be okay!" I say with excitement, before pulling back and looking at Harrison, watching the big smile come to his face, matching my own.

"That is great news!" he says, putting my feet to the floor now that we are back outside my dad's door.

"Beth?" the nurse says tentatively. "You can go back in now." I don't wait. Pulling Harrison by the hand behind me, I walk into the room and see Dad propped up, having something to eat.

"A grown man needs more than this poor excuse for Jell-O," he grumbles as I walk to his bedside.

"How are you feeling, Dad?" I ask, tentatively taking his hand. He squeezes my fingers and gives me a small smile.

"Fine. I'm sore, but fine."

"You scared me," I whisper, the thoughts of what-if still lingering in my mind. I feel Harrison come up behind me, his hand resting on my shoulder, giving me comfort.

"Stop, Beth, I am fine. By the looks of things, you two are not at all worried about the elections tomorrow if you are waiting around this old man's bed. How are you positioned for the election, Harrison?" he asks, switching the subject.

"Well, it is a tight race. I have a few more hands to shake, but essentially, there isn't too much else I can do at this point. It is now up to the voters."

"Beth, why don't you call Marci and Larry, then give your father a hug before you two go off and do whatever it is I know you should be doing for the election tomorrow. Because even though I appreciate it, I know staying at my bedside is not where either of you should be."

"Dad..."

"No, Beth. You need to go. I will be here; I am not planning on going anywhere."

Dad looks at Harrison and then me, and I sigh.

"Fine. Be good for the nurses," I warn him because he has a habit of getting snappy when receiving help from others.

"I will keep the TV on, so I'll see you on there," he mumbles to Harrison.

"I hope to do you and Beth proud, sir," Harrison says a little more formally, and my dad looks at him.

"You're doing fine just as you are, son," he murmurs, and I think I almost die with happiness at Dad expressing something other than grumbles to the man who still stands solid and dependable behind me.

It is quiet as I sit at home in the early evening. Harrison dropped me home after Dad sent us both away for the day, and while Harrison spent the afternoon shaking hands at a construction site and a business center, I took a nap, then started to clean. I cleaned every inch of this house because I have so much nervous energy, I can't sit still. My bathrooms and kitchen have never been this sparkly. The windows and doors glisten; the carpet is shampooed and already dry. The curtains are dust free, and the bedrooms all have fresh linen and are spotless. The house is ready for Dad to return, hopefully in another week or so, depending on how he improves.

Marci and Larry visited him today, but Jeff couldn't because of something happening at the center. Now as I stand in my living room, surveying the results of my labor, I take a breath and relax.

My cell phone rings, and I walk to the front of the kitchen counter and pick it up, seeing it's Harrison.

"Baby, open the door," is all he says before he ends the call.

I peek around the kitchen wall and see his shadow at the door and quickly skip to open it.

Taking up all the space is Harrison, looking tired but happy, and in his hands is the largest bouquet of red roses I have ever seen.

"Harrison?"

"These are for you." I step back to let him in.

"What for?"

"For just being you," he says, one hand passing me the enormous bouquet, the other snaking around my waist. He pulls me tight to him then, the stress of the last week now released from us both, and we stand there together, letting it all wash over us.

"You smell good," he whispers.

"Aren't you meant to be at a pre-election party or something?" I ask because it is election eve. I am sure his mother has thrown some bash for him.

"I hear there is a party for two right here," he murmurs, his lips brushing against my collarbone and the sparks immediately fly up my body.

"Is that right?" I tease him. "What else did you hear?"

"That you like it when I kiss you here..." he says as his lips nibble my neck, and my nipples peak. The effect he has on me is ridiculous.

"What else?" I ask breathily as I let my head fall to the side, allowing him access to my neck.

"That underneath these clothes is the sweetest pussy I have ever tasted..."

My breath catches before I continue.

"What else?"

"That I want to make you come on my cock all night

before I take you again in the shower in the morning. Because tomorrow, I will be elected governor, and whether you are ready or not, you will be my first lady..." he whispers, and my heart almost stops.

"Harrison?"

"I want to introduce you tomorrow. As mine. I want the world to know all about us, and I want to show them all how amazing you are," he says, pulling back to look at me.

"What about your mother?" I ask, holding my breath, knowing that there is still so much we need to discuss.

"Leave her to me. You don't have to worry about her. I know everything, Beth, and I am so sorry it all happened to you. But I want you to know that our lives are going to change tomorrow, and I need to know that you are with me, because I don't think I can do it without you." I feel the weight of his words sit on my chest, but they are not heavy; instead, they warm me.

"I'm with you," I whisper, happy to have him manage his mother and even more delighted to be by his side when he wins the election.

"Great, now where were we?" he murmurs as his lips find mine.

38

HARRISON

Her soft lips move against mine, and I wrap my arms around her middle, pulling her against me. I feel settled in the world once again. She makes everything alright, keeps my head above the water. The week has been explosive, but being here with Beth in her small suburban home is just where I need to be.

"God, I missed you. Missed this," I say, running my hands all over her, not sure how I can live another day without having my hands on her.

"I missed you. I never want to have a week like that again," she murmurs against my lips, as her hands shed my coat from my shoulders, after I take the flowers from her and put them on the side table.

"Never again," I confirm as I skirt my fingers around her waist, feeling her smooth skin, before I push them up her back, wanting more of her.

"I can't believe tomorrow is the night we have all worked so hard for," she whispers as my lips skim across her neck.

"There is no way I could have done any of it without you. You are my rock, Beth. I knew the moment I saw you, there was something about you. The moment we spoke, I knew you were special. Every minute of every day I spend with you is the best investment that I have ever made. I love you. I love you so much it hurts, and tomorrow I want to scream it to everyone. I want the world to know just how much you mean to me." I look at her, our mood now serious. I mean every word. The feelings I have for this woman are finally breaking through and my heart jumps in my chest, waiting for her response. Although, I can see it in her eyes before she speaks.

"I never thought I would find my person, Harrison. Never in a million years did I think I would have someone who saw me for me. Someone who cared, who could take everything that I am and everything that I carry. But you saw me. You saw straight into my heart and didn't stop looking. I love you, Harrison. You are my forever." Her voice is a mere whisper, her eyes glassy, and I can't take it.

"I want to worship you. Tonight it is just us, and I want to show you everything I have and everything you mean to me," I grit out, my need for her now stronger than ever, thrumming through my body, barely contained. I crash my lips into hers, my movement strong, but she matches my strength as her hands grip on to my shoulders.

"Fuck, I need you naked." I push her up against the kitchen wall, my hands now running up her back to unclip her bra.

"Harrison, too many clothes," Beth says as her hands

fly across my shirt, pulling at the buttons, tugging it from my body. I yank the sleeves down and throw it on the floor before grabbing her face and pulling her lips to mine again.

Our kiss is feverish, our tongues tangling, and my skin pebbles as I feel her hands move down my front, landing on my belt. She moans in my mouth, and I nearly come undone as she pulls my belt away and I make quick work of my zipper.

"Let me," she says, panting, pulling my pants down over my ass, her hands ending up on my cock, which is heavy and throbbing.

"Beth, baby..." My hands land on either side of her head, slapping against the wall, my forehead leaning against hers as she pumps my length.

"Are you ready for me, baby? This is going to be hard and fast." I look directly into her eyes, and she smirks.

"I can handle anything you give me..." Her confidence flips a switch, and I don't hesitate.

I push up her skirt and lift her body up off the floor. Her legs automatically wrap around my waist, and I feel her hot, wet center against my hard length as I push her back up against the wall, our movements so desperate, I hear the pictures rattling behind her.

"Harrison, I need you..." she begs, her voice so pretty it almost stops me in my tracks.

"These pretty panties have to go," I grit out as I pull the lace to the side and without waiting another second, I sink into her, sheathing myself all the way.

She inhales sharply, her head falling back and hitting the wall, and she moans, the sound hitting me directly in the groin. I feel feral, my desire for her getting stronger and stronger, and I pull out a little before slamming back in.

"You feel that, baby? You feel how needy you make me? How much I want to be inside of you, make you mine, mark you so deep?"

"Mark me as yours. I'm all yours, Harrison," she says as she claws at my shoulders, digging her hands into my hair as she bounces up against the wall, my thrusts moving her perfect breasts up and down and making my mouth water.

"Fuck, you are so beautiful, so fucking beautiful. You were made for me." I barely have enough air to breathe, my focus unrelenting on her.

"Harrison, I'm so close," she says as her head leans forward and captures my lips, and our kiss is just as hungry.

"Come on my cock, baby. Grind that perfect pussy on me; show me what I do to you." My words are demanding, and she clenches around me.

"Harrison... I can't... Harrison..." she pants over and over as I feel her nails dig into my bare shoulders and her head falls back again. I seal my lips around her nipple and suck, and then I feel her quiver. Her whole body shakes, her movements erratic, and she screams my name.

"Baby..." I pant, my movements now carnal as I pound into her, her wet pussy twitching around me, making me come undone.

"Beth, fuck, Beth!" I yell, my voice booming through

the room, as my hands grip her voluptuous ass, and I suck harder on her nipple, losing myself to her.

I hold on to her, both of us panting and leaning against the wall. I kiss her neck, tasting her salty skin that now is coated in a light sheen of sweat. It wasn't my plan to fuck her against the wall in her living room, but it couldn't wait. I pull away from her and love her flushed post-sex look.

"You alright?" I ask, knowing I was harder on her than ever. I am still inside of her and already want to go again, but I slowly pull away and lower her to her feet.

"Never better," she says, smiling. "Although I don't think I can look at this living room in the same way ever again." I swallow her giggles with my mouth, kissing her, keeping her close to me, never wanting to let her go.

"Come with me," she whispers, her eyes love drunk as she grabs my hand and leads me down the hallway of her house. I grab our clothes from the floor and follow her, looking around before she pulls me into her bedroom and closes the door. It is small. Her bed freshly made, I throw our clothes onto a small armchair in the corner and look at the few trinkets and photos she has around the room. She keeps it neat. There is a large floor mirror on the wall, and a soft table lamp throws warm light across the otherwise dark room.

"Hmmm, is this where you spend your nights without me?" I question, taking it all in.

"It is. But tonight, you are with me." She pulls her skirt from her waist down her body, throwing it across the room. She stands before me now completely naked, and I admire her.

"Do you see something you like?" she asks, flirting with me, toying with me, my dick liking it and already rising to the occasion again.

"I see something I love..." I tell her, walking toward her, wanting to feel her body next to mine. "And I love that you are all mine," I add, my hands resting on her hips for a moment before I run them up and down her sides. I notice her nipples peak, and her skin pebbles, and I love that I affect her so much.

"All yours tonight and forever." I see her eyes sparkle again for the first time in a long time. Pushing the hair from her face, I grab her jaw, wanting to see all of her.

"Forever mine," I grit out, loving hearing her say the words as my other hand skims up her back, leaning my body forward until her breasts push against my bare chest. Her hands trail down my torso, before cupping my hard dick and massaging me a little.

"Fuck, baby, I need you again," I groan into her mouth as I pull her toward me, taking her in a heated kiss.

"Better?" she sasses at me as she pulls away momentarily, and I fist my cock as I drink her in.

"You are being a very good girl tonight. Come here. I want to touch all of you while you grind your pretty pussy onto me," I say, leading her to the bed.

I sit on her bed, then turn her and pull her down onto my lap so her back is to my chest. I kiss her neck from behind, and my hands travel up her soft tummy to cup her perfect breasts, and I knead them in my hands.

"That feels so good..." she moans as her head falls back onto my shoulder, her body open and completely at my mercy.

"I want you to open your legs wide and let me sink into you," I grit out to her, my dick getting harder and harder by the second.

She lifts a little then, and I fist my cock, positioning it for her, and she sinks slowly, taking me in. Inch by inch, I feel her pussy clench around me.

"That's it, baby, take all of me," I say as my hands curve around her waist, and I pull her down, pushing into her at the same time.

"Now bounce, baby. Bounce on my cock. Grind your sweet pussy on me," I moan into her ear as I bite her neck a little. She starts to move then. Her hips swiveling, taking me in, then out before I push back in again. The two of us move in tandem, finding a sultry, slow rhythm that works for both of us, and she leans back against my chest with a whimper.

"Look how fucking pretty you are," I say to her as I look at the large floor-length mirror that is directly opposite. I watch us in the reflection, her body moving on top of mine, my hands caressing up her body again to grab her breasts.

"Harrison..." she moans, and I know she loves it. Whereas before we were hard and fast, this is slow and sensual. My eyes are glued to us in the mirror, watching her body grind up and down on me, my hands skimming her perfect curves, her hands still above her head, wrapped around my neck, keeping us close.

"Fucking look at us. Look at how perfect your body is with mine," I groan again, this visual something I know is going to live in my memory bank for years.

"This feels so good, Harrison..." Beth pants as a light

sheen of sweat builds again on her body. We are running a marathon this time, the feeling of our two bodies joined not something we want to hurry.

"You feel good, baby," I say, moving my hand lower across her stomach and down until I find her center. I circle her clit and feel the connection of our bodies as we move together, her clenching and unclenching my dick tighter and tighter. Faster and faster.

"Jesus, baby. You are beautiful." I put pressure on her clit, moving my hand swiftly, creating friction for her, and she begins to moan on the most breathtaking loop.

"Harrison, that's too much... that's amazing..." she cries out as my finger continues its torture and my other hand runs up her back and grabs her hair. Pulling it down, I arch her back even more, the new position sending her hips forward slightly, taking me even deeper.

"Fuck, Beth. Baby... that's it, grind on me. I fucking love seeing you like this." I already feel my balls tightening. I am definitely going to be ordering a floor mirror for my bedroom, because this is most certainly going to be happening again.

"Oh my God, Harrison! I'm coming!" Beth's moans get louder, and her hips move a little faster. My dick pistons, matching her pace as my hand moves on her clit to push her over the edge.

"Me too, baby. Fuck, me too," I pant out before we explode. The buildup and tension of the week leaves me in an instant as our orgasm rushes through us.

"Fuck," I groan into her neck, and her hands grip my hair tighter as she screams out her release. Our bodies wet with sweat, we are both now bone-tired, and Beth lies back onto me. I pepper her shoulder and neck with kisses as we both try to catch our breath.

My hands travel slowly up and down her body. I watch us in the mirror again, her naked body still on full display.

"That was intense..." she murmurs, her head turning to capture my lips.

"So fucking good." I continue to feel her body, never wanting to stop.

"All yours," she whispers, and my heart clenches.

"All mine," I say with a kiss.

39

HARRISON

It's early. But I need to get out of this bed. It is the biggest day of my career, and I would be lying if I said that my stomach didn't feel like lead. But I don't want to move. It has been too long since I watched Beth sleeping in the early morning light, and while her room and bed are too small, none of that matters like I thought it would because we are together. My fingers trace the small line of a scar that runs across her shoulder and down her chest, the small sliver of silver catching in the morning rays, the mark now holding an entirely new meaning for me.

My girl is a survivor.

The storm she has weathered is astounding, and it's my key motivator today as I embark on a journey that, if successful, will totally change my life. And hers.

Because Tennyson is right. She needs to be my wife.

"Hmmm, good morning," she murmurs in her soft, sultry tone that makes me want to tie her to this bed and do ungodly things to her.

"Morning. How are you feeling?" I ask her.

"My body is sore in places it hasn't been for a while..." she says, a seductive smile gracing her lips. "My mind is acutely aware that I should be asking you that question. So how are you feeling?"

"Excited, confident, nervous, so many things..." I say quietly, never admitting anything like this to anyone before. Us Langford men are strong and stoic, with our charming smiles. But Beth sees the real me. I can't hide from her. I grab her hand, lifting it above us where we lie, my mind full of thoughts about today, about us, about the future.

"Whatever happens, I want you to know I am proud of you. You have run an excellent campaign, and I am proud to be by your side for all of it," she whispers, her eyes piercing my heart with an arrow a million times over. No one has told me that they are proud of me since my dad died.

"Win, lose, or draw, I want you by my side," I say, knowing that she has a million other things to do today with her father in the hospital, but I'm not sure I can do this day without her.

"Well, we will be at the Four Seasons so that is not going to be a hardship," she says, smiling, her joking making me feel lighter.

"I canceled the Four Seasons," I tell her, having not informed her of my new plan yet.

"What? What do you mean, canceled? Where are we spending Election Day?" she asks, turning her head, looking at me in shock. I don't blame her; The Four Seasons has been booked for my team for months.

"The community center," I state, watching for her reaction.

"The community center? My community center?" she asks, shocked.

"Yes. *Our* community center."

"What? Why?"

"It is where it all began. Where I announced my intention to run for governor, where I saw you again, where your life is, where I want our life to be..." I say, taking in her awed expression. She is quiet for a second, then her sparkling blues get glassy.

"That is brilliant," she whispers. "The perfect location for it. I bet Jeff is already in a scramble."

"No doubt. What is his problem, anyway? He sure is protective of you. I don't like it," I say, the honesty and jealousy seeping out of me a little too strongly.

"He means well. He has latched on to us all at the center. While annoying, he is a good friend."

"I don't like the way he looks at you," I grumble, the feeling in the pit of my stomach something I have rarely felt before. But he is trouble. I already know it.

"Do you like the way anyone looks at me?" She toys with me, her fingers strumming my chest, and I feel like purring like a kitten.

"I want to kill any man for looking your way. It is a constant battle every day," I growl.

"Well, you can rest easy. One governor is enough for this woman to handle. I am not interested in anyone else but you," she says, leaning forward, kissing me softly, and I can't think of a more perfect way to start the biggest day of my life.

As we wrap up our last visit for the day, I have an energy humming through my body that I find difficult to contain. We are all at our last canvassing location, another elementary school, our campaign focusing heavily on education. I am tired after staying with Beth last night; our nighttime activities kept us both up too late. They were worth it, as I look over and see her laughing again, making me smile.

I haven't made any announcements today, and I won't be yet. But it is clear from our body language that she will be by my side if I am announced governor tonight. The media are circling us both closely, photographers grabbing all kinds of shots of us together and separate, her friend Max watching over her, making sure she has space and isn't overwhelmed, while I walk and talk with people.

"Okay, so I think we are all done," Oscar says, breezing up to me.

"Really? I can't believe it," I say, looking around the room, my smile the most genuine it has been for the entire campaign. This is it. This marks the end of campaigning, and the start of the waiting.

"Me neither. It has been a big journey, but I think your life is going to change tonight," he says, his smile wide as well.

"It isn't over until the fat lady sings..." I warn. Before Oscar can reply, I hear her. Laughter fills the small schoolroom, Beth's giggles interrupting all conversations as the kids join in and the laughing becomes contagious. All the adults who were standing on the outskirts talking politics stop and stare at my girlfriend who is in fits of laughter, her arms wrapped around her middle and with bright-blue paint on the tip of her nose and down the front of her dress. The culprit, a young boy holding a paintbrush with blue paint on the bristles, looks horrified, until Beth's laughter puts him at ease, and he is soon in fits of giggles as well.

The cameras flash like crazy, capturing the moment, and I watch them all for a minute, then I walk over, and the kids all scatter after being pulled away by their teachers.

"Got a little something on your nose," I say as I walk up to Beth as she is wiping the tears of joy from her eyes.

"Really?" she asks in mock surprise.

"And a little something on your dress..."

"Oh, I hadn't noticed." She smiles as we say our good-byes and start to leave the school. I shake the last few hands and wave to the group of people who are seeing us off, then I fall into the car with Beth.

"So I think I need to go home, get changed, and maybe meet you at the center later?" she says, taking in her appearance.

"Let's drop Beth home, and then get straight to the center. We need to lock ourselves in for a bit now and make a few phone calls," Oscar offers, reviewing his very tight schedule.

"I've left a present on your bed at home. Wear it tonight," I murmur in her ear, kissing her cheek. While I know that she doesn't want me spending my money on spoiling her, I hope she'll like her surprise.

"Okay. Thank you. I just hope this paint doesn't

stain..." she says, and I pass her my hanky to wipe her nose. She succeeds in smearing it across her cheek, making me chuckle.

"Is it gone?" she asks innocently.

"You look beautiful," I reply, because blue paint or not, she does.

40

BETH

As I zip up a new black dress that, along with some matching black heels, was left in a gift box on my bed today, I look at myself in the small mirror on the back of my bedroom door and smile. It was nice of Harrison to select an outfit for me today, but he didn't need to. He hasn't provided clothes for me since the kickoff party his mother arranged back when I first started working with him. The night we both put caution to the wind, and I ended up in his bed.

A smile comes to my face as I relive the memories. While the dress and heels are nice, they are not what I would assume someone like Harrison would normally buy. The dress is lovely and from Target, the shoes stunning and fashionable and look to be from Walmart. The tags are still on and they are thrown onto the bed like someone was in a hurry. I wonder if this is something Dad did and had Marci shop for, and the gift Harrison left is somewhere else. Looking around, I can't see anything else, though. Regardless, I am grateful as I look at my reflection, pleased with how they fit.

My eyes roam my face and body. *Do I look the part? Can I pull this off? Will people like me? Accept me?* Flashes of Mrs. Langford's face come to my mind, and I sigh. I know I am not for everyone, and I know that bonding with that woman is going to be like climbing Mount Everest. I am expecting to see her tonight. I will be nice and civil, much more than she deserves, but I will be the bigger person.

I will do it. For Harrison. Tonight is all about him, and as I take one more sure and steady breath, a feeling of calm comes over me. For the first time in my entire life, I feel like the steps I am about to take with Harrison are where I need to be.

My cell phone pings from the bed and I grab it quickly.

Tom: Stuck in terrible traffic, running late.

Not ideal, but noticing the time, I run around and grab the rest of my things, and with one last look in the mirror, I leave. I have too much nervous energy humming through my body to just sit here and wait. I slip outside, locking the front door behind me, and even though the weather is crisp, I decide to start walking. Tom can pick me up on the way.

My new shoes click on the sidewalk, the hard leather pinching my toes a little and the backs rubbing my heels. As I near the end of my street, I am already regretting my decision to walk and stop for a moment, trolling through my handbag, wondering if I have a Band-Aid to put on my already raw heels.

Coming up empty, I contemplate staying where I am to wait for Tom or walking the fifty yards to the bus stop. Still too nervous to sit still and wait, I slowly step toward the bus stop, grimacing with every step.

Crossing the street, I see the bus shelter up ahead, but a car pulls up right beside me.

"Oh, thank God, I was..." I start, grateful that Tom has arrived. But it isn't his car.

"Need a ride, Red?" Max, my photographer friend, yells from the driver's seat.

"Oh, I have a car coming," I say, not wanting to put him out.

"I think we are probably both going the same way, and those shoes don't look like they are very comfy."

As he says it, my feet pinch even more, the throbbing already having me at breaking point.

"Well, if you are sure you don't mind?" I say as I tentatively walk toward the car door.

"No problem. Get in. All the roads are blocked off within a few hundred yards of the community center, so traffic is a nightmare!" Max exclaims as I sit in his car and put on my seat belt. I have never felt more relieved to be off my feet, and I sigh as the pain starts to subside.

As Max concentrates on the road, I look around his car. It is small and dirty. Takeout containers fill the floor behind me. But what is odd is the big designer bags in the back seat. One branded bag houses a box of shoes that look like they are the expensive red soles everyone loves, the other Prada, Harrison's favorite brand. It makes no sense, since the car is old and rusted in spots, but I try not to judge or think too hard about it. I know how hard it is to make ends meet, and I have no idea what Max's lifestyle is like.

"My town hasn't ever seen this level of police presence before," I state, making conversation as I clasp my hands together on my lap so I don't get myself dirty on the dust that is thick on the center console.

"There sure is a lot," he says, and I notice him sweating, even though it is cool out.

"Oh, we should have turned down that street!" I say as I notice he missed the turn.

"Nope, I need to go the long way around, to get around the police barricades; otherwise, it will take us hours."

I nod in understanding. Although I have my ID to wave us through any police checkpoint, I don't say anything, just grateful for the ride. I notice he leans in and turns up the air conditioning in his car, the cold blast chilling me to the bone. I rub my arms to fight the chill.

"Sorry, I have trouble regulating my temperature," he offers.

"It's fine, no problem," I say with a small smile. While I know Max, I don't know him well, and sitting in such close proximity makes me feel a little awkward. I stare out the window and watch the world go past, noticing that he really is taking the long way around, as we are now on the total opposite side of the city. The air conditioner is blowing directly in my face, and my throat dries from the blasting air. I swallow, but it gives me little reprieve, and I start to clear my throat and cough a little, trying to find some moisture.

"Sorry, let me turn it down. Here, have a drink." Max offers me a bottle of water, and I take it, thankful to have something to quench my parched throat as he turns the cool air off.

"Ahhh, thank you. I don't think I have had a sip of water all day!" I say as I take another big swig of water, then another. Mentally noting that I need to increase my daily water intake, I scold myself for not sticking to a healthy habit that is so simple.

"No problem. I am just going to head back into the center this way," he says, turning on his indicator to turn left, when he should be turning right.

"No, Max, I think you're meant to turn that way," I say, pointing as my vision gets fuzzy.

"You look good in the outfit I picked for you..." Max says as he pulls the car to the side of the road. He stops the car and looks at me.

What did he say? My head feels like it is floating... I can't hang on to the words.

"Max... I think. I can't... Max..." I say as the world spins. My body starts to sweat, and darkness consumes me before I can hear his reply.

41

HARRISON

W_here is Beth? She should be here by now,_ I think to myself as I tread a very well-worn path into the thin carpet in Jeff's office. The community center is overflowing with people. The caterers are buzzing in the kitchen; the media scrum camped outside is ten people deep, and as Beth predicted, Jeff is running ragged, trying to manage everyone. In fact, I haven't seen him for hours.

Umbrellas are being handed out to everyone outside as the rain has started. The thick gray clouds rolling in as they often do this time of year. Tom arrived an hour ago without Beth. She wasn't at her house, and no one has heard from her. I pull out my cell and dial her number for the hundredth time as I look out the window at the ominous weather. Her phone rings and rings, but she doesn't answer.

Beth. Where are you?

"Any word?" Eddie asks from behind me, where he sits with Ben and Tennyson.

"Nothing," I grit out. The feeling in the pit of my stomach is back, my body filled with panic I don't want to expend in front of anyone yet.

"Maybe she decided it was too much for her?" Ben asks, looking at all angles like the lawyer he is, and it isn't as though I haven't thought about it. It is a big life decision to go public with me as I step into the shoes of governor. But she isn't a runner. She has been with me up until this point. The next step is big, but one I know she was willing to take.

"No. She wouldn't run." I hate this. I know deep within she wouldn't run; she is mine, and I am hers, and I want her here. I want her with me.

"And she hasn't shown up to the hospital?" Tennyson asks. My brothers are all aware her father is now in the general ward and recovering, but neither her father, nor Marci, who is by his bedside tonight, have seen or heard from Beth. Both are now starting to worry. Like I am. I have my security team positioned at the hospital, at her house, and here at the center, their sole focus looking for her or any evidence of her.

I look out the internal office window to the growing crowd inside and see Larry talking with some people from the center. Leaving the window, I say nothing to my brothers as I step out of the office and through the cheering supporters, plastering my face with a fake smile, making a beeline for him.

Larry looks at me with a smile, which soon fades.

"Still no word?" he mumbles to me as we shake hands and both smile for the flashing camera that has suddenly appeared before us.

"No. She was meant to be here hours ago."

"It's not like her to be late. Is she at the hospital?"

"Not when I called fifteen minutes ago," I say as I subtly move my head to the side and crack my neck. Tension builds in my shoulders. My body is agitated.

"Let me call Marci again..." Larry offers as he steps to the side to make the call.

I stay rooted where I am, as person after person comes up and shakes my hand, the men giving my shoulders a hard slap. My opposition hasn't conceded, but there is no denying the numbers. I will be announced as the new governor of Maryland later tonight.

"Nope, they still haven't seen her and have been calling her, but no answer," Larry confirms as he steps back to my side.

I look out to the sea of people, spotting everyone and no one.

"Have you seen Jeff?" I ask him, because I haven't seen him for a few hours, leaving him stressed about the lack of toilet paper in the bathrooms earlier.

"I haven't seen him for a while," Larry comments as we both start looking around the room for any sign of him.

"We need you for a live cross with the night news programs..." Oscar says, slipping up to my side. I nod, forcing another smile to my lips as I leave Larry, my legs feeling like they're weighed down as I sidle up to the camera. A microphone is shoved under my chin and bright lights shine in my eyes, and I put on the charm. My body language is at ease, my smile well manufactured, and my brain remains focused on the questions until the bright light switches off and the cameraman lowers his lens. Then I am back to worrying.

"Where is she?" I bark at Oscar and Eddie as we walk back into the office. I clench my fists, taking another look at the storm outside, and I know deep in my gut things are not right. Everyone is running on nervous energy, waiting for the call from our opposition to concede while frantically trying every avenue we know to find Beth. This is the most important night of my life, but I don't feel joy, not like I was hoping. Just as I thought this night could not get any worse, the door to the office opens, and I whip around, all eyes on the person who enters. In a cloud of perfume, my mother walks in with Lilly hot on her heels, looking at everything and everyone with disgust.

"Hi, darling... I can't believe you picked this place over the Four Seasons. Have you totally lost your mind?" she comments, her hand waving around the room like she is trying to prove a point. Typical. The first thing leaving her lips is a complaint. No *congratulations on a successful campaign, early voting is looking good*. No, *I'm so proud of you*. Beth's words of support from earlier ring in my ear.

I look at Eddie, the two of us having a silent conversation over Mom's head. I chose to ignore my mother and turn back to look at the darkening sky out the window. Pulling my cell phone from my pocket, I dial her number again. It goes straight to voicemail. It is not ringing anymore. It is either dead or has been switched off.

Now I am really starting to worry.

42

BETH

My head is throbbing as I slowly try to open my eyes. I feel groggy, and my body feels weak. *Did I fall during my sleep and hit my head or something?* I think to myself as I swallow, my throat dry, my lips chapped.

I go to rub my eyes, but I can't move my hand. *Do I have a migraine? Am I dreaming?* I hiss a little at the sharp, intense burn that I feel on my wrists every time I try to move my arm. It feels real.

A TV is blaring in the distance. News anchors are talking about the campaign. *Harrison.* Wait, Harrison is in the lead? My mind is now a little more awake, and I open my eyes, the bright lights of the TV making me squint, my eyes watering a little as they start to get used to the brightness in the room.

"Harrison?" I croak out, wondering if he can get me a drink of water. Why does my bed feel so hard?

"Harrison?" I say again, a little louder.

My eyes adjust to the room. *Where am I?* I slowly look

around the large bedroom that doesn't look familiar. The curtains are drawn, but I can hear the loud rain outside. The bed is dressed in crumpled gray sheets, with timber bedposts, and as I look at them, I notice my feet are tied with rope to each corner.

"Harrison!" I say again even louder as I look up to my wrists. They are both tied to each corner as well, the rope burning a mark into my skin. My heart starts beating faster as I turn my head around the room and see Harrison being interviewed on the TV. He is at the community center. My memory comes back to me, knowing that is where I am supposed to be. Eyes widening, I look to my other side and see a large wall covered in photos and clippings.

I try to remember how I got here, but the last thing I remember is saying goodbye to Harrison at my place because I had paint on my clothes. Looking down, I see I am in a black dress, which has ridden up my thighs, leaving me exposed in the pretty black lace panties I put on for Harrison.

The bedroom door opens, and I still.

"Max?" I say his name as the vision of him comes into view.

"Hello, Beth," he says, his voice no longer the happy-go-lucky tone I remember him having.

"Where are we?" I ask, looking around the room again. I try to move, wriggling up the bed to cover myself, wondering why he is not tied up like I am.

"My place," he states as his gaze stabs me with disgust.

"What are we doing..." I start to ask as I lift my hand,

forgetting I can't move it. I try again and my wrist burns, my eyes latching on to the knotted rope. Whipping my head back to him, I begin to panic.

"Max. *Max*! Who did this? We need to get away!" I yell, my body ready to run, if only I could. I start pulling at my legs and arms, still not comprehending the situation. Until he laughs. A sinister laugh dripping with contempt falls from his lips, and I still.

"Max?" I ask, genuinely confused and a little scared. I know him from around the work events I do, a regular in the media pack I manage, but I don't know him well outside of that.

"Oh, Beth, you are so stupid sometimes. Although you do look lovely in the new outfit I got for you. You look just like my mother the night she died. The night they all did. I have waited so long for this moment. I have been watching you for years, eager for my chance," he says, and I scrunch up my eyes, trying to make sense of what he's saying.

"What do you mean?" I stutter out, fear starting to crawl up my body, my heart racing and my head continuing to thump in pain.

"You never asked about me. Not once. Never asked if I was okay..." he says as he starts to pace the small bedroom at the foot of the bed. I try to pull my legs together, acutely aware of how vulnerable I am right now. The dress is now up around my hips, my black lace underwear not really covering me much at all.

"Max, untie me," I almost plead with him. His hair is everywhere, his eyes red-rimmed, and I wonder if he is on some kind of drug.

"You didn't care at all, did you, Beth? You didn't even look into it," he says, before he starts muttering to himself, pacing the floor, his fists curling at his sides before he digs them into his hair, grabbing the ends and pulling.

"Max, please, untie me?" I say again as I begin to sob, knowing that I am in big trouble. He ignores me and continues to mutter to himself, and I decide to keep him talking.

"Was it some event, Max? Did you not get the right shot?" I ask, wondering what the hell he wants with me.

He stops dead in his tracks and looks at me. His spine-chilling expression is enough to make my heart thump out of my chest before he starts to laugh. A big belly laugh. I watch as his curly blond hair bobs up and down against his forehead as his head shakes. His mouth turns up in a wide smile, but not a happy one. It is something much darker than that. He has no charm. My eyes flick to the TV, where I see Harrison finishing his interview before the news anchors come back on the screen.

"You don't remember, do you? You don't know who I am?" he questions, getting my attention again as he slowly stalks toward me.

"You're Max, the photog." I try to lean farther away from him, wanting as much space between the two of us as possible. My eyes look over his shoulder, and I see the wall of photos again and one catches my eye. I squint to look closer and see it is a photo of me, in the beautiful evening gown from Harrison's launch party months ago. My eyes skip quickly to the next one, which is of me again. This time in my work outfit at an event in DC about a year ago. My eyes graze over the next one and the next one. They are all of me.

"Do you know what it was like growing up in foster care?" he asks, as his knees hit the side of the bed. I swallow quickly as he stands there, waiting for my response.

"No. I don't," I say quickly as I continue to curl my hands around, trying to loosen the rope that is restraining me.

"Do you have any idea how my life has been?" he yells at me, and my body jolts. I move my hands faster, even though the rope burn is killing me.

"No, Max. Please, Max, don't hurt me..." I cry out, tears falling down my cheeks, but my body is feeling the slack of the rope on my wrists. I start to gain some confidence that I can get out of this situation.

"I knew I had to make my move soon, since our new *charming* governor was sniffing around you. What better way to end your life than to do it on the biggest night of his life. In a thunderstorm too!" he spits out at me, and I still. I look at him wide-eyed as my brain finally catches up with his words and understanding washes over my face.

"I'm the little boy you left in the wreckage. I'm the little boy without any parents. Your mother killed my family that dark, cold, rainy night, Beth, and now I want my revenge."

43

HARRISON

"I t's over. He conceded. You are now governor of Maryland," Oscar says as he hangs up the phone with a broad smile.

One I don't match.

"Call the police chief," I bark back at him, and I watch his smile fade a little as his eyes flick to Eddie. My brother already has his cell to his ear, the chief on the other end. After our meeting with him last week, we have protocols in place, security everywhere, yet no one is on Beth. Guilt wraps around my spine. I should have had security on her. I should have made sure she was okay.

"Didn't you hear Oscar?" my mother scolds me. "You are going to be governor!" she exclaims, clapping her hands together, her jewelry around her wrist jingling. Her bright-red lacquered nails reflect the lights from the ceiling as the large diamonds decorating her fingers glisten. I have never craved the plain pink short nails of Beth more. The long talons my mother has now are the kind that give me nightmares.

I look around the room. I want to be happy. I want to celebrate. But I want Beth more. We are still holed up in Jeff's office, where I have been for most of the night. Oscar taking the official phone call that I have just been voted in for governor now puts us firmly in the spotlight. I can hear my supporters outside in the large hall, and even more gathering around outside. Choosing the center for my election night headquarters was a great idea, something that the local community welcomed. But Beth still isn't here. My eyes home in on Jeff, and I watch him out in the hall, running around, ensuring things are running smoothly in his center. He turned up about an hour ago, having gone out earlier to grab more supplies. We have double the number of people here than we were expecting.

Eddie and I both grilled him when he returned. But he came up clean. He doesn't know where Beth is and he, along with everyone else in this office, is deeply concerned for Beth's well-being.

Aside from my mother, it seems.

"Seriously, Harrison, you need to go and make your acceptance speech," my mother says, and my eyes flick to her. I love her, I do, but right now, I hate her. Hate her with almost every fiber of my being. I don't say anything to her. I don't have to. She knows. It is rolling off me more violently than those thunder clouds outside. She can feel it. Everyone in this fucking office can.

"The police chief is sending a specialist team, but they might be a while. Tonight is crazy for them," Eddie says, and I nod.

"Maybe..." Oscar starts, and my eyes flick to him.

"Maybe what?" I snap at him to hurry up and spit it out. I'm on the edge, barely hanging on. My need to snap is simmering at the surface.

"Well, you need to do a speech. The entire state will be listening in. Maybe request their help?"

"Oh, you cannot be serious? She has probably gone off with another boyfriend or something," my mother chimes in again, starting to huff and puff around the room.

"Get out," I say calmly. I can't even look at her.

"Oh, Harrison..." she starts.

"I said, *get out!*" I yell. I raise my voice for the second time this week, all at the same woman.

I watch her stand there, looking at me, her eyes wide as she swallows the words that were about to come flying back out at me. She purses her lips then, before grabbing her luxury leather bag, and teeters on her heels out the door. As the door closes, I breathe out and rub my forehead. This night is not going anything like I had imagined.

"Right, I will make my speech and talk to the press. Set it up," I say to Oscar, and he rushes out the door to organize the crowd. I can hear them out there, cheering and clapping, excited that their man just won the position of governor, while I am holed up in this small office, trying to keep it together.

I run over a few things with Eddie, gathering some key points before I walk out to address the crowd and waiting media. As soon as I am out the door, the cheers go up. I give a small smile and a quick wave before I walk up to the podium.

"Thank you, everyone," I say as I wait for the noise to die down a little.

"Today, we won." As I wait for the clapping to cease, I look over the crowd, seeing the familiar faces of my brothers, some friends, business acquaintances.

"Thank you for championing for me, canvassing for me, highlighting the very important causes we commit to now that we are in power. I could not have done this without you," I say to another cheer that on any other day would fill me with joy.

"I want to thank my brothers for their unwavering support." I look at them all, deliberately not mentioning my mother.

"I would also like to thank Oscar, my campaign manager." I wave my hand in his direction and give him a brief nod in acknowledgement. We are all happy, but reserved, the feeling of dread too close to the surface.

"I also want to make special mention to my girlfriend, Beth," I say and pause, because there is a frenzy as soon as I mention her name. Cameras flash incessantly, the crowd cheers, and people holler and whoop. I smile a little because the acceptance of her is immediate.

"Beth and I met a year ago and have become close over these past three months as I started the campaign. Without her, none of this would be possible. But she isn't here tonight." The crowd goes silent.

"Beth was due here five hours ago after I dropped her at home earlier today, and she hasn't been seen or heard from since. None of her family or friends have seen her, and she is not answering her phone. We have fears for her safety." Shocked faces and quiet murmurs are the first response. This is not how I expected my first speech to go. I look around the crowd and see the paparazzi on the outskirts. I look for his unique yellow hair, but I can't see Max, his curly mop nowhere in the crowd. That's when the penny drops.

"Beth, if you are listening to this tonight, please know that I love you, and I will find you," I state through gritted teeth, angry that I didn't notice him missing earlier. Max has followed my entire campaign. On the biggest night of it, he is suspiciously absent.

I step away from the microphone, the blinding lights of camera flashes going off in every direction, and I walk off the stage and back into Jeff's office to chat with my team.

"I know who has her," I state, fully convinced of it.

"Who?" Eddie asks as all three of my brothers crowd around me.

"Oscar, get me the media list," I bark at him, my patience now all out the window.

"What have you found?" Ben asks, stepping up to my side, the four of us boys together giving off a commanding presence.

I tell them all about Max. Once I give them his description, Eddie nods, clearly remembering him as well. Oscar scans through our media contact list to find any details we may have of him.

We have none.

"Fuck!" I yell as I start to pace the office, running my hand through my hair for the hundredth time tonight.

"Wait! Her work cell. We have access to her location via her cell," Eddie says, grabbing his phone out and tapping into the app. Why didn't we think of this earlier? I rush to his side, looking over his shoulder, and wait as the map pulls up and a little blue dot appears.

We have her last location. We've got her.

"I have a car waiting out the back," Oscar says, having already organized it for us.

"We are coming," Tennyson and Ben say as they sidle up to Eddie and me.

"Take security," Oscar pushes, and I shake my head.

"I have no time," I say, already walking out the back door.

"Harrison. Let the police handle it." Oscar follows the four of us boys down the hall, the only secure exit for us in this entire building.

"Call them. Tell them where we are going and why. But if they are not there when I get there, I am not waiting."

I am not waiting a second longer.

44

HARRISON

BREAKING NEWS

There is disarray in the Maryland Governor elections tonight as new Governor Elect Harrison Langford has delivered his acceptance speech.

After the obligatory thanks to his family and team, Governor Langford shocked onlookers with the news that his new girlfriend, Beth Longmere, has gone missing. In what appears to be a kidnapping, Miss Longmere hasn't been seen since earlier this afternoon and was due to arrive here at the Riverside Community Center hours ago.

Local law enforcement, county police, and the security team of our new governor are all scouring the streets looking for clues.

We will have more details soon.

The storm is raging outside, but that didn't slow us down as Tennyson pulls up outside the dilapidated house.

"Is that it?" I growl from the front seat, looking at the overgrown garden and the front gate, which is off its rusty hinges.

"Her phone was last located at this address," Eddie confirms, and as soon as he does, I am out of the car.

The street is dark and quiet. It is almost midnight, and a few neighbors have soft lights coming from their windows, but not many. The darkness of the street matches my mood. With the police presence following me, I know it is about to get very bright here in about five minutes.

"Harrison! Don't go in! Wait for the cops!" Eddie yells at me over the rain, but I pay him no mind. I stalk across the street and up the front path. The house is old, barely standing. The lawn out front is in need of maintenance. And as I run up the front steps, I don't need to look behind me; I already know all my brothers are following me.

I bang on the door, my fist hitting so hard the wood almost splits, bits crumbling underneath my fingers. Even though my gut is telling me that Beth is in here, I still can't go barging in. It could be a false alarm, a warm, loving family home, but I doubt it.

"Jesus, this is a shithole..." Tennyson murmurs, already rolling up his sleeves. Out of all of us, he is probably the best fighter. Constantly suspended from school as a kid, and now as an adult, his temper always gets the better of him. He was closest to dad, and his death hit him hard.

I bang on the door again, impatient, as Tennyson looks into the front window, trying to look through the cracks in the curtains.

"TV is on..." he comments.

"I have photographed the car in the driveway and sent it to the police. It is a shit heap, but there is a Prada bag in the back," Ben says from somewhere behind me, him and Eddie tied to their phones. His mention of the Prada bag reminds me of the outfit I purchased for Beth. The one I left on her bed earlier today.

My fist clenches and I thump on the door again. I am about to push this fucking door down, when it swings open. Max comes up to my shoulders as he stands there, looking warm and dry and toasty. His eyes widen when he sees me, and I don't hesitate. I grab his collar and push him inside, just as I see red and blue flashing lights come down the street in my peripheral vision.

"Where is she?!" I push his body against a wall, slamming his head into the plasterboard so hard the wall crumbles, a small head-shaped dent now behind him. He laughs and tries to push me away.

"Governor, so nice of you to push your way into my home and assault me, unprovoked. I am sure that will be a fantastic piece for the front page of the newspaper in the morning. Why don't you hit me as well, and maybe I can get a good shot of you leaving a jail cell in the morning," he teases.

I pull my fist back and throw it into his cheek. My knuckles collide with his chin, and the laughter slides from his face, obviously thinking I wouldn't do it. His face is now smeared with blood, his teeth chipped, his eyes angry.

"Where is she?" I yell again, my face right in his. The venom of my words spit out onto his skin.

"You hit me?" he asks in shock, the look on his face now completely changed from snide snickering to devastation. What is it with this man? He is a complete psycho. My grip on him gets firmer, the material of his shirt becoming tighter around his neck as I slowly cut off his air supply.

"You fucking asshole. Where is Beth?" My nerves are running rampant through my body, my voice shaking the walls of this dilapidated house.

"Harrison!" Beth's voice is barely audible over the pouring rain and sirens from outside. But I whip my head toward the hallway.

"Go, I've got him," Tennyson says, having heard it too, and I release my grip on Max's shirt briefly before Tennyson's hand replaces it. As I move down the hallway, I see Tennyson kick Max's legs out from under him and knee Max under the chin, his head snapping back and hitting the wall again before his body slumps at his feet. Good. He deserves more, but that is a start.

"Beth?" I shout, my body now moving on its own, my chest heavy, my teeth grinding. My adrenaline has kicked into overdrive, the hard rain on the tin roof and my thumping heart making it almost impossible to hear anything. I run down the hall, throwing each and every door open, looking inside, seeing nothing but mess and filth in each room.

"Harrison!" I hear her again, and I run to the last door at the end of the hall, pushing it open and falling into a bedroom. The lights are bright, the TV blaring. It is old, smells musty, and I see Beth, tied by her legs to the wooden posts of the bed, looking exhausted and weary. Bleeding from both her hands, her ankles no better, I rush to her.

"Beth!" I breathe out, as I jump onto the bed, pulling her close to me as her tears coat my shirt.

"You're okay. I'm here. You're okay," I repeat as she looks up at me with relief, sobbing.

"Untie me. Please, untie me," she says through her tears, her body shaking, her voice no better as I pull away, seeing her hands free from the rope, and her ankles still tied.

"What happened? What the fuck did he do to you?" I grit out, barely containing my anger as I get to work trying to untie the rough rope that grips into her skin.

"I got out of the wrist ropes, but I was struggling with the ankles," she says, her tone panicked as she continues pulling at one leg while I do the other.

I yank at the rope, tugging it to open the knot, and blood, her blood, is smeared across her skin, her ankles and wrists red and raw. My blood boils.

"He is going to pay for touching you," I grit out, barely containing the rage in my body I never know I possessed. Even over the loud TV, I hear sirens and men yelling at the front of the house

"He gave me something, a drug, and I passed out. I woke up here, tied to the bed about an hour ago," she says through shaky breaths as I untie the last rope and pull her to me.

"Police are here, paramedics. You will be okay. We're going to get you out of here."

"Is he... is Max..." she murmurs, and as I look over her face, I can see her eyes roll a little, the drug clearly not out of her body yet.

"Beth? Stay with me, baby. Stay with me," I say to her as police fall into the room. Men shout and guns are raised, before they realize who we are, and as Beth's body feels heavier in my arms, I look down and see her out cold.

45

BETH

"**D**oes he always snore like that?" Harrison asks me as I lie in the bed, the starched hospital linen scratching against my skin.

"Every night." I sigh, looking at my dad, who is finally asleep after I was wheeled into his room during the early morning hours under observation.

My hand remains in Harrison's, where it has been since we arrived.

After the police stormed Max's house, I passed out in Harrison's arms and I am told he didn't let me go until I was safely and securely with the paramedics, and even still, he sat by my side for the entire trip to the hospital. When I woke up at the hospital, he was here next to me and has remained sitting on the hard plastic chair all morning, his thumb stroking my hand.

"Isn't your body sore from sitting in that chair all night, Governor?" I ask him, a small smile coming to my face as I use his new title for the first time. His win last night was totally overshadowed by my kidnapping. Max's face is now all over the news alongside Harrison's and mine.

"I can't feel my body. My ass is numb. But I am not moving," he says, giving me a look indicating I am not to push him on that. I have a feeling leaving Harrison's side any time in the near future is going to be hard.

My eyes flick across to my father. He is out cold, having not slept a wink until they found me. Harrison pushed the hospital to put me in the same room as him, knowing that both me and my father would want to see each other. Dad only fell asleep a few hours ago, after we told him about the whole ordeal, none of us quite believing any of it still.

Security men block the entrance to the room. I see them both standing there, solid and strong, in black suits and slick hair. Harrison's men, who I also know will now follow me everywhere from now on. There is a media pack waiting outside, the TV in the room has quietly been on all night, and we have been watching the rolling coverage in between lightly napping from exhaustion. All of Harrison's brothers have already checked in on us, and now they've all gone home for some sleep of their own after the police finished with them all. My interview with the police will be today sometime, but they have a lot of evidence already.

The room Max held me in was his bedroom and the wall of photos was explained to me as a shrine. He held a two-decade long vendetta against me. Wanting to get revenge for his parents' accidental death in the car crash my mother caused. I didn't see the photos. Not all of them. I didn't want to. But Harrison did. His team will go through each and every one of them, plastering Max with not only kidnapping and assault, but also stalking, harassment, and even down to driving without a license, drug possession, breaking and entering, and the list goes on.

I look at the drip in my arm, the clean saline solution pumping through my body, pushing out any remaining drugs from my system, and aside from my wrist and ankles that are now bandaged, I am relatively unscathed physically. Mentally and emotionally, I think it will take me some time.

Harrison and Ben, along with their team of lawyers, will continue to work with the police to obtain all records of the accident and build a timeline. They want to throw the book at him and will stop at nothing to ensure he stays locked up for a long time.

But guilt still sits heavy in my chest. Guilt from the accident all those years ago. Guilt at ruining Max's life back then, and maybe being a contributor to his mental state now. I watch the new governor, as he sits next to me, lifting my hand and kissing each knuckle. Something he has done periodically all night. He is completely lost in his thoughts, no doubt reliving the evening, the events leading up to it, and thinking of a plan forward, past all of this. His new position starts immediately. He will have to walk out and face the media today at some point. Even though his hair is a mess and his suit is crumpled, the show must go on.

The small wrinkle between his brow hasn't disappeared all night, so I reach out with my other hand and rub it. He looks up, his eyes catching mine, and I give him a smile.

"I was so worried..." he starts, before dropping his head.

"I know. Me too," I whisper, feeling my heart breaking all over again. I thought I was as good as dead last night. I managed to loosen my wrist ropes, but it took a long time, and when Max left to answer the knock at the door, I rushed to escape the ankle ropes, but couldn't. The panic I felt at being tied up and not able to get out of it still runs through my body every time I think about it.

There is a small knock at the door, and we look up.

"I don't want to intrude..." Oscar whispers as his head pops through the ajar door, his eyes flicking to my snoring father before a small smile graces his lips.

"Harrison, I need you to make a statement this morning. The crowd is insane at the front, almost blocking hospital access, and the hospital security are struggling," Oscar says, and I see Harrison hesitate.

"You should. Go. Give them your time, show them you are a strong and capable leader. They want to hear from you," I encourage, squeezing his hand, knowing that he needs to leave me at some point and start his term in office.

The wrinkle between his brow returns, and I plaster on a big, bright smile. "I will watch," I state, pointing to the small TV flickering in the background.

"Fine, then I am coming straight back here," he says to Oscar, offering no room for alternatives.

"No problem. I have cleared everything from your calendar today; just tomorrow is a little hectic," he says, and we both know it won't just be tomorrow. Our lives are about to become very busy.

"Alright," Harrison says, standing. "Rest, baby. I will be back soon." Kissing my forehead, he walks to the door. He stops as he reaches it and looks back.

"Do I need to invest in one of those sleep apnea machines, because your father..." he starts, and I giggle.

"Go!" I say, pointing to the door, and I see a small sheen of glee in his eyes; meanwhile, I am horrified my father will wake to hear us making fun of him.

"Fine. Just asking," he says, his smile now wide, putting his hands up in mock surrender, and I watch him as the door closes and I can't see him any longer.

I sit up in the bed, feeling better and more together. Life goes on. It always does. I grab the TV remote and turn up the volume, not wanting to miss seeing him. I missed so much last night. The night of his dreams was obliterated, but this morning will go a long way to cementing his position.

"What's going on?" my father grumbles from across the room.

"Harrison is making a speech this morning," I tell him, and I notice he sits up as well. My father is now very fond of the boy from Baltimore, it seems.

"Good morning, everyone," Harrison's voice starts, his posture straight, solid, dependable. I see cameras flash and microphones move closer to his chin. Oscar is right; the media pack looks even bigger than normal today.

"Thank you to all of you for your kind support in the past twenty-four hours; it has certainly been an unprecedented way to start a governorship, the first of its kind," he says, smiling, and a few chuckles are heard in the crowd. I clench my sweaty palms together, my father silent, taking it all in. He is aware our lives are about to change, neither of us sure what to expect other than we know it will be impactful for us. But we are ready.

"Firstly, I want to thank the voting public. You have put your trust in me to run the state on your behalf, to look after not only Maryland across all areas, but to also look after you. The people. Each and every one of you have placed your trust in me to deliver a prosperous and safe state, one that thrives in the face of adversity, one that delivers on goals and promises, and one that will continue to be successful in this great country we call home. You are important to me. Your families are important to me. Your schools, hospitals, safety, and health are important to me. As are businesses, commercial success, and climate responsibilities. There is a lot to manage; there is a lot to deliver. But as I stand before you today, I promise to deliver on each and every one of my commitments. I promise to lead this state forward, to ensure that Maryland is seen as a leader in this country, and together, with Beth who is your first lady, and my team, we will make you proud." He pauses then, looking over the crowd, and for the first time ever, the media pack claps. It is slow to start, but as Harrison stands solid in front of the camera, a small smile comes to his face, and the media start cheering.

The camera pans out to the crowd, and I still. It is huge. Not only is it the full media pack, which we were expecting, but there are people. Masses of people standing outside this very hospital. Some holding signs, many with hearts, some with *I love you* written on it. It looks like my entire city has come out to hear his message today.

I see Oscar and Eddie standing next to Harrison, both smiling, no doubt happy with what we have all achieved. Even though I know Eddie is leaving us next week to start managing the family real estate portfolio, he looks at his brother proudly.

"Looks like the two of you have a big job to do," my dad grumbles from his bed. I look at him, still in awe, shocked almost at what I am seeing.

"I have no words," I say quietly.

"Well, you need to find them, Beth, because they," he says, pointing to the crowd on the TV, "need you. The people see Harrison today, but it is clear they want you as well. I know you will be a fine first lady. The best. Now you just need to show them all." His face is awash with pride.

I look back at the TV, watching Harrison again.

"Before I wrap up, I would like to take this opportunity to thank the county, the media, the emergency services, and the strong, smart men and women of our police force for their assistance and dedication in helping find Beth last night. I know many of you shared my concern overnight, and I can tell you she is resting comfortably and being well looked after here at the hospital. I am hopeful that I can bring her home in the next few days," Harrison says to another few cheers and whoops from the media.

"Together, Beth and I hope to make this state proud. We promise to do our very best always, and look forward to leading Maryland together into prosperity. Thank you." He nods his head in thanks to the sound of cameras and bright flashes. I smile wide, as does he, and at that moment, I know everything will be alright. Maryland, my father, and us. Together, we can do anything.

HARRISON - SIX MONTHS LATER

I look out the window, noticing the clear blue sky, birds chirping, and flowers in full bloom. We are at my brother Ben's estate. The only one out of all of us to have a secluded mansion on the outskirts of the city, with lawns that stretch for days. Something I think I may invest in soon too.

"I can't believe you have this place," Tennyson says from the side of the room where he is sitting with a whiskey.

"You could too," Ben quips, and he is right. We all could have something like this. But Ben invested in this early. He is the thinker of us boys and while he still spends most of his time in the city penthouse with us all, this estate is here when he comes to think.

"I'm looking at investing in that new building down on the east side. Trollo," Eddie quips, his mind now always on our real estate business. For a kid who pushed against our wealth for most of his life, he is certainly making a lot of it for us now as our real estate empire has really skyrocketed.

"Nervous?" Ben asks from the sofa, looking up at me, assessing my response carefully.

"I thought the election night was the biggest event of my life, but today... Fuck, give me that, Ten." I march across to Tennyson and grab the crystal glass from his grip, downing what's left of his whiskey.

"What do you think Mom is doing?" Eddie asks, and the mood in the room lowers.

"Probably yelling at someone about something," Tennyson mumbles as he snatches back his now empty glass and refills it at the bar.

"I'm just glad the doctor forgave us for nearly killing him with that fucking seafood sauce," Ben says, sighing. That was a tough negotiation that took multiple conversations over many months. But Doctor Warner is a good friend, and although I know never to invite him to a dinner event again, he understands that Mother had an *episode* and is not in a good place right now. Unfortunately, she hasn't learned, is still vindictive, and I wonder how any of us boys will ever be close to her again.

"So you decided not to invite Lilly today?" Eddie asks, looking at me in question as he stands and fixes his tie.

"No. Beth and I wanted today to be small. Family only. We didn't want the usual society circus," I tell him as Ben stands and comes over, pinning the flower to my lapel.

"Breathe. You look like you are about to throw up," Tennyson remarks as he slides his glass across the bar and walks over to where we are all standing together.

My brothers. We have always been close, but now

Eddie is back and Dad is gone, and our connection is stronger than ever.

There is a knock at the door, and Oscar pokes his head through. "Time to go," he says, as he looks over us four, giving his nod of approval. He is in charge of me today, Beth not trusting anyone else to get me to the altar on time.

"Ready?" Ben asks, and I look over them all.

"Let's go get married." I say the words that I never in a million years thought I would say. My palms sweat as the four of us walk out. I lead us down the hallways to the garden outside. My mother sits stoically at the front on one side, next to Oscar, who must have run out of the house to beat us here. Beth's dad, Marci, and Jeff all sit proudly on the other side.

I stand at the front next to the celebrant who gives me a big, warm smile.

"You ready?" Larry asks, smiling. Beth and I were both surprised to learn that Larry is an authorized wedding celebrant, something he obtained during his years in the military. We couldn't think of anyone better to help us commit the rest of our lives together than one of our own.

"Absolutely," I say, my smile in full effect. And I am. I have spent my entire adult life repelling against the idea of marriage. I know too many people who end their marriages and I never thought it was something worth investing in.

But then I met Beth. She turned my world upside down and helped me land on my feet again. She is stable. She gets me. She is beautiful and all mine.

I look over at my three brothers who all stand next to me. Us Langfords are a commanding bunch, and my eyes flick to my mother, who offers me a rare soft smile. She nods at me, and we have a silent acknowledgment that she knows I am doing the right thing, although she would never admit it out loud. I nod to her in return, before I hear the first few notes of music, and my eyes lift, seeing Beth standing a few yards away, looking breathtaking.

At the sight of her, my heart rate becomes steady, my sweaty palms recede, and my balance is restored.

I watch her walk to me. My eyes are laser-focused on the woman who looks radiant in her soft-pink gown, her red hair flaming down her back, her curves on full display. My eyes do not waver as she stands before me, and I reach out my hand, helping her up the step to the altar.

"You didn't trip?" I whisper. Her biggest fear of today was falling on her walk to me.

"The day is still young," she quips with a smile, one that is contagious.

"Are you ready to be Mrs. Langford?" I ask, and even though I know she is, my heart still stutters, waiting for her answer.

"I think the question is, are you ready for me?" she sasses, her blue eyes sparkling at me just like they did years ago.

"Always," I say, smiling brightly as our eyes stay locked on one another, and I give Larry a nod for him to start. I barely hear his words, my thoughts totally consumed by the woman in front of me.

Beth.

She is my heart, my soul, my everything. Including my lucky charm.

GRAB your bonus epilogue to see where Harrison and Beth are now!

ALSO BY SAMANTHA SKYE

The Arrogant Billionaire

The last thing I need in my life is another suit. Especially the tall, dark, arrogant kind.

Single mom life is hard enough without worrying where my next paycheck is coming from. Which is why I don't hesitate to step out of my comfy teacher shoes and into lawyer heels to help my school when the rich city billionaires try to buy our land.

I just didn't expect to go head to head with Benjamin Langford.

The complete opposite of me in his designer clothes and expensive cars, Ben is the billionaire every woman is trying to catch. But when a persistent ex becomes a problem, he puts a ring on my finger instead.

Our engagement is as fake as my smile, but I am determined to protect my students and their haven. I didn't crawl through the depths of despair to lose it all again. The school is all we have got and it is up to me to save it.

Even if that means I dance a little too close to the devil.

www.books2read.com/arrogant-samantha-skye

ALSO BY SAMANTHA SKYE

The Billionaires of Whispers

Tanner

Hudson

Connor

Sawyer

Sutton

Griffin

SCROOGE: A Billionaire Christmas Story

Under The Mistletoe: A Billionaire Christmas Story

The Baltimore Boys

The Charming Billionaire

The Arrogant Billionaire

The Damaged Billionaire

The Secret Billionaire

The Bossy Billionaire

The Billionaire Babe

Men Of New York

My Legacy

My Destiny

My Fight

My Chance

Boston Billionaires

Coming Home

Finding Home

Leaving Home

Building Home

ABOUT THE AUTHOR

Samantha Skye

Samantha Skye is an international bestselling author. A country kid turned city slicker, she writes spicy and suspenseful contemporary romance novels that leave you hot under the collar and on the edge of your seat.

Samantha lives in Melbourne, Australia and when she's not plotting her next novel, she can be found travelling, drinking margaritas and enjoying a sunset or a stargaze somewhere.

To join in the conversation join Skye's The Limit Facebook group here; https://www.facebook.com/groups/skyesthelimitbooks

To learn more about Samantha and what comes next in her author journey you can find her on;

Website: samanthaskyeauthor.com

www.ingramcontent.com/pod-product-compliance
Lightning Source LLC
Chambersburg PA
CBHW061937130726
47909CB00013B/2028